A CYBIL LEWIS NOVEL

SILENCED

NICOLE GIVENS KURTZ

Silenced: A Cybil Lewis Novel

Published by Mocha Memoirs Press, LLC

ISBN 978-0692718865
ISBN 0692718869

Second Edition

Credits
Cover artist: Adrijus Guscia
Formatting: JimandZetta.com

Printed in the United States of America

Praise for *Silenced: A Cybil Lewis Novel*

"Silenced" has all the hard-boiled elements of sex, violence, crooked politicians and dishonest cops and a story told by an engaging but difficult heroine. It is an excellent start to what promises to be a very interesting series." ***--Fred Cleaver, The Denver Post***

"Nicole Givens Kurtz is a gifted sci-fi writer with a wonderful imagination…And with the extra benefit of a strong African-American woman as the main character, this adventure captures the essence of the future." ***—Affaire de Coeur, 4 1/2 Star Review***

"A missing-persons case takes us into an action-packed story. Cybil is no shrinking violet, and the tale is vivid enough to keep the reader looking forward to the next chapter in this new series. This is a fast-paced, enjoyable ride." — ***RomanticTIMES Book Reviews, 4 Star Review***

"Nicole Givens Kurtz has written an enjoyable sci-fi mystery that displays her active imagination and her ability to build a storyline around believable characters in an advanced time setting. I found Kurtz's heroine to be interesting; however, buy-in took a minute due to the character's brashness. Once there, I was able to understand her motives and mode of operation. SILENCED is being dubbed as the first in the Cybil Lewis series. Now that my appetite has been whet, I am looking forward to the next installment." ***—The RAWSISTAZ(tm) Reviewers***

"For top-notch suspense, edge-of-the-seat breathless anticipation, and reeling denouements that never stop, run to your nearest bookseller and pick up SILENCED!" ***—Dark Angels Review, 5 Angels Review***

Other Cybil Lewis *Titles*

Cozened: A Cybil Lewis Novel

Reunited: A Cybil Lewis Story

ACKNOWLEDGEMENTS

Writing is often a lonely experience; however, I would be greatly remiss if I didn't acknowledge the talents, assistance, and support of the following people to help Cybil make her way from my imagination to the page. First, Kymberlynn Reed, who first accepted Cybil Lewis for Parker Publishing, LLC. Her enthusiasm and love for Cybil would stroke the flames of creative fire. Secondly, Michael Larocca's editing kept Cybil's tongue sharp and her action swift for the first two novels. Without this, Cybil wouldn't be as refined. Thank you for your support, your candor, and your talents.

Nicole Givens Kurtz

SILENCED

silenced- to suppress the expression of something or stop a person or group from speaking out.

CHAPTER 1

Late for work again, I set down my *wauto*, a four-door wind automobile, in the lot outside my office building and hurried inside. Gusts of poverty-infused wind forced my jacket to flap about in earnest. If someone watched close enough, they might've gotten a glimpse of my gun. The weapon couldn't be seen otherwise, and normally I didn't sport it out in the open so much. With the temperature down in the thirties, I should've been buttoned up, but then I couldn't reach my piece without unbuttoning. Though I could undo them in about a minute, it only took two seconds to squeeze off a shot to kill me. Lately, people have tried to do just that. It didn't leave room for me to be fashion conscious or stylish.

I never really bought into the whole beauty before death idea of life.

Greetings, I'm Cybil Lewis, private inspector and all around snoop.

Already Tuesday's noonday sun sprayed the handful of vehicles sprinkled throughout the parking lot with sunlight that wore down the paint job and gloss, baking them like little biscuits in an oven. Way off in the distance I could make out a patch of clouds, puckering up and waiting to deliver a downpour of snow later tonight, perhaps first light tomorrow.

Sweating despite having gotten out of a warm, climate controlled vehicle, I knew the unbuttoned coat was a no-no. Icy blasts tore through my sweater, right to my skin. Chills scaled up my back and blanketed my arms. I shuddered. Yet I couldn't walk around the better parts of D.C. without concealing the gun. Well, I had a choice. I could leave it home or take it with me.

You already know which option I selected.

As I crossed the threshold into the building, I headed straight for the elevator. My office was located on the East Side of D. C. From my private office window, I could see the bits of the now ruined former capitol of the United States. According to the news files, a committee had been assembled to see if they wanted to convert it to condos or rental meeting rooms.

Downtown D.C. was a ghost town on the verge of resurrection. Hallmarks of our territory's past sprinkled the ten mile area like hollowed husks of once fruitful glory. The governor of the district and the senate council operated out of the district's building on Pennsylvania Avenue. The White House had been obliterated and the capitol, although still standing, had been assaulted and abandoned.

My slice of heaven wasn't in the best neighborhood and definitely not on the up and up, but I couldn't beat the rent.

Cheap.

Sure the vagrants made their presence known by soliciting funds, exposing worn, ragged, desperate faces, but they were harmless.

To be honest, the violence that occurred on this area's twelve-block radius was a result of yours truly.

As I rushed into the building, I caught the elevator before the doors closed. Shoving my bulk through the diminishing gap, I discovered I wasn't alone. I shared the funky carpeted and wood paneled compartment with an insurance salesman. With the trenchcoat, withered gray cardigan and hat, he looked the part of salesman. He didn't speak to me and I didn't speak to him. He kept his eyes averted and his hands folded in front of him. A little man, with a head the size of a cantaloupe and stringy hair, he seemed to be a part of the ancient, grim interior of the building. He didn't smile or even wink at me.

Definitely a strange one.

He got off at the fourth floor.

Two floors later, I fled the tiny space and moldy air for the somewhat cleaner breeze of the air-conditioned hallway. As I approached my office down the sixth floor corridor, I noticed an armed bodyguard posted outside. He wore opaque, sunglasses and a big navy blue jacket that could have been used as an elephant tent. I caught a brief glimpse of my reflection in his glasses as I passed him and entered my office.

His post outside my place of employment didn't work well if he wanted to be incognito.

But with bleached blonde hair, a turquoise blue sweater and shiny black shoes, perhaps incognito wasn't what he was going for.

Let's not overlook the big-barreled Bronzing laser gun he held over his chest like a crucifix.

Now everyone who passed my office would know that someone who *thought* they were important was inside.

As you walk in from the hallway, the lobby's layout consisted of Marsha's desk in the center. Her desk was flanked by the door to my private office on the right and Jane's, my inspector in training, desk on the left

Immediately I didn't like what I saw.

Seated in the two visitors' chairs were two more goon-heads like the one outside, each wore navy-blue jackets and turquoise sweaters. They smelled like honeysuckles mixed with gun cleaning oil. One of the bodyguards, a male had a serious hair loss condition and the other, a rail thin female of no older than eighteen reached for her weapons when I entered.

Jumpy and possibly trigger-happy?

Tuesday was already looking up.

Marsha's empty chair had been moved over to join the two visitors' seats and there sat Mayor Christensen, of the Memphis Quadrant, in all her polished, political glory.

Jane, my inspector-in-training, looked up from her desk

and stood, a look of complete angst on her face. Oh, Jane, what have you been up to?

"Cybil..."

I'd never met the mayor before, but I had seen enough of her grinning picture in the hordes of Internet jpegs and e-news files to know her upon sight. Pretty and well dressed in a manner consistent with those of power and privilege, the mayor of the Memphis quadrant was a media favorite. Every little detail, down to the most meaningless of things, was reported with fervor all over the online tabloids. The Internet mags thrived with coverage of her triumphs, failures, and risky political moves.

"Good afternoon, Mayor Christensen. What brings you to D.C.?" I ignored Jane. She could explain it later—although I was curious to see what spin she would put on *this*.

Jane sat down at her desk, her hands twisting together in front of her as she kept her eyes on the mayor and me. Already a thin line of sweat decorated her upper lip and even from across the room, I could see her eyes flittered around, unable to focus on one thing.

Yep, she had done something she knew I'd be pissed about.

I don't like being ambushed and despite what Jane would tell me later, the situation definitely felt like an ambush. If it quacks like a duck, walks like a duck, and looks like a duck, then it surely is a duck.

Ditto the ambush.

Mayor Annabelle Christensen, *Belle* to Jane and other family members, was as Southern as grits and bluegrass music. She had occupied the mayoral seat of the Memphis quadrant for at least ten years. The Memphis quad extended up as far north to what was once Louisville, Kentucky and as far south as the modern day Jackson, Mississippi. The quad's eastern border stopped at the far mountainous border of what was once Tennessee and dipped down to the former Mississippi. The Mississippi River served as the western border to not only the Memphis quad, but also the entire Southeast Territories to which Memphis was the largest quadrant.

She rose from her seat like a queen, with grace and an air of royalty. Her media smile stuck to her face like glue. The room smelled like sweet southern honeysuckles and was thick with humidity. The mayor had been waiting a long time since her scent seemed infused into the office's atmosphere.

"Ms. Lewis, so good to finally meet you. I've heard so much about you and your work." Her voice dropped on me in heavy globs, like syrup, thick and sugary. "I wish it could be on better terms. I assure you that what I have to say will not waste your time."

Jane fidgeted in her seat as if she wasn't sure about her aunt's claim.

I didn't look over at her, but I could feel Jane's uncomfortableness. We'd been partners long enough that I didn't need to see them to know what they were thinking or feeling. I just *knew*.

"What do you want?" I asked, ready for the game to be over and failing to keep my irritation out of my voice. Mind games, pomp and circumstance didn't suit me well. My immediate dislike for the mayor didn't help the situation either, and beneath my attempts at professionalism, I think she heard it.

Her eyebrows rose and her mouth made a small little 'o'.

She recovered and her media smile was back on, full blast as if I hadn't said anything. Despite the grin, a smarminess seemed to radiate out from her heart-shaped face as if she was restraining her own dislike for me.

Sometimes, a person doesn't have to do anything to you for you to dislike them. It had to do with chemicals and personalities and other biological complex stuff.

I didn't know the exact chemicals, but I knew I didn't like Mayor Christensen.

Moreover, I didn't trust her.

Already pain nibbled at the edge of exploding along the

base of my neck. Stress. I didn't feel like bullshitting around with the mayor and her entourage of goons. Had the clientele been a little seedier, I'd shot someone by now.

I have only so much honey in my system a day. Nice people, sometimes-even clients (when we get one) received small doses of my honey. My mother used to say I had an overabundance of vinegar. Of course, bees liked honey, and no one liked vinegar.

Right now, my honey supply of kindness was ebbing away faster than the eastern coastline.

The two bodyguards reached into their jackets threateningly, their eyes narrowed and attached to me. I fought the urge to smile and wave back at them.

Mayor Christensen's red painted lips opened to speak, but instead she waved the goons into submission. A reddish flush appeared on her cheeks.

"May I speak with you in private?"

I shrugged and headed to my private office with her in tow. I unlocked the doors with a lick of my thumb. After a DNA confirmation check, they slid open. I dropped my satchel on my big oak desk as I stepped into the room and remained standing behind it. It had a big, open surface for all of my belongings. I loved the desk more than some men I've known.

Mayor Christensen didn't sit in my only visitor's chair.

With that well-bred posture, she remained standing as she scanned the walls of my private office taking it in. I knew what she was seeing, and I didn't really care. Everything in the office came secondhand or was here when I leased the space eight years ago. The walls were adorned with newspaper and electronic clippings of various cases I had either been involved with or solved. The yellowing on some of the actual paper ones had chipped and split along the edges. New jpegs had been enlarged and added with updated electronic articles about recent cases. They scrolled upward in slow, casual, read-me-if-you're-bored cadence.

"Mayor, why are you here?" I asked tightly, my voice edgy and impatient. With amazing effort, I tried to hang on to some professionalism. It slipped out of my hands, like sands through an hourglass. "I do have work to do."

I had a good idea of what the mayor wanted. Still I wanted her to say it, to speak it out and to ask. There was something naughty in the smile I gave her. The edges curled up in a dark satisfaction of knowing that I'd refuse her request anyway. Beg me, baby! Wait—hold for the rejection.

She brought her eyes back to mine and pressed her lips together before talking as if trying to keep her mouth from saying things she might regret later. With three more attempts, her words finally managed to clear the gate.

"Miss Lewis, I am from tough southern people who aren't bothered by mosquitoes, wauto wrecks, or mouthy inspectors."

Her voice lost its sweetness and turned hard, like wet sugar left out in the cold. In place of the soft, worried mother, was now the voice of a seasoned politician who thought I would cower and obey her every whim.

Obviously, she did not know me very well.

"The Memphis regulators are idiots," she was saying, her hands folded neatly in front of her. "They have bungled my daughter's missing person's case and I want the bastard that took Mandy found," she finished, her voice demanding, her eyes seething with anger and raw emotion.

Will the real Mayor Christensen please stand up? There is something knowing, hell creepy, about someone who could flip the coin of her personality like that. It made me want to lock my satchel in the safe, and nail down the valuables.

She stood there in her immaculate gray suit that cost more than my monthly food budget allowed. The layers of make-up didn't hide the bluish circles under her eyes, or the new crop of wrinkles along her forehead the photos and media coverage seemed to have missed or airbrushed.

"In case you haven't noticed, this is a long way from

Memphis," I said, my temper escaping into thin strips of exasperation. "And I don't respond well to threats and name calling."

The mayor's eyes held mine.

"I apologize," she said forcefully, as if she didn't really mean it. "You're the best in this business, or so I'm told." She crossed her arms over her chest. "You solved the case that sent Governor Price packing to Alamogordo Cradle a few years back."

"Yeah, I did. But the answer is still no," I said back, inserting my own steeliness into my voice. The Change met with certain death and several key political figures were apprehended, killed, or promoted depending on what side of the case they landed on. It garnished me some publicity and the client list swelled after that, a fat monsoon rain, drowning me in fresh currency, vile human actions, and a shower of gun play.

It had since dried up.

I came around to stand close to her, to face her so that she knew she wasn't intimidating me. I was taller by about three inches and weighed more than her for sure, which somehow didn't make me feel all that great.

The doors to my private office slid back in a hush. Jane came in, cautiously. She stood inside the entranceway. She opened her mouth to say something, but quickly closed it.

Smart girl.

Mayor Christensen ran her hand through her light brown Afro, ruining its puffiness.

"Miss Lewis, I have come all this way through the territory. The regulators are no closer to solving this than they were four weeks ago! Time is ticking away, and my, my baby is out there somewhere. These are dangerous times, as you well know. Help me find her, please."

Suddenly, she was the sweet, southern girl from Memphis, twang and all—the distressed parent, not the bullying politician.

This one was quite the actress.

I shrugged. "As a rule, I don't investigate cases where the regulators have already been called in."

My friend Daniel Tom, a regulator and the only one competent on the D.C. staff would kill me for meddling in his case without his permission. I'm sure the Memphis regs felt the same way.

She stared at me, aghast. "As a rule? This is my *daughter*, Miss Lewis, surely..."

"Yeah, a rule. You should know about those. They're kind of like regulations...back in the day those were called laws. When you are self-employed you can make up rules for your business. That's one of mine."

I did not dance to the beat of anyone's drummer, but my own, especially not that of some big shot politician. She could bring all the muscle she wanted, but I wasn't budging unless I wanted to.

Call me stubborn. Call me cautious. Just don't call me dead. I didn't like the way this whole thing was unfolding.

"I will double your usual retainer," she said as she looked around the office. "It seems you can use it."

Jane winced, but still didn't speak.

"No," I said, struggling to keep my displeasure from going nuclear. "I just explained it to you. I don't do regulator ruined cases."

"Miss Lewis-"

"No."

My voice was louder than I wanted. Could it be that she just didn't get it? I wasn't taking her on as a client. Was it because she was a mayor and no one in the Memphis quadrant ever refused her, so that *no* was a word she didn't understand?

Or could it be that she was so desperate to find her daughter, *no* was unthinkable?

I wasn't quite sure yet, but I did know one thing...I didn't like the ambush and it had put me in a bad mood.

Mayor Christensen stiffened as if slapped.

Jane finally spoke. "Cyb..."

I waved her off. My ire boiled beneath my somewhat awkward grin. I didn't take to people barging into my office with a trio of paid thugs to flex on me. If you truly wanted my help, there were better ways to ask than to come armed. Yeah, I had a reputation. And sure, she required protection, who didn't in this age? Still, the entire affair could've been handled differently. Way different.

"Excuse me, Mayor Christensen. Jane. I have work to do."

What work? I had no idea, but I wanted them both out of my office and fast before I lost total control. I hunkered down at my desk and turned on my computer. I played around with the mouse, gliding my fingers across the metallic square as if I had something important to read or type up.

I didn't look up as the doors opened and closed after them.

CHAPTER 2

I remained at my desk for a few more hours, trying in vain to balance my incredible shrinking checkbook. The register flickered in scarlet angry protest on my monitor like a neon sign on the brink of permanently going dismal. No matter how I figured it, the result was the same.

I was broke.

My screen buzzed and in bright pink letters, the word "call" appeared. The buzzing continued twice more. The corresponding *ding, ding, ding* were the only sounds in the office and lobby where the sound could also be heard from Jane's computer.

"Jane!" I yelled through the partially open door to the outer office where Jane's desk was located.

Since Marsha's death some two years ago, I hadn't found a new receptionist I trusted enough to pay to fill in the vacant spot. The string of temporary employees from the temp agency across town took one look at the office and fled in fear. A few couldn't take the hazard that came with the job. After a client shot at his wife inside the lobby, the temp agency refused to send anyone else.

I teased Jane about hiring a young, handsome stud. The office could use some sprucing up... nothing like youthful beauty to add spark to office parties.

She preferred someone of the other gender.

No answer from the lobby…just the thick swell of complete silence.

I clicked off the banking program and got up slowly, my

pug in my fist and my heart doing its thump-one, thump-two routine. My pug was a laser gun with a small barrel and a short robust cylinder. The power might not have been there to catapult someone, but it still tore through bone and muscle with disastrous effect.

I gently slid out of my office and into the outer lobby area. Marsha's desk lay empty, deserted. With the gun held closely to my face, I crouched down and glanced over to Jane's desk.

It too was empty.

Where did she go?

The lobby doors were still ajar and hastily closed. Someone (or someones) had come into the office. I could feel another's presence like a hair on your face. You could feel it, but it took you several attempts to actually put your hand on it. The scent of some male cologne hung heavily in the warm forced-heat air. Outside snow drifted down to the landscape without pause in huge wet flakes.

Nothing moved.

"Come out! Now! Whoever you are! I am armed!" I yelled. My heart sped up its thump-one, thump-two routine. Adrenaline seeped into my body forcing everything to become crisp and sharp in focus. I took in a deep breath and released it slowly, trying to settle down.

Didn't want to shoot the maintenance person.

Jumping the gun, excuse the pun, and shooting some harmless civilian would not be a good thing right now. The D.C. Regulators would be all over the place...swarming like angry bees.

Ugh.

"I-I'm sorry," came a whimper from an elderly, rather portly man who stepped out from behind our coffee machine's alcove. He wore a red and blue plaid (I kid you not) suit, including a vest. In his hands, a matching red hat that contained wool covered earflaps. The alcove behind the machine held supplies for coffee, some rather expensive chocolates imported from the Northern Territories, and basic medical supplies.

"Who are you and why the hell are you in my office?" I demanded as I pointed the pug at his chest. "Now!"

He jumped and fumbled for words. His dense glasses seemed to be too heavy for his round face and his hairline was in the back section of his head. Wisps of white hair circled his dome of exposed scalp like a halo. His moustache dipped down on both sides of his rather thin lips in a fall of hairy whiteness.

"Oh, I-I am Mr. Schmuckler and I represent, well, I guess it wouldn't be prudent to speak of them here, but then I have come all this way..."

He rambled on to himself like this for the better part of a minute, and several times he yanked on the bushy moustache as if for emphasis to some point he'd made against himself.

"Mr. Uh- Schmuckler, did you say?" I asked after a sharp clearing of my throat. "I have a gun pointed at your heart. Don't know what territory you come from, but here in the district things are done different about breaking and entering."

Technically, he hadn't broken into the office, nor had he stolen anything that I could see. The threat sounded good, and I was already weary of entertaining people.

His beady eyes rose in surprise and he glanced at the gun (okay I know it's small, but it is still effective) as if he'd never seen it before and then back at my face. He coughed nervously, his eyes back on the floor.

"May we discuss this in private?" he asked, his voice shaky, his hat making a complete circle rotation in his nervous hands. His long fingers ideally brushed against the wool-covered earflaps.

"Look around. This *is* private. Tell me now what this is about or I will shoot you."

This guy had used all the honey in my system. After Christensen's visit, the only thing I really wanted was to go home, have a beer, and a shower...in that order too.

He fumbled around with his hat, whispering to himself, heatedly.

"How about I give you to three, and then I start shooting?" I said, shoving iron into my words. "One."

"I am here to discuss..." he said quickly. His head shot up and he stared at the pug. Already beads of sweat dotted his freckled forehead.

"Two."

"...the...group...oh, fine, Trey Ohornon!" he spat. He breathed a sigh of relief and wiped his face with a handkerchief.

A handkerchief!

Who still used a handkerchief in this day and age?

"Trey?" I said and lowered the gun to the general area of his midsection.

Trey Ohornon was a hatchling, a genetically engineered human. He was perfect in every single way except he did not have much of a sense of humor. Not many of the hatchlings did. It seemed the engineers had screwed that up, but then again, do you know any funny engineers?

"Sit! Now!"

I gestured to the two visitors' chairs in front of Marsha's desk with the pug. "How long have you been hiding out in my office?"

Just then the office doors slid back and Jane came in carrying a rectangular plastic box and a bottled drink. Wet patches of melted snowflakes dotted her coat and she stopped abruptly when her eyes landed on Mr. Schmuckler. She shot me a glance.

I shrugged.

"Who are you?" she asked, her eyes narrowed and back on Schmuckler.

Jane wasn't one for mincing words. No doubt she saw the pug in my hand and knew that this guy wasn't forthcoming.

Or perhaps she ate something bad and was just in a terrible mood.

"This is Mr. Schmuckler. Where the heck have you been?" I asked her, a little miffed that she'd leave the office without telling me.

She placed down her drink and lunch on her desk. Careful and slow, as if thinking of a significant answer to present itself.

"I told you that I had a lunch date at one. It's in your calendar. You acknowledged it and I told you before I left today."

"You did?" I frowned at her. My calendar automatically voiced the appointment when the time came. With the reward money and several other hot cases after the incident with the Change, I purchased new items including new doors, new computers and new software. I also updated the telemonitor system.

"Yeah, I did," she said, a little irritated herself. "What do you want Mr. Schmuckler?"

Mr. Schmuckler, who sank into one of the visitors' chairs, glanced up at her startled. "I am here to speak with Ms. Lewis."

"You can speak to the both of us," I said. "Or neither. You choose."

Aside from the pay out of the Change case, I also came away with Trey's heart. He had mine for a while. Unfortunately for him, happily-ever-afters and me don't usually gel for too long. It's like leaving ice cream out in the sun. Within minutes, it starts to melt and run off into the sidewalk cracks leaving a sticky sweet residue that's hard to wipe off.

Trey's presence still coated much of my heart, my thoughts, and my libidio with sticky resistence.

Mr. Schmuckler searched my face and then he said, "I am here on behalf of the Territory Alliance. Trey Ohornon has been released from our employ some three months prior. It recently came to our attention that Mr. Ohornon may have been kidnapped. He has been missing for several days."

I felt like I had been punched in the stomach. All of the air left my lungs and a tight stitch took up residence in my chest. Nausea swirled around in my stomach and threatened to zip up my throat. I swallowed hard forcing the acidy mix back into its proper place

Missing.

"He's missing?"

I forced myself to concentrate on the issue, and not on the knot of emotion in gut. My mouth went dry like I was chewing cotton balls. I had not seen Trey since my birthday, Christmas Day, when our relationship crashed and burned like a faulty transport trip

That parting wedged a stony place between us. Doesn't most break ups? I shoved the memory of our own fiery end out of my mind, but to this day, months later, the separation still hurt.

It hurt like hell.

"I am afraid, Ms. Lewis, that during his tenure with us, he made many enemies—as most of the agents do," Mr. Schmuckler smiled, revealing tiny, nearly child-like teeth. "Employment hazard, you can say."

Why Mr. Schmuckler thought this was something to smile about bothered me. I didn't like this guy and his personality was shoving his likeability meter well below zero.

"She told you we haven't seen him," Jane said from the spot by her desk.

She opened the bottle and sipped the bluish fluid inside. Her eyes however were on Mr. Schmuckler. Her posture might have fooled him into believing she wasn't paying attention to him because she leaned back against her desk. Even while still drinking her bottled drink, Jane could kill him with the very bottle from which she drank.

It was glass, and Jane had a way with glass that gleaned muscle from bone with such fluidity and grace, Mr. Schmuckler would die with a grin on his face.

Mr. Schmuckler shrugged. "I am not here to take a statement, but rather to ask your help in finding him."

"Why?" Jane and I asked in unison.

Embarrassed at the jinx, Jane sat down at her desk, and took out her lunch, boiled eggs on rye it smelled like, as if her contribution to this was over. She didn't like hatchlings anyway.

Schmuckler smiled broaden, --a close secretive smile…like he knew something I should know, or worse, something he didn't want me to know.

"Namely because you know people we do not. People of questionable occupations," he said stiffly. "Secondly, those people will talk to you and not say, someone like myself. His eyes scanned the floor with sudden interest. "Finally, because Trey was your lover."

"Why is the T.A. interested in finding an ex-agent who you released from employ?"

I let the comment about Trey being my lover go and routed the conversation back to the topic at hand. The T.A. knew many things and most of it violated civil rights on numerous levels especially when it came to morality and ethics.

Not that there was anyone who could monitor the Territory Alliance's behavior. The other quadrants, fragmented into sections like a gigantic puzzle, had a grueling time taking care of the violence, violations, and civilian strife staining the lives of their own politicians and people.

"That is classified," he said back stonily and this time he looked me in the eyes. The "aw-shucks" act vanished into the air like fading smoke rings.

And dammit if he didn't want me to jump through them.

"Fine. Then the answer is no," I said solidly, giving him a one-shoulder shrug. "I don't work for the T.A. and I'm not doing their job for them. You want Trey, *you* go find him."

Even as I refused, my stomach balled into a knot in protest. I didn't like him being missing. Schumuckler's act left a bad taste in my mouth. Trey's disappearance was foul.

Mr. Schmuckler rose from his seat. Before he came to a full standing position, Jane had her gun out and pointed at him. Startled (or pretending to be) he blinked repeatedly as he stepped back to the office's doors, still facing Jane's gun. His lips pressed together in a line of irritation. The T.A. wasn't used to people telling them *no* or pulling guns on them.

Was it me or was I suddenly bombarded by authority figures needing my help, but failing to understand the word *no*?

Why these types of things came in clusters must be one of Murphy's less popular laws.

"Do not come back here," Jane said, for she had enough of him apparently. "No means no."

"Good day then Ms. Lewis." There was a flash of something on his face, the real Schmuckler peeking through. It contorted his features into another face, one filled with something like disappointment or pity. He left.

As soon as the doors quietly closed, Jane turned to me and asked, ""What the hell was that all about?"

She slipped her gun into its hiding place as smoothly as it appeared. With a swift shake of her dreadlocks, she freed them from their band and whistled through her teeth.

" A nutter for damn sure."

"I have no idea, but I can't get involved. I don't like being brought in like the third string quarterback in the Super Bowl, I said, putting my weapon back into its shoulder hostler.

She gave me a funny look before turning back to her computer, having only read about Super Bowls in electronic books. I bet Mr. Schmuckler managed to reduce her appetite, like he did mine. Her meal grew colder by the minute, but she could always nuke it in our microwave if, or when, her appetite returned.

I felt drained. The after effects of an adrenaline rush made me feel like I'd just run across the territories in a distance marathon. I went back into my office. I plopped down into my comfy office chair and stared at the telemonitor.

Trey is missing. Where and why would you disappear, Trey? Where have you gone?

The message window box on my screen didn't flicker or blink, but its very presence meant that someone had left a message. I'd forgotten the call in all the ruckus of Mr. Schmuckler's arrival.

Before I could click the message box, Jane stalked into my private office.

"Aunt Belle..." she said, her pitch higher than I'd like, her hands in fists and her lips a rigid line of fury. "She asked you, and..."

"Whoa, Jane."

I needed to slow her down, for she threatened to explode in raw, ripped out emotions, and once that happened, I wouldn't be able to talk to her logically for she'd be flooded with feelings.

She paced around the small section between my visitor chair and the shelves that lined the back section of my private office. Her arms folded defensively across her chest as if protecting herself from my words...my answer...my explanation.

I decided to give it a go anyway.

"You know I hate cases where regs have messed it up."

I knew she'd be angry about me not taking her aunt's case, but I had rules and procedures to which she was aware. The storm had been brewing since Christensen left and now the downpour of blame and accusations were about to commence. I'm sure she'd been thinking about all day. The anger had been stirring and now was the time for it to overflow.

Her lips trembled. "Cyb, this is my *family*!"

"I know that," I replied, much too quickly.

"Stop! Think about this!" she shouted, her fury at my rejection rising to the surface like boiling water. "Damn it! It is my cousin!"

"Family or not, you know the rule!" I said, firmly back, my own temper mounting. I hated it, but anger reared its red-hot face. "Besides, it gave you no right to ambush me! You work *with* me, not *against*!"

Jane's eyes grew wide and she punched her thigh in a huff. I rose from behind my desk, and with concentration, placed them both on its cool surface. Jane's hands were moving in time to her speaking, visual aids for her angst.

"I didn't ambush you. I didn't know she'd be here today."

I stared at her, studying her face. Her hazel eyes shined brightly and her lips were white with irritation.

We sat in the quiet heat-blown hush of my office for a few seconds glaring at each other. Neither of us was willing to look away, to blink first.

After several tense moments, Jane blinked and her gaze dropped to the floor.

"I can't believe you think I'd do that," she added, her voice small and hurt.

"You know the rules," I said softly, my fury disappearing like the smoke on an extinguished fire.

Jane perched down in the visitor's chair and leaned forward, her elbows on her knees. Her hands twisted together. "You were the one who said we needed a case. Aunt Belle is willing to pay twice the retainer."

When trying to woo me, money is almost always an option.

"Look at you, Jane. You're way too close to this. It's too personal," I said, lowering myself back into my chair, closing my eyes to the shattered and emotionally fragile woman in front of me.

Personal cases had a way of ruining an inspector's objectivity. Not to mention, during the course of an investigation, all kinds of nasty things come out like pus from a sore, painful and gross. Family cases were the worse for learning long hidden secrets, stirring up dramas, and ripping the scabs off of old wounds.

"You've taken personal cases before," Jane said, her voice quieter, farther out of reach.

"Yeah, but I don't like them." I opened my eyes and they fell directly on her.

Her eyes filled with tears, but none fell. She was way too tough for that.

"Cyb. I'm askin'. Me. Jane."

I thought about it.

She'd never really asked me for anything.

And I did need the funds.

On the other hand, four weeks had passed, trails were not just cold, but frigid. If we solved this case, it could take years, if ever. Was I prepared to devote that kind of time to it?

My eyes met Jane's and her need reached out to me. It claw at my clothes, desperate and sharp, urgent with need.

I thought then of my niece, Nina, whose birthday was only a few weeks away.

If she were Amanda Christensen, would I feel as Jane did now: Powerless to stop her abduction but devoted to finding her?

Yes, I would. She was my family.

This *was* personal.

I knew Jane well enough to know that if I said no, she'd leave my office and investigate on her own. I suspected she'd been doing that for several days already. She'd leave the office early and on some days spend a lot of time at her computer, surfing for clues. Not that she had told me. I just knew.

Without me, she may be killed inspecting on her own.

"Cybil," she said, her voice strained eyes wide with raging pain. "She's my cousin, but she's more like a little sister…you know?"

"All right!" I snapped, knowing in my gut that regret was stamped all over this thing. "I'll take the case."

What else was I going to do on weekends?

Defeated and weary, I wiped my face in aggravation. Once

I got home, a beer was definitely on tap. Heck, I may even have two.

Jane released another sigh…this one as if our argument had exhausted her too.

"I'll tell Aunt Belle."

"Tell her that I want to meet with her tomorrow at one," I said. "I'm sure she's still in the area."

Jane caught my tone, and blushed. "I swear I didn't ambush you, Cyb. I ain't like that."

"Save it, Jane," I said, not looking at her and trying to cool my irritation at the idea. "I'm going to do what she wants, so the rest is immaterial."

She nodded before leaving.

My door slid closed with a hushed click.

My stomach growled in protest to the already stress-filled day.

I glanced at the door Jane had just disappeared through.

"You're welcome."

CHAPTER 3

On most days, I tried to leave the office before the sun sinks into nightfall. Too many people wanted yours truly permanently out of business for me to be hanging out at night. The evening's velvety darkness hid most of them or so they thought. It's easier to hurt someone in the darkness. The dark shadows cushioned the intense effects of blood and goriness, making it less real. Unlike daylight which revealed the true horror of violence, shadows shielded it from view.

Tonight, however, Captain Hanson's rushed email files of Amanda Christensen's case kept me glued to my seat until well after five.

Not that it was riveting reading.

It was more *necessary* reading, like an English assignment given by a professor. In order to progress or pass the course, you had to read the text. Notes I'd made from Amanda's regulator file lay sprawled in my handheld. The midnight-bluish tint of twilight brushed the lower section of the horizon when the files arrived into my email box.

Now the entire sky was cloaked in deep blue.

I started reading, feeling like I was back in high school with an assignment to write about later. Grudgingly, I read through each attachment, looking for something the Memphis Regulators would've missed, or had in fact screwed up.

My experience with regulators was one of mutual loathing. They considered private inspectors second-class citizens, below even an average civilian. No one liked people stepping on their toes, and the regulators were no different. So, p.i.s and regs, well, couldn't all get the glory. I was certain the Memphis Regs disliked my meddling into their case.

When I looked up, it was around six-thirty.

My eye caught the message left hours earlier that I hadn't had time to play. I desperately needed a receptionist, not that our telemonitors were lit up with incoming calls from potential clients, but I just wasn't good at this secretary stuff. Give me something to shoot or kill from several hundred yards away, I could do that. Locate missing people, items, and such, I did as a job and normally without complaint, but this office manager routine was simply too much.

I clicked the message box and it played in audio only. The caller elected not to leave a complete message with a video feed, just audio.

Wautos horns could be heard and the caller's raspy breathing. There were faint voices in the distance, of conversations and huge guffaws, but other than that there were no words.

I listened, straining my ears to hear the background noise or something distinctive that could id the caller. My telemonitor i.p. was non-public. A caller didn't get my number by mistake too often. My trusty caller id only read the number as *payline*. That meant it came from a public telemonitor somewhere in D.C. The caller could have truly been anyone.

Intently listening, seconds passed before my private office was engulfed with horrifying memories and a chilling message.

"Sweet Cinnamon, this is…well, you know who it is now don't you my favorite inspector? I've got information on your *perfect* boyfriend," he said, his voice a warm, awful sound. "I will be in touch, and I know you miss my looooooving touch. It's a killer, isn't it Cinnamon? Later..."

The message ended and not too soon. As I listened, I already had my pug pointed at the screen, ready to blow the voice…to bits. He had no right to contact me. The restraining order demanded he stay away from me. Not to mention the fact that he should still be locked in a cradle cell at prison entertaining his dreamlike fantasies until he died...or was paroled.

"Cybil!" Jane screamed as she bustled into the office. A look of confusion wrinkled her face. "What are you doing?"

Her scream brought me back to the room and from that terrible time—place where Jarold Montano had reached out, touched me, and dragged my ass close to death.

I blinked rapidly. "Did you hear it? It's him!"

I didn't have to say whom, she knew. Remember what I said about being partners?

"It can't be. He's dreaming away thirty years," Jane said as she struggled to take the pug from my hand. "He's not even due for a parole hearing for twenty years."

I kept the pug and slapped at her hand. Just to appease her, I tried to calm down and put the weapon up for the second time today. "It's his voice. I'd know it anywhere."

With the click of the mouse I had the computer run a trace on the voice message to match it to a list of known violators in the D.C. area. The screen whirled until it located the match.

Just as I knew it would.

The mug shot appeared and Jane gasped.

"It's him. Jarold!"

His cold, black eyes stared back at me from his cradle photo. Beneath the picture in artful comic sans white font was the word "match."

"Damn," Jane spat angrily and leaned back against my private office doors. "Do you want to call up to Frazier's Cradle House to see if he's still asleep?"

"What do you think?" I said, bitterly, touching the screen and closing windows. "They'd cart *me* right off to the nut house."

Since the war, the territories pretty much did whatever they wanted with regard to regulations, sanctions, trade, etc.

During the war that separated the once United States, jewels and other fine goods like paintings had been stolen and sold on the black market or added to private collections. Rioting and looting occurred on a universal scale. That's how I met the infamous Jarold Montano or Phish. His pet name for me had always been Cinnamon. He said that my skin reminded him of it and he wanted to eat my flesh.

I shuddered at the memory.

Jarold Montano stole a bunch of jewels belonging to a family that hired me to recover them. I successfully did, but not before he'd put me in the hospital with a concussion and a blast hole two inches away from killing me. I had a mound of scar tissue that adorned the area just under my left breast.

Sentenced to sleep thirty years in status, Jarold occupied a cell up at Frazier's. Cradles are what were once called jails and prisons. Jarold went for attempted murder and theft. His hatred for me was so great that he requested his dream sequences all include images of me so he could kill me over and over again for his thirty-year sentence.

The judge declined.

I had to admit, he wasn't my favorite violator either. He had a snowball's chance in the ghetto of getting out clean from the cradle on parole or otherwise. He liked being mean, evil, and moreover, he enjoyed hurting people the way some people enjoyed making blankets or fixing aerocycles.

Tonight he had called and he said he had information about Trey. My precious perfect boyfriend, he said. How did he get communication privileges? How was he awake?

Nevertheless, he knew something. The very usage of the word *perfect* told me he knew Trey was a hatchling. Societal punching bag, hatchlings were often tortured, mutilated and killed by various extreme groups scattered throughout the territories. Hatred on a grand scale, just because of the way hatchlings arrived on the planet. They weren't born; they were created in laboratories.

Thus they couldn't truly be human, could they?

Jane subscribed to this theory as well. Another area to which we did not agree.

"Look, I've got something to do, so I gotta go early," Jane said, breaking my concentration. "See you tomorrow. Aunt Belle said she'd be here at one o'clock."

"Sure, take off. I'll see you back here," I said, my thoughts straddled between her and Jarold. "I can't worry about Jarold right now. We've got to find Amanda."

With a thumbs-up gesture, she disappeared through my private office doors.

The doors hissed softly at her exit.

CHAPTER 4

Fleeing the office shortly after Jane, I hurried to my wauto only to sit in traffic a few minutes later. Grayish clouds had turned the sky a smoke gray against the heavens. Threatening snow. The network of highways weaved through the quadrants slick metallic skyscrapers. The former law forbid buildings to be taller than the capitol had been vanquished. The traffic lanes were jammed with wautos, aerocycles and cargo crafts and I spent most of the journey home listening to the news on the in-flight radio.

On the West Side of D.C. a serial rapist preyed on elderly women. The news rambled on about other violent, vile, and vagrant acts humans committed against each other. I lowered it to a low drone in the background.

My internal dialogue was much more entertaining.

Jane's actions this afternoon nagged at me. Up to this point, I had always trusted her with a faith reserved for religious figures. Now, I wondered. Did she or did she not know her aunt was coming and when her aunt did appear? If she did, why then hadn't she contacted me at home to warn me?

Could it be she cared more about finding her cousin than her duties to inspecting?

Now that I've taken the case, I'd have to watch for similar actions like this from her. Personal cases drove me nuts. Emotions blurred perceptions and caused errors. One error could get one if not both of us killed.

According to the Memphis regs, Amanda was last seen leaving the mansion in Germantown, headed for her boyfriend's, Nathan, house in Memphis proper. She didn't return home that night and she didn't answer her personal telemonitor. Mayor Christensen grew nervous when Amanda didn't show up before she left to go to work the next day and contacted the Memphis regs.

A teenager not coming home wasn't the norm where I came from, but the Memphis regs didn't seem to take it too seriously that the girl was gone.

Mentally, I reviewed the case file over and over again, making sure I understood the facts, or what was presented as facts. Committing them to memory helped me separate the truth from lies when I started questioning people and digging around for information.

I finally arrived home around ten minutes after eight.

My apartment smelled dry and musty from being locked up all day. I crawled onto the sofa, reached across the sofa's right pillow, picked up my satchel and carefully pulled out my portable, handheld computer. Tiny, compared to most home computers, it was a third the size of laptops—my own little PDA. Ideas and questions popped up as I pondered the files Hanson sent. I wanted to get those down before I forgot them.

Sighing, I pressed my thumbprint into the space in the structure for thumbs and said, "Cybil Lewis". It booted up and a white, electronic blank sheet appeared. Using the attached pen, I dated the top of the electronic page, March 10, 2147.

As I did with every new case, I started taking notes almost immediately. I wrote about the client, my first impressions and the assignment chosen.

Well in this case, *forced* assignment.

Information dumping helped me when trying to piece together clues and impressions. It also served to keep me on track and made great material for client progress reports whenever I got around to actually writing them. It also showed the client that I didn't spend my time at my desk eating sandwiches. Fieldwork being what it was, the progress reports weren't always regularly scheduled or timely.

Not only that, but when I retell the story to you, I'd have accurate information. My memory isn't all it used to be, and surely you didn't think I was making this up?

My telemonitor buzzed, pulling me back from my thoughts into the icy splash of reality.

I didn't bother to check the call identifier.

"Yeah," I said as I hastily put the handheld away.

I pressed the receive button, a big red R and the screen brightened. Malcolm Moore's beautiful brown eyes loomed out from a pile of arrow-straight raven hair. Somewhere in his family genetic-tree was a fine, handsome Scot. A smile graced his face and that usually meant trouble (or work) for me.

"Cybil. My, my, my," he said in a voice that was so damn soothing. "It's been what? Two years?"

Malcolm worked for the e-news crime section for the *D.C. Mirror* "How come you don't call me, anymore?"

He wore a cobalt blue button down shirt, a black tie and a black blazer. A silver-earring dangled from his left ear and his clean-shaven face made him look younger than his thirty-six years. The earring contradicted his polished shirt and tie, but I knew that beneath the monitor's camera, he wore jeans and cowboy boots.

"Busy with work, you know," I said, but I knew Malcolm wanted something. No point in wasting time. "What do you want?"

He laughed, forcing his hair to shimmer under the fluorescent lights of his office. Behind him the sounds of typing, data drives saving and conversations provided background noise. The *D.C. Mirror* was one of the city's best newspapers.

They were still called newspapers although paper itself was rare thanks to pollution. Mutated trees made very poor stock indeed; so all newspapers were files. You could get them as attachments in email or as virtual newspapers sent to your handheld or personal telemonitors.

He cleared his throat as if sweeping out the remnants of laughter. "You were always a direct girl. I'll come to it then. The mayor of the biggest quadrant in the Southeast Territories came to see you. Why?"

I smiled as I shook my head. Unbelievable. Asking him how he knew would have been a waste of time. Malcolm's snitches numbered in the hundreds in D.C. alone, which is why he made such an excellent reporter.

His attention to detail was also brilliant.

And that made him an excellent lover.

"How is that newsworthy for the *Mirror*?" I asked as I stalled for time.

Should I tell him the nature of Christensen's visit? Why does he want to know anyway? Normally Malcolm wanted to know so he could have the information. It had nothing to do with news, necessarily. On occasion, he liked knowing things that other people didn't know.

A trait we both shared.

He grinned, flashing his white, strong teeth. "We know her daughter's missing. I covered it in last month's violators section. If Christensen is doing anything, it's automatically newsworthy. Besides, if you toss in your name and hers…the news-factor goes up from somewhat interested to damn, there's a story here."

The case was still young. To be true, I haven't even started. I could honestly (a rare event) tell Malcolm I didn't have anything for him. On the other hand, Malcolm probably knew stuff about Christensen that wouldn't be in an official regulator report.

We've traded favors before…

"So tell me what's going on," he said smoothly with a wink. "I need an exclusive. Readers are bored with the vigilante justice blood sport. But politics, abduction and sex, let's say. That sells as you well know."

I shook my head. "No, I can't tell you. I got nothing."

"After all we've been through together," he said softly, his eyes roaming over my body, passing his heat from downtown across to my living room. "You look tired. You know I can fix that..."

When Malcolm pulled out his bedroom eyes there was more to his call than he let on. He didn't only want information from me. He wanted an exclusive, which meant he thought I had more than I was giving. As I said before we have bartered and exchanged, uh, favors in the past.

"Play it straight, what are you really after?" I said, ignoring his tugs at my lust strings with amazing difficulty. My body seemed to rise up in attention to his lustful looks. Already parts of me were tingling and hardening in response.

His eyes clicked with mine and he held my gaze. The lust spilled out of them, like water released from a dam. He stroked his chin where his beard used to be. The hard edge reporter was back.

"Hang on a sec," he said thickly. He got up from his office leather chair.

I watched his perfectly tight rear-end as he got up. Then he disappeared from the telemonitor screen.

He must have shut his soundproof doors because the office din instantaneously sliced off.

Within moments, he sat back down and leaned in to his monitor, his face suddenly serious. He ran his fingers through his hair and smirked at me, fleshing out a lone dimple.

"You know the deal, Cybil. This goes no further than you and me. The cost is the same as always. Do you agree?"

"Shit, Malcolm, you called me!"

Malcolm's smile reached ear to ear. His eyebrows relaxed and he said, "You know my price. Do you want the information or not? I dunno why you're acting like you don't want to pay me."

Oh, I wanted to pay him, but my horniness was beside the point.

ꝏ

"Yeah," I said, swallowing his bait. His price meant an exclusive and some hanky panky. What he knew was worth his price. Besides, I was single and free again to exchange my time with whomever. "Deal."

"Word from Memphis is that the mayor is looking to be the next governor. Elections are in November."

I shrugged a little disappointed that it wasn't juicer information "She's good for it. Ten years as mayor. Memphis is one of the safest quads in the divided states."

Malcolm sighed, his eyebrows raised. "True, but the daughter's extracurricular activities kind of put a damper on those plans, according to some in the know down there…"

"What extracurricular activities?"

I read the regulator files on Amanda's vanishing and recited them all the way home, but there wasn't any mention of Amanda's hobbies or a criminal violation record of any kind. Even still, Memphis regs worked for Mayor Christensen. A few things may have been neglected or outright omitted to prevent scandal for the mayor, her office, or her future campaign for governor.

He continued to stare at me as if sizing me up to see if he could believe me. After a few minutes, he continued.

"The daughter, it's rumored, frequented a dance club on the moon colonies. She and her mother despised each other…something to do with the father though I can't seem to nail down the father or any stuff about him. Perhaps the girl has run off with say, an older man. Looking for daddy or a father figure?"

The moon colonies? The war-ravaged moon was no place for a young girl, especially some dance club. Come to think of it, strip bars masqueraded as dance clubs on the moon. They peddled prostitutes, pot, and pills of every kind and shade. Definitely *not* a place for a teenage girl of privilege like Amanda.

"I'll be in touch. Thanks," I said sweetly.

"Come over to the house," Malcolm said, his voice low and once again full of heat. "I'll fix you up. You know I can."

I laughed. "Malcolm."

"I'm serious." Once glance at his face and I could tell he was very serious. "You're not still dating that hatchling are you? For goodness sake, drop him. I know you miss my magic fingers…"

He raised goose bumps across my arms and I had to fight not to fall in to his web. The look he gave me now wasn't one of coy flirting; it was pure, unrestrained, fiery, I-want-to-fuck you passion.

"I'll have to take a rain check," I croaked, my throat dry. My heart slammed in my chest and I desperately wanted to feel his magic fingers dance across my back, relieving stress and stirring up desire as only Malcolm could.

"Suit yourself," he said with a deep sigh. "You still owe me."

He blew me a kiss with his thin, pink lips and the telemonitor faded to black.

CHAPTER 5

Important decisions shouldn't be made at night. The menacing gloom made thoughts monstrous and more sinister. This case rose up, full of teeth and fire, spiraling flames from its nose, threatening to devour me. As I thrashed about in tortured slumber, I dreamt of a hand closing forcefully against my neck, squeezing the air from my lungs—the nails digging deeply into my flesh.

Wednesday morning's sun invaded my bedroom like a seasoned thief, silently and effortlessly, spraying me right in the face, forcing my eyes to flap open. Under the ray's illumination, the case retreated to a tiny, harmless thing, and nowhere near as frightening.

Relaxed, I fell back into a light doze. The sun's rays warmed my face. I slept until my alarm blared.

I jumped and regretted the sudden movements. I buried my head under the pillows and again swore at whoever invented alarm clocks. I'd forgotten to turn off the blasted bleating beast, but now that it had gone off, I was fully awake.

The buzzing of the telemonitor infiltrated my pillows' defenses and groaning I clambered out of bed, dragged myself into the living room to answer the call.

"Hello," I said, seeing Jane's face on the caller identifier.

Her face failed to hide her surprise, and her eyes roamed over my scanty clad pj's, before meeting my eyes. "Aunt Belle will be here in twenty minutes. You're goin' to be freakin' late again!"

My recently cut braids were tied back in a ponytail. They

used to be waist length, but I found it distracting, heavy, and time consuming. It was like walking around with a small child hanging on your neck. Now they reached just past my shoulders. My black pj's fit like a glove, exposing a lot of leg, arm and belly. Barefoot, sleepy, and annoyed, I sat down Indian fashion on the sofa. "So…"

"So you said you wanted to meet with her today at one," Jane said back. Already awake and dressed in a black sweater with muddy brown corduroys, her sullen expression matched perfectly. Her dreadlocks, free and unrestrained, spilled over her slender, athletic shoulders. "It's already noon!"

A smile tugged at the corners of my mouth. I didn't do mornings. That didn't stop Jane from trying to rotate my internal clock to an earlier hour. I'd forgotten about the meeting with Christensen, which I made for the afternoon. 12:01 was technically no longer morning.

"I'll be there," I sighed and rubbed the sleep from my eyes. "Give me a few minutes. I did say one o'clock. If she shows up at 12:20, I'm not late. She's early."

I opened my eyes soon enough to see Jane's eyebrows rise in question.

"A few minutes?" she scoffed. "You're practically naked."

I laughed. "Okay, about twenty minutes. I'll be there before one. How about that?"

8

Half an hour later, I walked into the office. Mayor Christensen stood in front of Marsha's desk, her arms folded over her blinding winter white suit. Her deep, blood red nail polish glistened under the room's lights. Her media perfect smile greeted me and I tried to force the grimace from my own face.

I gave her my best, professional smile, devoid of meaning as a wauto's headlight, but sparkling.

"Miss Lewis, we meet again," she said coolly, her breath smelling strongly of mint. "Thank you for accepting my daughter's case. I trust Captain Hanson forwarded you the necessary files?"

"Yes, he did. They arrived safely." Detesting her again as if yesterday wasn't enough, I fought to keep myself in line. "He was quite prompt in getting them to me. Thank you."

I walked around to Marsha's desk and pulled out a contract. Contracts helped with clients because they outlined what I would and would not do and what to expect. The handheld weighed less than three pounds and provided a video explanation of what to expect. Contrary to some legends, I am not a miracle worker. There are limits on my abilities and time.

She took the handheld and watched the video clip. When it ended, she typed her name briskly and signed the contract, her nails clicking on the metal device. Her signature was comprised of several illegible loops and spirals.

"You do understand that I may not be able to find her, especially if she doesn't want to be found?"

The last point I said firmly and clearly courtesy of Malcolm Moore. The idea that Amanda may have simple run away from home should be a possibility and one that Christensen should entertain. I was.

But I wasn't the girl's mother, either.

"What is that supposed to mean?" she balked, her eyebrow arched in surprise. "Mandy never would have left on her own! She loved Memphis!"

It struck me as odd that her mother said Amanda loved Memphis, not "me". I wanted her reaction and I got it although I couldn't tell is she was acting or truly disgusted by the implication that Amanda didn't like being at home. Mayor Christensen was used to playing a role.

And I was good at spotting cracks in those performances.

"All I'm saying is that when I call it quits, it's quits," I said, making sure to look her in the face so she knew I was serious. "No questions, no threats. It's done when I say so."

"I watched the video, Miss Lewis," she said, her hazel eyes narrowed. "I am not a simpleton."

With that said, she opened her purse and tossed the hard plastic currency card onto my desk.

I opened flipped the card over .4,000 non-district currency. The silver pressed across the back was the Southeast Governor's seal. His broad nose and fuzzy eyebrows had been streamlined and artfully corrected so that he looked less like a brute and more like a politician. I'd be able to convert it to district money, though I might get burned on the exchange rate.

"You'll be in Memphis tonight."

It wasn't a question.

It sounded more like a command.

You know me and authority.

"Remember, *mayor*," I said icily, my voice unkind, my gaze penetrating hers. "I am the inspector. I'll be in Memphis, but it won't be tonight."

She actually had the grace to blush. Her light, cream-with-coffee, complexion became rosy and she straightened her jacket. "Yes, of course. So… contact me and let me know when you arrive so that I can coordinate your efforts with Captain Hanson."

With a wave goodbye, she disappeared through the lobby's doors.

Jane's throaty voice met hers in the hall and echoed into the tight space. It was full of southern twang. Amazing how Jane could make that accent reappear and disappear like some sideshow magic trick. It usually cropped up when her family was around, which wasn't too often.

The door shut on their conversation, no doubt discussing why I wasn't going to Memphis tonight.

The throbbing, at the base of my neck, inched upward toward my head. I walked around to the area behind the alcove where Mr. Schmuckler hid, to the medicine box and took out the pain patches. The nanos in the patches had one duty—deliver the pain relievers to the central nervous system and the nerves closest to the area of injury

I smiled down at the strips. *Hurry, hurry little nanos.*The doors opened and I heard Jane come into the office. She reeked of beef and beer. Another lunch at the bar across the street. The thin kick of cigarette smoke also draped her person. Smoking wasn't allowed for those under the age of something like forty. Jane wasn't even close to that number, but it didn't stop her from participating in sucking down tobacco.

"It's about time you dragged your carcass in here," she said roughly, with a hint of humor. "I didn't want to be here when you came in so you couldn't accuse me of plotting with her."

I laughed because I deserved that jab. "Yeah, well, she didn't wait long. Plus she was early, and I wasn't late."

"Says you." Jane barked out a laugh.

She put down a plastic container. Grease stains smeared the inside of it. She came over towards me and leaned against the post. "You busy?"

I shook my head no. "I planned to go back over Amanda's files. What's up?"

"I was wondering why we couldn't leave for Memphis now," she said with a shrug as if she didn't really care when we left.

"I want to go when no one knows we're coming," I said, my patience waned. "Off balanced is how everyone should be, including your aunt, until we get a handle on who's involved and who isn't."

"Enough time has already passed!" Jane snapped. I could almost see her frustration spewing out her ears. "The trails..."

"...are cold," I said, finishing her sentence. Didn't I mention that to both her and Mayor Christensen before I took this case? "I know. Remember what I said about regulator ruined cases."

I took a deep breath and let it out leisurely. Jane has never questioned my decisions before with this vigor and frequency.

See why I detest personal cases?

"You need to remember this is a caselike any other," I said through clinched teeth and shoving my irritation into a far away emotional place. "Or else you won't make it through this. Not only that, but you might get us both killed. We have no room for error and that's because we're playing catch up."

No one directed me. I followed my own drummer girl.

That wasn't going to change because of Jane.

She stared at me a moment. As if noticing my struggle not to smack her, she rolled her eyes. "Keep your panties on, I know."

"Good. We'll leave tomorrow around two," I said, pushing past her and going to my private office to dig once again into Amanda Christensen's life. "Be ready."

Memphis, here I come.

CHAPTER 6

I removed my laser gun 350 from the wall safe hidden in my private office. The safe confidently ejected from the wall when I gave both a retinal scan, DNA via saliva, and a fingerprint confirmation. Not that I felt this kept my prized possessions totally safe. The unsettling thought that my dead body could be used to give all three sometimes kept me awake at night. I placed the sack from Mayor Christensen in the box and that's where it would stay until I used it all.

The gun had more firepower than the pug...almost too much. Crafted by Smith & Wesson, it punched large, gaping holes in people and obliterated small animals. The laser gun 350 was a bit too big for my hands. I almost never use it, but keep it locked up so that no one could break in and pawn it for silver, drugs or other more lethal weapons.

With the pug in my ankle holster and the 350 in my new shoulder holster, I was feeling all right and protected. Fate smiled on me. I managed to escape the office before the sun fully sank into the horizon. It sprayed the sky with a reddish pink that reminded me of watery blood. With any luck, I would beat the traffic over to Padre's Gym. I glanced once more around the darkened office before locking up. Almost immediately, my thoughts returned to Amanda Christensen as they had done for the last day. I didn't want to think about Montano right now. It could have been a crank call he made from the cradle, or someone who had pieced together his voice clips into a frightening harmonious message to terrorize me.

I had plenty of enemies.

The T.A. had people who specialized in doing that very thing. And if Mr. Schmuckler didn't believe that no meant no, he might succumb to strong-arming me via terror tactics.

It wouldn't be the first time someone tried to bully me into doing what he wanted. Not that it happened often, but it did happen.

With these cheery thoughts, I entered the elevator and pressed the number one button. No one got on and it did not stop until I reached the first floor. As I exited the building, wind whipped with whistling sounds as I walked across the lot to the only remaining wauto. Mine. A whirlwind of garbage tumbled by like urban tumbleweeds. The odor of urine, grime and trash scented the air. Ah, eau de East Side D.C.

My coat billowed outward because I had only buttoned the bottom three buttons. I wanted to be able to get to the 350 without difficulty in case Montano was out through some big ass loop hole in the justice system.

My eyes watered up from the damn cold, but better to be cold now than dead later.

Nervous? Who me?

Nah, just prepared.

As I reached my vehicle, my skin itched as if someone was watching me. It prickled and the sensation blanketed my arms and legs. I searched the area around me in the fading sunlight as I took out my 350. I climbed into the wauto, and checked the backseats for possible, uninvited guests.

No one.

Nevertheless, I closed and locked the wauto's doors and flew over to the gym with frequent glances back in the rearview mirror. The 350 rested on the passenger seat, within arm's reach all the way to Padre's. The wauto's shield iced up with regularity and limited my ability to see clearly. I lessened my speed to only ten over the speed limit to be cautious. I cranked up the heater in an attempt to melt off the ice.

My thoughts slid from Amanda to Mayor Christensen. At

some point, it would be necessary for me to get unbiased information about the good ole mayor. Jane usually scoured snitches and the world wide web for information on suspects and clients. She couldn't be trusted with this one. Her "Aunt Belle" was a role model of sorts.

Night came swiftly and with its arrival came bitter cold. March in DC. meant black ice, frigid temperatures, and taxes. The howling wind outside contributed to the ice-cold temperature. I could feel the arctic weather through the wauto's windows like invisible fingers stroking my face with cold tips.

The new year had arrived with the usual ruckus of people making absolute fools of themselves along with the predictable resolution making. This year, I vowed to do more exercise (doesn't everybody?), and that meant working out six times a week instead of four. I'd been pretty consistent due to lack of really daring, time-hungry cases.

A few blocks from my apartment was a man-made beach. It was more like a pile of dirt and a sunken water hole. Some of the real oceans and beaches had either been swept away over time or were so contaminated that to inhale the air around them would kill you. A short distance off the beach, the city resurrected a park. I guess to allow the neighborhood residents to participate in nature's glory. The park came complete with a little creek and an abandoned trail. The trail snaked upward to the local Trillian Hills, an area of steep hills and woodland. In the summer, spring and warming part of fall, I jogged through the park.

But in the frigid winter weather, I worked out at Padre's gym. A sleek, new arena devoted to the chore of exercise. Padre's membership fee ranked among the ludicrous, but it sure beat icicles hanging from your arms and nose when trying to jog.

Not that I was vain or really concerned about my looks. Anyone who has seen my wardrobe knew that. No one would ever accuse me of being petite or skinny, no matter how much weight I lost.

For me, exercise wasn't about weight loss. I stood at five feet ten inches. I had large bones and a well-defined waist. Back in time when food was scarce, I would be considered an ideal mate for I was filled out in all the right places. The African in my bloodline gave me a rear-end that would have been worshiped for its fertility in my ancestors' lands.

Riiiight.

For me exercise was about strength training and endurance. In this business, I often found myself up against bad guys who didn't think twice about punching, slicing or stabbing a woman. I considered my workouts defense mechanisms. Occasionally, I could outlast and out maneuver a bad guy (or naughty girl).

Padre's took up most of the block between Fifty-first and Summer. They had replaced their indoor pool with a larger one that contained illuminated, underwater lap lanes. Just thinking about it made me speed up. Swimming was a pleasant, full-body workout, and one that I enjoyed immensely.

Outside snow fell softly to the ground creating a hush among the streets. The area resembled a Christmas card, with everything covered in pristine snow. Piles of snow towered along the sidewalks and street parking spaces in city snowdrifts. I sat down my wauto next to this rather new model Honda wauto with sunless tinted windows and nice, shiny blasters, the color of silver.

The 350 went back into my shoulder holster. I didn't want the wauto's windshields broken by some ack-addict yearning for a fix to break in and pawn it for district dollars.

Quickly, I pulled up my braids into a ponytail and wound them into a bun with a thick rubberband, leaving the back of my neck exposed. I climbed out of my wauto, determined to sweat or swim away the day's drama. Moments after my door went *click*, I felt the frosty metal lips of a gun on my neck.

A hand grabbed my elbow, as I went for my gun.

"Tsk, tsk, Cinnamon," said my attacker and instantly I felt my blood pump harder. "Wouldn't want to hurt an old friend, would you?"

"Nothing, I'd like better," I muttered back. The taste in my mouth turned sour. Fear laced my tongue, metallic, thick.

"Hands up!" he barked, slamming the gun into my neck for emphasis.

I clinched my teeth in fury. Slowly, I removed my hand from my coat and held my palms up and out to my shoulders—ready for the crucifixion.

"What do you want, Jarold?" I asked, as I turned to face the demon that haunted my nightmares and forced me to awake in a cold sweat. My voice was thin with panic.

The streetlight showed his face tight with threat. He reeked of marijuana and beer.

Great. Not only was he armed, but he was high and possibly drunk.

He swayed with the wind, his funky brown hair, curly and short, stood out in odd angles, and his eyes held that glassiness that came with drug usage. A faded, stained sweatshirt and dirty jeans were not trademark issued from the cradle. They looked like they'd been removed from a neighborhood garbage can.

And not the wealthy neighborhood either.

With a grin, he said, "Didn't get my message?"

"No," I said sharply, perhaps too sharply for he laughed again.

Or it could be the wacky weed gave him the giggles?

He pressed his forearm against my throat, while his free hand slid under my coat, searching for my weapon. Once he removed it, he took his forearm away.

He held it high in the air. The moon's silvery light reflected across the area. "This is a big gun for such a fine woman as you Cinnamon. A 350!"

He put my gun in his belt like some western cowboy. The skin around his mouth at the corner began to pulsate, as if he was nervous.

Despite the iciness of the night, he didn't wear a coat.

His grin widened and he slipped his hand in my coat and under my shirt. The feel of his fingers on my skin made me nauseous. His dirty fingers traced circles across my stomach and up and around to my back.

"I'm here to give, Cinnamon," he whispered and licked my face. "Maybe to *take...*" He pressed closer to me, his hips grinding into me. His phallus grew hard against my thigh, rubbing without pause, forcing me to gag into the cold air.

Repulsion and burning hate propelled my arm and I swiftly took my right hand and shoved his face backward as hard as I could. "Bastard! Kill me and get it over with!"

He stumbled and then regained his balance. With a shaky hand he pointed his gun, a laser gun 325, maybe smaller, at me. "What's the matta? I ain't perfect enough for you?"

Cautiously, he inched closer to me. A drop of sweat slowly ran down his face.

Once he came within arm's reach, he said, "Dangerous, ain't you? I loooove it when you struggle."

"Jarold," I said softly. Forcing myself to stay cool, I puckered my lips and said, "Let me make it better."

His eyes narrowed to suspicious slivers, but he couldn't resist himself. He hadn't been with a woman in what, five years?

Once he leaned in to kiss me, he closed his eyes. A natural habit.

I grabbed a handful of his greasy hair, feeling its sliminess in my hands, and bought my knee upward, smashing his face into it. His eyes flew opened in shock.

Blood spurted out like a faucet from his nose. He wildly pointed his gun back at me. His eyes were black and alive with fiery coals of pain.

"Oh, oww, you broke it you nasty bitch!" he growled.

The broken nose should have stopped him long enough for me to go for the pug.

But it wasn't.

Jarold's smile, bloody and sinister, widened. His weapon fluttered in his hand like a captured bird.

"Nervous?" I asked.

"No, oh, no," he said dawdling. His face sobered swiftly, like the sands of an Etch-a-sketch. "Anxious, Cinnamon. Do you know how long I dreamed of this? Of my beam piercing those beautiful brown breasts and your heart? Watching you take your last breath?"

He licked the blood from his chapped lips.

My eyes drifted down and the animal still had an erection!

"Jarold, listen, whatever you know, I don't care or want it," I said slowly, giving him my its-your-lucky-night smile. The anger from a few moments before receded and in its place was icy-cold fear. "Can I just go?"

"No, oh no, Cinnamon," he leaned in and pressed the barrel to my heart. His hardness rubbed against my thigh and I had to quell the urge to vomit. My stomach did a flip-flop, and I swallowed hard.

My mind whirled for ideas, strategies for I had been here with Jarold before. He still had my weapon and his…

Outgunned.

Damn.

I did have the pug in my ankle holster. Hmm…he didn't pat me down.

"Oh, how easy it would be," he whispered, his eyes swimming in their sockets. "But it ain't to be tonight, Cinnamon."

"My name is Cybil," I said, my voice like ice. My rising rage melting my terror. "Either shoot or allow me to leave. I'm late for an appointment."

He frowned. He head did this jerky shake as if he hadn't

heard me properly. He laughed a rich sound that ended with a hysterical, coughs that had him bent over, shaking. His gun remained trained on me, pressed into my chest. I thought about smashing my knee into his face again, but he spat a wad of phlegm onto the street and he righted himself up so fast I missed my opportunity.

"Believe me, if it was up to me, I'd lick your blood as it pumps out after I shoot your lovely ass. But, I got orders to follow."

At the mention of this, he glanced back quickly over his shoulder into the smoky night.

"What? Somebody finally put you on a chain?"

"You could say that," he replied. He pulled back a few steps and without warning punched me in the face.

Spots littered my visions as my head whipped to the right. I shook it off as best I could as I turned back to him. I swallowed and tried to breath through the pain. A left hand hook...closed fist. Bastard. Damn, that was going to leave a mark.

"Now listen, your boy, Trey, is in deep shit. You know where he is?" Jarold's eyes took on that far away look those who are bored get.

"For starters, he isn't my *boy*. And no, I don't know where he is." I braced myself for another punch from him. He couldn't do it for long because we were on a public street. Someone was bound to pop out of the shops and see him.

A romantic couple we weren't.

"You ain't tellin' the truth," he said. A loopy grin appeared on his face and he slapped me.

My left cheek seared with sharp pain. I could feel the inside of my jaw scrape against my teeth. I didn't see it coming and I fell to the ground, overdoing the actual impact of his strike. I lifted my pants' leg, took out the pug, my body blocking my actions as I collapsed to the icy ground.

What was I saying about being prepared?

"Get up, bitch!" he shouted. "Don't fuck with me Cinnamon. I'll beam your ass!"

I caught a quick look at him as he reached down to grab me. I swung around, swinging my left leg outward, knocking his legs from underneath him.

He fell with a loud *crack,* my 350 scattered across the frigid pavement, out of his waist.

I shot up and stepped on his wrist until he let go of his 325.

"Who sent you?" I asked, my resolve shrinking. I could kill him and have legal justification too. He deserved it if anyone ever did.

But vigilante justice wasn't my thing. Justice system may be flawed, but it was some sort of attempt to put away the bad people.

Somewhere in the surrounding scenery, doors hissed closed. I heard giggling, but I was too distracted to look up or around.

I kicked his piece far away from his reach. He growled and hissed at me, spittle ran down his chin. "You're going to be sorry, Cinnamon..."

My ears burned with icy numbness and my fingers stiffened around the pug.

"Who?" I demanded, applying more pressure, rubbing my heel into his flesh. "Talk, Jarold...you seemed so damn eager earlier."

His lips trembled and the blood formed tiny clumps of reddish ice on his face. "Screw you. She'd kill me and it ain't worth it."

"She?" I hissed as I leaned down closer to his face. I flipped my pug around and raised the butt of it up into the air. "She who?"

He moaned, but did not confess his employer, how he got out of the cradle or why he thought I knew Trey's whereabouts. But he was going to tell me, even if it was through broken teeth.

"What are you doing?" called a man in a brown coat and hat. He emerged fully from a coffee shop that looked closed. He resembled the insurance salesman in my building, but from here he could've looked like Elvis.

I looked over to the man.

Dumb move.

Jarold punched me from the side—mind you the same left side—sending me reeling sideways to the unyielding asphalt. I could feel the blacktop strip away flesh as I used my face and hands to break my fall. I rolled over and groaned. My hands seared with pain. My fist still gripped the pug as layers of skin were scraped off my knuckles, hands and face.

I landed awkwardly on the right arm. It tingled and then went numb. The sharp pain drilled into my upper torso.

That definitely was going to leave a mark...Correction, *marks*.

Jarold laughter was bitter, like broken glass. It seemed to come from way down the block.

"Miss, are you okay?" the man hurried toward me, his steps sloshing in the brown slush of snow.

"Yes, no thanks to you," I said, bitterly. I jerked up and pointed the pug at the man's scarred face. He looked like he didn't get many dates. "Don't come any closer, you punce. Back the fuck up!"

Startled, the man ran away, slipping and sliding, up toward Padre's.

When I glanced back to my wauto, Jarold was gone.

CHAPTER 7

Sweaty partially clothed bodies continued to workout in bliss, oblivious to my attack. The boom of the music's back track pounded from beneath the glass like a hyped up heart beat. It then burst into a pulsating frenzy. From here, the spaces in the frosty glass windows revealed several women running on the treadmills that overlooked Fifty-first. Their make-up applied perfectly as the perspiration glistened from underneath.

My face hurt and knuckles ached.

Slowly, I picked up my 350 from its end destination several feet from the wauto. I reholstered the pug for the third time in two days as I wondered who sicced Jarold on me. Every inch of my body screamed in agony as I opened the door with my left hand. My right still tingled and I could see reddish-white patches from where the skin had been scraped clean off and only the muscle, tissue remained.

Female. A she, he said. He was even ready to take my beam rather than tell more. High as a kite and more than a little drunk, Jarold may have been blowing smoke, but someone with clout and power got him out of Frazier's.

Great. A free roaming psychopath psyched out on drugs plagued the streets and innocent pedestrians.

The bigger question, as I carefully climbed into the driver's seat, was how did he get out of Frazier's? His sentence carried a minimum of thirty years. He'd served less than ten. The parole board would have notified me if they knew he'd escaped.

I sighed and again felt the sting of every single abrasion. I leaned over to press the button above the glovebox and felt gritted my teeth as my muscles moaned in protest. The glovebox gradually lowered as if it hadn't been oiled in ages. Inside were a medical kit, a box knife, and a back up battery to my handheld.

In the hush quiet of the wauto, I could feel my body groan in anguish.

The wauto's doors clicked as they automatically locked and I opened the medical kit. I surveyed my hands. They didn't look as bad as they felt. Inside the glovebox were bandages and an extra large pain patches. Already my cheek swelled and threatened to force my right eye to close. A dark, nearly midnight colored bruise appeared. Great, tomorrow it would be good and black.

I peeled back two patches and gingerly placed them on. Putting the adhesive across the bones hurt too. Hell even swallowing burned due to Jarold's forearm pressure.

The sharp pain between my shoulder blades stretched outward like a butterfly's wings, wide and colorful. I couldn't see them, but I knew a startling array of bluish black bruises dotted my back too. Each inch of my body wailed in sharp smarting agony.

All I wanted was to go home and soak in a hot, soothing bath.

I patched up my right hand and forearm, making sure to be gentle. I looked like I had stolen a mummy's right arm. My face was another matter. The ground had scraped off thin strips of flesh from my right cheek. So I had a bruise on the left and nail thin scraps on the right. My face had definitely seen better days.

Padre's, the office, and my apartment all resided on the East Side of D.C. I pressed the start button and ignited the flight sequence. Lifting the wauto into the air, all I could think of was home and getting to safety. Thinking I would be home in minutes made me smile despite the stinging to my face.

Icy flecks of snow melted and zipped down my back, creating chills and reminding me of where Jarold had touched me.

Shivering, I turned up the heat to six, but I still felt clammy and really pissed.

The illuminated lanes hovered in the air and provided a clear path home.

The drive to my place went painfully slow despite the clear lanes. Driving with my left hand isn't something I do everyday, and I kept checking my mirrors and circling the block, trying to shake any possible T.A. henchmen or worst still, Jarold. He wasn't a complete idiot.

The automatic pilot function was offline, busted by a hacker who I was investigating. He successfully fried my autopilot's system.

Finally, I arrived at home and set down the wauto in the space assigned to me outside my apartment building. I hurried across the lot to the entranceway between corridors that covered the vehicles from the ills of the elements. My building missed some of the last one hundred years of technology. Sure it had an elevator, but only a few doors were automatic and nothing was computer automated.

I took the creaky, decrepit elevator up to the fourth floor. Alone, no one entered the elevator, which was a relief. I despised elevator conversations. Sometimes, I'd get the new male renter looking to fulfill his fantasy of having sex in the damn contraption. Other times I'd get stuck with the lonely grandmother whose kids have moved to other territories and only sent her pictures and emails.

I exited and walked down the hallway to my apartment.

The trek seemed longer than usual due to my aching, throbbing body.

At last I reached my door only to find Jane leaning against it.

"Been waitin' a long time for you," she said. She wore her

glossy black bomber and black, steel-toed combat boots she kept from the Marines. Her eyes were puffy and the inside of them was lined in red. "I see you've been busy."

I laughed and immediately wished I hadn't. My face erupted into painful flashes where the temporarily formed scabs scrunched down and ripped open.

Jane moved away from my door. "So, what happened?" she asked.

We went inside and I dropped my coat onto the sofa. The cold, closed in air hurt to breathe and I hurried to switch on the heating unit's weak system. Almost at once it started wheezing out puffs of cool streams instead of the warmth I sought.

"Jarold Montano jumped me outside Padre's gym."

"What?" Jane balked as she sat down on my big orange sofa. "He's out!"

My living room consisted of a sofa, a rustic wooden rocker and a glass coffee table with metallic legs. Two floor-to-ceiling lamps occupied the left and right side of the corner walls. And mounted to the wall between the lamps was a new 27" telemonitor. It was a mere four inches wide and the plasma rippled in crisp waves.

With the pay out and reward money for the Change case, I updated my place a little too. After all, some goons trashed it during the course of the investigation. Therefore, the upgrade included a new security system.

I headed to the kitchen and pulled a bottle of Peck beer out of the refrigerator. It relieved stress, but I was solely a two bottle a week girl. No lush here.Only your friendly neighborhood inspector with a buzz.

"Yeah, he's out," I called back to Jane. Even to me I sounded tired. Raspy, my words escaped in scraps against the air—nothing solid. Damn, it hurt to talk.

I went back into the living room and carefully lowered my throbbing body into the rocker. It belonged to my grandmother and it was rare. Cradling my beer and holding my right hand high in the air, I closed my eyes to await the need of the pain.

"I hate to add to your lovely night, but I've got problems," she said.

I opened my eyes. Couldn't she see I did too?

Jane shoved her hands into her dreadlocks and gave them a good shake. She'd recently had them cut so that now they reached the small of her back. They were sprawled over her shoulders like a jet-black and blonde shawl.

I twisted off the bottle's cap and took a long drink. The living room lay in partial shadowiness. Only a small circle of light from the left lamp arced across Jane, casting her into silhouette, the other part in the spotlight. I waited for her to tell me her professed problems.

Nothing. She stared up at the ceiling.

"Anything you want to talk about?" I asked, prompting because I didn't want to be up all night waiting for Jane to get around to it.

She smelled like cigarettes and food. Her sunglasses were perched back on her head. With a long, slow sigh, she said, "No."

"Sure?" I asked, keeping my voice even although fatigued threatened to lure me to sleep and my bath called to me. "You did say you had something like problems to talk to me about"

"Yeah."

I wasn't convinced and she knew it. Only in her early twenties, Jane flat out rejected any attempts at love, but family, she kept them even closer to her vest. She seemed to prefer apathy and solitude although she did spend a lot of time with me.

But that was work.

And all work and no play made Jane a dull girl.

Although friends, she wouldn't have come clear across town to sit in my apartment.

"You might as well tell me," I said lightly with a grin that stung like the dickens.

Her face crouched down in a mash of fuming attitude.

"All right," she said as she flopped back to the sofa. "Aunt Belle called. The Memphis regs have escalated Mandy's disappearance to critical. They found her shirt, the last one she was seen wearing, balled up in a bag outside the mall she frequented. There are blood droplets on it."

"How'd they know it was hers?" I asked. "Must be hundreds of girls wearing denim shirts these days...unless they matched the blood."

"Aunt Belle didn't believe either...at first. But Mandy had her initials embroidered on the sleeve and yeah, they pulled her DNA from the blood and sweat found on the shirt," Jane said, her voice breaking. "It's hers. No doubt."

I sipped the beer, feeling the knot in my stomach twist tighter as I listened. I didn't like where this was going, but the forces-that-be gave me a hard nudge.

"We need to get down there. Let's leave tomorrow at seven," I said, hating the early time, but feeling the pressure to be in Memphis soon. Droplets of blood were definitely not good.

"Fine," she snapped, her head down. Her dreads acted as a curtain between us.

"What else is eating you?" I asked, a little disappointed that my suggestion to get up early didn't make her feel better. After all, I was sacrificing my sleep. I bet she wanted to leave tonight, but tonight I needed to recoup. Fix my arm and get myself ready for the trip down. Leaving D.C. might not be such a bad idea since Jarold was out.

"I'm pissed," she finished abruptly. "I tried to call you, but got worried when I didn't get you. So I came over. And you were out dancing with Jarold Montano."

She stood up and put on her sunglasses.

It was about nine o'clock at night.

"You look like crap, but you're alive."

"Thanks," I said.

I watched her leave, knowing inside that she hadn't told me everything.

CHAPTER

After Jane left, I lay down on the sofa and tried to get a handle on the day's hairy sequence of events. For months, I was doing nothing more than boring work that involved wayward husbands and or boyfriends (sometimes girlfriends and wives). Nothing exciting, simply capturing images and reporting them like a first year newspaper reporter.

Then BAM! Everything erupted and demanded my immediate attention.

I got up from the sofa to get another beer and some more pain patches. If the nanos didn't kick in hard enough, I was going to have to inject the acetaminophen. Normally, I didn't take so many of the things, but this week was already shaping up to be quite the bottle opener. I located my private stash of needles and neat, cute clear liquid-filled bottles and loaded up one of the needles before having a second cold beer.

As I stood at the sink, waiting for the new patches to kick in, I filled it with soap warm water and removed the bandages from my right hand. They were bloodied anyway. Without thinking about it, I shoved my hand into the water with the hopes that soaking it would somehow make it better.

Searing pain shot through me. Gritting my teeth, I kept my hand in the water, watching it shake uncontrollably from the raw agony and feel my knees weaken against the flooding anguish.

My kitchen wasn't big enough for a dining table and I wouldn't know what to do with one if it was. I did have a small, round breakfast table with two mismatched chairs. I removed my hand and with a towel, dried it off carefully. I sat down and closed my eyes as I felt the tiny nanos slither across my fingers.

My new sink was gray and clean.

Gray like Trey's eyes.

Trey. Perfect hatchling and T.A. agent.

Missing.

&

Christmas night in the desert was both warm and scary. The Southwest Territories loomed in a warm spell because of an extremely kind breeze from the Pacific Ocean. The usual dry heat had been peeled back to a comfortable 75 degrees…almost beach weather.

Paper snowmen danced in the breeze and appeared to fly from Trey's backyard deck. Lanterns and luminaries illuminated the twilight, with help from the full moon above. The smell of popcorn and candy canes scented the atmosphere. Trey's cottage lay tucked in a thicket of trees in the middle of some wooded acreage sprouting from the usual arid land. All around darkness provided a tapestry of beauty...crickets sang, copper and reddish turned leaves rustled, and music filtered out, soft and soothing, from hidden outdoor speakers. Out here, I could see the stars twinkle and wink down from the heavens. No light pollution in the wide, open spaces of the Southwest high desert. You could look up into the midnight-blue and see all the way to other worlds unknown and undiscovered…almost. The low roar of wautos and aerocycles could be heard like the buzzing of bugs far off in the distance.

Trey wore rugged jeans and a soft, cable knit gray sweater that made his already smoky colored eyes more gray like the fog that rose from the hills in the morning. His full lips tasted like candy canes and his hands felt like rose petals.

We reclined in an oversized loveseat on his deck overlooking a tiny, man-made pond. I drank warm cocoa and thought that life couldn't get any better than this.

Because of the nature of our professions, our schedules rarely synced, and this sliver of time belonged solely to us. I relished it, reveled in it, and wore it about my shoulders like a favorite sweater, close and tight.

His hand held mine, my gun rested in my ankle holster, as we studied the sky.

This indeed was the life.

I shifted to get more comfortable and my gun peeked out from beneath the coal belt of my charcoal trousers.

"Do you have to carry your gun everywhere?" he asked, his voice velvety soft. "You're not working now are you?"

"My gun stays whether I'm working or not."

The breeze kissed my face that was suddenly damp with sweat despite the cool air. I could feel it coming, and I didn't want to engage him in this kind of conversation. I'd had it with other lovers in the past and I thought Trey was above it. The over protectiveness that men seemed to whip out against women they deemed incapable of protecting themselves, lay unspoken between us.

"Why? I'm here. You're safe," he said, his voice turning hard.

"I don't need you to protect me," I said. I tried to keep the defensiveness out of my voice. Still his face wrinkled in annoyance.

I sat up and removed my hand from his. The gun wasn't new to him so why the argument? Did he want to fight with me on purpose? Why?

If he was over the relationship, which I admit was strained by distance, by devotion we shared and by desire that erupted with fervor when we were together, then why not say that? I was a big girl, and I could take it.

"I know how tough you are, but we're here, relaxing," he explained, eyes on something far in the distance (or right beside him). "And not even for a few minutes, you could remove the bloody thing!"

It went on like this for the better part of an hour with the both of us escalating in both temperament and accusations.

I could forgive many sins and mistakes, except two: infidelity and overprotectiveness. My job rested on my ability to keep sharp, and I've crossed many bad people and violators in my long past as a private inspector. My gun stayed closer to my heart than most lovers I've held in my bed.

Crowding made me feel trapped. Relationships and I danced in an uneasy swing, not really touching or succeeding to the point that we were close enough to embrace.

What was it about men that they couldn't accept a woman doing things for herself?

"If it bothers you so much that I don't fit your rosy-colored vision of a traditional relationship, then we shouldn't date any more," I said angrily. As soon as I said the words, I wanted them back.

"Done!" he said, his eyes round and full of hurt. He got up from the seat and disappeared into the house. The outer doors making a quiet hush as he cleared the threshold. His mug of cocoa long since cold rested on the deck's railing…abandoned.

I didn't mean to hurt him. I liked him very much, but he wanted the image, the dream girl that depended on him to provide a house, to marvel at his abilities, and to be a good wife.

That's never been me.

༄

And it wasn't me now. I thought of the image of Holly Homemaker packing a gun and a black belt in karate.

Yeah, right.

CHAPTER

9

I snapped awake when I heard my door slide open. Or was I dreaming?

I must have dozed off as I sat at the kitchen table. My whole body felt stiff, and the soaking didn't make my hands feel any better. It felt like I was peeling the skin off my fingers. Nevertheless, I had put an antibiotic ointment on them and wrapped them back up in bandages before sitting down at the table to finish off the beer.

Exhausted, I slept while sitting up. The bruises on my face and ones along the right side of my body pulsated in some brain choreographed performance.

The lights were out and the place lay in darkness. The kitchen clock read the time as a little bit before midnight. I knew I hadn't shut them off before going into the kitchen and dozing on the table.

So who did?

I reached down and gently took the pug out of my ankle holster. I crept into the living room. Humbly and a little irked by the fact that someone had already picked my lock and beat my upgraded security system, I winced against the smarting twinges. Cursing to myself, I frowned, irritating my scabs.

I slipped into the room, my pug held high and my body sluggish and stiff.

Immediately I realized it didn't feel right. With a hurried leap, I reached one of the two living room lamps and flicked it on to reveal an uninvited guest.

"Stop!" I shouted, my heartbeat mounting into a frenzied

gallop. I tried to swallow the large, sudden lump in my throat. Droplets of sweat appeared on my skin. My tongue moved lazily as if swollen.

No one broke in.

The idiot still had his key.

"Were you followed?" I asked cheerlessly over the pounding of my heart. "Were you?"

He shook his head no. Along the left end of the sofa, he rested, his head reclined against the sofa's burnt orange cushions, and his legs crossed at the ankles. His eyes closed as if for once he lay at peace.

"Trey," I said, my hands sweaty, the gun swinging from my left hand. What could I say to him? "What are you -"

He sat up. Dressed in all black, he still managed to steal the breath from my lungs. The v-neck sweater revealed his double helix tattoo that branded him a hatchling. The strong sent of musk and old sweat filled the apartment. A little tattered around his edges, Trey protruded the unmanaged sexuality of someone confident and accustomed to it.

"Cybil, I would not have come here if I had some place else to go," he said, his voice soft and amazingly tranquil. "My underground escort won't be available until tomorrow. All I need is a night, one night to lay low. You can't give me that?"

His bright gray eyes studied me and lingered on my face, trailing over the bruise on my cheek and along the edge of my jawline, the scratches across my right cheek. They zipped down to my battered hand, and across to the other, equally injured left.

The lines around his mouth deepened, and his eyes narrowed.

"What happened to you?" he asked, voice tight with anger.

"Not your problem," I said, trying to stop him from changing the subject. "Tell me what's going on. I haven't seen you in months."

The rocking chair was opposite the sofa, so that I could see him. Sitting next to him was out of the question. One touch from him would be too hard to resist.

Right now I needed to focus on what he told me. The fact that a T.A. agent came to my office searching for him, only reinforced that they wanted him too. His whereabouts ranked as important or imperative to them.

Normally, lying was a habit, and something I did well. I didn't want the T.A. thinking I'd lied to them about Trey. They simply had too much power. Couple that with Jane's pulling a gun on one of their agents, and I was already in hot water with them.

Trey had lost some weight, but not much. His ability to heal was serving him well.

"I was fired by the T.A...It started about ten months ago. Been a crazy few months. First you dump me and --"

"I didn't dump you," I interjected. The words were out of my mouth like horses at the Louisville Quadrant's Derby of Roses. Fired up and anxious, I tried to breathe out slowly to keep my mouth closed. Talking wasn't nearly as necessary as listening.

"...and then I get fired," he said as if he didn't hear me.

Butterflies fluttered in my stomach. I held my hands together to keep them from trembling or from reaching out to him. He seemed so doleful and scared. My arms wanted to hold him and to pull him close to me.

Focus, Cybil, focus...why is he here?

I took in one deep steadying breath and waited for him to continue.

He briskly rubbed his face, but did not say anything else.

"Would you like something to drink?" I asked him, feeling an overwhelming need to get out of the room. "Beer, water, and, well, that's it."

"Water," he said as he closed his eyes again.

Fatigued? Probably. How could he rest when several groups were out to kill him?

I fled into the kitchen, my hands shaking as I grabbed a bottled water from the refrigerator. As if prompted by my movements, the butterflies whipped around in unrest. I took more cavernous breaths, trying to calm my rapid heart rate.

My libido had kicked in to overdrive. The sound of his voice had reactivated my lust. Already my stomach tightened and that special, moist warmth which came with being horny caused me to perspire. Hell, I was panting like a mutt in heat.

With carefully placed steps, I walked back into the living room and handed the water to him. His fingers brushed mine causing my stomach to quiver all the more.

He drank huge, thirsty gulps of the water. My eyes watched those long drinks glide down—gulp after gulp of ice-cold aqua—his throat, forcing the flawless skin to move up and down as lovers under covers do. When he sat it on the coffee table, it was three-quarters empty.

"Ahhh. That hit the spot. Thank you," he said, his eyes skipping over my face and around the apartment. "Haven't done much with the place."

"No, I'm too busy," I said sharply, feeling the hair on my neck rise up. "Tell me what's going on. Quit stalling and spill it. This isn't a casual visit. Stop pretending it is."

He grimaced and stood up. As he walked around the sofa, I thought he was going to leave, but he didn't. He pivoted around and walked back to the end of the sofa. Pacing, he folded his hands behind his head.

"The agency received some complaints about me," he said dully, his voice extremely low and quiet. He paused long enough to toss me a a glance. He commenced at once.

I bent forward to hear, straining my ears to capture each word.

"The people were high up in quadrant governments."

"Governor level?" I asked, interrupting his explanation. The highest level in all the quadrants was governor.

He shrugged his brawny, square shoulders, drawing the

sweater fabric taut against him. "Don't know. The complaints were anonymous and false anyway."

"What kind of complaints? Sexual?" I felt like I was interrogating a witness, which gave me an odd feeling, for Trey had done nothing wrong.

Right?

Sure he hadn't done anything wrong, but his presence in my apartment surely wasn't right. He didn't knock or ring the bell, he'd used his key...even thought he knew I wasn't expecting him. We weren't a couple any more.

I guess it could also mean we weren't a couple any *less*.

I grinned at the joke, a small one, with my lips moving upward in a grin, nothing more.

Besides, I wasn't getting the entire story from Trey and that alone killed any amusement.

He smiled. "That would be the first choice wouldn't it?"

"It's how my mind works," I said back almost playfully, almost like we were before...almost. "As you know."

He nodded. "No, let me explain."

Finally.

With his smooth, caramel complexion, baldhead, and sturdy build that was engineer perfect, Trey looked good enough to eat. I fought back my naughty thoughts and focused on his tale.

"...I was undercover out in the Southwest," he was saying. "Deep cover, when suddenly I was exposed. Two days prior to meeting the head honcho of the Raymen Cartel. Rumor was that the leader was one of the governments' officials."

"Exposed? By who?" I asked, surprised. "And you weren't killed?"

"I overhead Buzz on the telemonitor giving the thug-party the heads up. I disappeared before they got to me. Someone in T.A. blew my cover."

I've heard of the Raymen Cartel, but for the life of me couldn't remember where I'd heard it. Drugs. Prostitution. The usual violantions, but the Raymen Cartel rang a bell I couldn't silence at the moment.

"Raymen Cartel…who are they?" I asked finally, revealing my ignorance.

He finished pacing and came around to the sofa. He sat tittering on the edge of the sofa, his hands holding his head as if it was too heavy to hold up any longer.

"The Raymen Cartel runs drugs like AckBack and Zenith out of the Southwest into the other territories and down to Mexico. As you know, Zenith is one of the deadliest drugs this side of the twenty-second century," he explained in a careful, weary manner. As he relaxed, black circle appeared under his eyes and large, heavy bags hung from beneath his eyes.

How long had he been without sleep? Days? Weeks? Months?

"At first glance, the Zenith pill is an unassuming, harmless pink pill. The cherry taste gives the user visual flashes or what is known on the streets as "cherry blasts."

I remembered now where I'd heard about the Raymen Cartel. Malcolm Moore had done a long investigative story on Zenith use with students at Old Montgomery College not too long ago. The piece had mentioned the Raymen Cartel, and how its tentacles reached into some of the most powerful political places in the many territory governments.

Figures—it takes a violation enterprise to unite governments who normally are at odds. These days, only the violators had much of the currency to support the various economies—except in Teriad's dictatorship in the Northwest and the Cali district.

"Like the Biblical Moses who went to the zenith of Mount Sinai to speak with God, cherry blasts allow the user to see his or her future, or so the myth goes. Once the visions are over, the person has a sexual release, and then he passes out," Trey continued, his voice lagging in excitement, as if he had given this lecture before and was bored.

Yes, that's what Malcolm's article stated and several experts agreed.

"The sexual element alone would be addictive, but the future visions were equally appealing. The added cocaine kick in the pill made it physically addictive," he said. "The visions aren't revelations of the future, but images stimulated by the chemicals in the designer drug…hallucinations brought on by the drug's peyote ingredients."

"As I recall if taken too much, the user could go blind, mad or into cardiac arrest," I said. "It not all three."

He nodded. "So the pressure is on the Territory Alliance to stem the flow of both Zenith and Ackback, especially now that it's the latest party drug for college students."

Right, only the government officials' kids were allowed to go on to higher education. No wonder the T.A. was catching so much heat and pressure. The generals, governors and territory dictators won't stand for their kids being used as drug bait.

The other drug, Ackback, although not as exotic as Zenith, contained deadly agents in its composition. It worked like crack and was a derivative of cocaine.

"Are you sure it was someone in the T.A.?" T.A. was the sole regulating authority left after the wars sliced up the former United States. "This is serious."

"Yes, it is," he said with a yawn. "As soon as I reported in, Captain Montague fired me. Said I was endangering his career."

"Did you explain your cover had been blown?" I took off my boots and removed my ponytail tie carefully as to not aggravate the bruises. My braids spilled over my shoulders like chestnut licorice.

We sounded like an old married couple and we weren't even a couple. A few days ago, I thought our breakup was for the best; painful, but what we both needed.

Now, I wasn't so sure. Seeing him again and in such a difficult position had conjured up feelings that I thought I had buried and deserted in the New Mexican high desert.

"Yes, yes," he groaned as he threw his hands into the air. "I did. He was enraged with me."

"So who's after you? The Raymen Cartel?"

"Yes," he said, his face sagged. "They are ruthless, callous people—some are hatchlings. The hired muscle that is, I believe. They would kill my family, if I had one. They would slaughter anything, *everything* I held dear if they couldn't get to me."

He got up and stood by the telemonitor. "Including you."

"Why me?" I asked, scowling and ignoring the flare of stinging needles at the action. "I'm not in your life anymore, remember?"

He sighed, but didn't turn around. "I didn't say those in my life, Cybil. I said those I hold dear."

I left the rocking chair and sat on the sofa, folding my legs under me. So, he still held me dear to him. He counted me amongst the people he cared for, but what did that actually leave for me? What did I feel about all this? Drama brought to my doorstep wasn't a way to get back into my good graces.

Montano's attack might have been an attempt by the Raymen Cartel. Didn't he demand to know Trey's whereabouts?

Why did Trey think the Raymen Cartel would go to such extremes to see him dead? He did say he'd risen up through the ranks to meet the head of the organization. But he hadn't actually gotten a chance to meet the leader.

Maybe that didn't matter.

Surely he'd seen procedures, faces of people who could spend a lot of time dreaming about pink bunnies in the cradles chambers. Was it worth going to these lengths to delete one person?

Trey gazed across the coffee table at me. "Fathers, you are so beautiful when you're lost in thought. Even though you looked like you lost a fight with a razor bot."

Husky and heated, his voice awakened my dormant longings and they shrieked for him. He stepped over the coffee table, pushing the table backward with his sneaker to give him space. Once comfortable, he kneeled in front of me. His hands slid along my thighs, brushing the bruises and caressing, giving me pain and soothing pleasure at the same time.

"So, tell me what happened?" he whispered, his voice like velvet, gliding along my skin and across my face, rubbing against my back and up my spine.

"Nothing I can't handle," I said softly, not wanting to talk about work. Not wanting to talk at all, but to act. Already every nerve in my body eagerly sought his familiar touch. Despite the complaints from my battered body, I wanted his hands all over him.

"Why won't you let someone help you," he said as his hands interlocked with mine. Calluses dotted his left hand. "I've badly missed you."

He leaned in and kissed my cheek gingerly. "Cybil, about our break-up…"

"Trey," I whispered hotly back as his full lips brushed mine, leaving them tingling and wanting.

"Yes?"

"Go take a shower. You stink," I said with a deep laugh, my motives to see him naked, clear and exposed.

“Come with me,” he whispered back, pulling me off the sofa with him.

“Owww…”

“Sorry.”

He navigated the apartment as if he had never been away from it. We slid together into my closet sized shower. With a laugh, he turned on the water, howling at the cold water and shielding me from it until at last it warmed up.

Taking my liquid soap, I squeezed tropical breeze all over his chest and busily rubbed my hands across it, turning the liquid into lather and loving it. Without waiting, Trey grabbed the bottle from me and squeezed the cold soap over my shoulders and back. His hands felt heavenly on my skin as he massaged in the soap. Even the bruises he touched seemed to sear and fall in response to his touch.

I closed my eyes and leaned back against the shower's wall, while his hands made their way from my back to my front and engaged in sensual circular patterns of warmth. I leaned back, palms against the shower's damp tile, and letting the water wash over us in scalding rivulets and streams of steam.

I couldn't tell if the shower clouded up from the hot water or from our own steamy embraces.

CHAPTER 10

Thursday morning came way too soon. Annoyed and sleep deprived, I clumsily got out of bed, slamming my toe on the bed's frame as I hobbled through the living room and on to the kitchen to start a cup of coffee.

There was nothing like waking up the morning after a good ass whipping.

People had this habit of underestimating bruises. They freakin' hurt. After you sleep and have sex with them, they tend to be more painful. Too much touching and biting, and smacking and grabbing—I felt like I'd been in another battle.

The apartment lay in semi-shadow. All of the curtains had been drawn throughout the place, except for my bedroom. I must have forgotten to close them last night. The nightlights, strategically placed in each room offered small circles of illumination, giving rise to shadows and dusky corners.

"Coffee on," I said with a throat as dry as cotton. The scabs on my face itched. I fought back the urge to scratch them, knowing that wouldn't satisfy the itch, but would make them bleed again.

The click of the coffeemaker confirmed my command. Not unlike most people, my coffeemaker resided in the kitchen, but only made cups individually. Not fifteen cups or twenty, one cup of hot java at a time. The machine held two containers, one for coffee and the other for water. The computer controlled the mix, the fulfillment and creation of my morning wake up.

I had to speak clearly to the coffee maker or I'd get something else like water with coffee grinds or coffee mud, a black sludge of bitterness. I leaned back against the fridge while the coffee hissed and whirled.

My heavy eyelids closed.

The telemonitor buzzed, forcing me out of my sleepiness. Groaning, and wishing it were a wrong number, I headed to the living room.

It wasn't.

I saw Tisha's face on the caller identifier and I wanted to scream. I hovered around the screen and tried to decide if I should answer it or let it go to video mail.

She was my sister.

I picked up the remote and clicked the telemonitor fully on.

"Hello, Tisha," I said as the video filled in the telemonitor's screen. My enthusiasm for the day continued to plummet like a rock thrown into the ocean.

My sister's face frowned, wrinkling the expensive and expertly applied cosmetics. "You're awake?"

"I am now," I said somberly and trying to not groan out loud. My body simply was smarting.

The volume immediately balanced so I caught the complete effects of her displeasure at finding me at home. If she could help it, Tisha would only leave messages. Talking directly to me might mean she'd have to have a conversation with her only sister. Which in turn meant she'd have to face the fact that she wasn't an only child.

Tisha's face relaxed into a visage of arrogance and mock importance.

Thursday was definitely not getting off to a good start.

"How's the shoulder?" I asked, failing to hide my own irritation at her call.

It was only six a.m. The time was even earlier out in the Southwest…by about two hours, which meant at four a.m. Tisha looked as fresh as blooming flowers. She was as poisonous as belladonna.

Even though I couldn't see the scar now, for she wore a

long-sleeve mauve shirt, I knew it was there. The scar on Tisha's shoulder would forever remind her of how dangerous my job was and the fragility of her own life.

And for that, she would never forgive me.

"Never mind," she spat. "I was calling to say that Nina's birthday is coming up."

She said it as if I didn't know my favorite (and only) niece's birth date. The unspoken accusation stirred up old feelings of rejection and competition. Instead of cursing a string of intelligible words at her, I smiled.

"She's having a party and wanted to-"

Tisha's voice trailed off. Her eyes moved over to someone or something out of picture range. She whispered furiously under her breath words that I could not catch. Her artfully plucked eyebrows crouched down in a menacing look, before finally saying, "Fine!"

She stepped back and Nina stepped into view, her braids pulled into two side-long ponytails. "Can you come, Auntie Cyb? Can you? To my party?"

Ah, now everything became clear. Tisha didn't want Nina talking to me. If I hadn't been home or answered, Tisha could have told her that I never responded to the message, thus painting me as a naughty, neglectful auntie.

As it were, I was home, and now faced with a difficult decision.

"Well, I'll try, but I'm working a case," I said, my heart twisting in agony. I'd missed so much of her growing up already because of the distance between D.C. and the Southwest Territories. Missing yet another milestone forced my heart to wring itself in indecision.

Her crestfallen face stabbed at my emotional center. Once one of my cases put her in danger. In fact, it was the same case that gave her mother the shoulder scar.

I couldn't let that happen again.

Because next time, Nina might not be so lucky.

With any luck, she might be out of therapy by the time she reached forty.

"You're working?" Nina asked, her eyes shimmering with unshed tears. She was stiff-upper-lipping it and for that I was proud. Her eyes betrayed her outward stance of understanding.

"Yeah," I said back, swallowing the lump that had risen there. "I am working a really tough one too."

"In your pjs?" she snickered and erupted into giggles. Her cheeks filled out in a cocoa-toned, chubby cheer. Still, disappointment lingered in her eyes. She knew my job and I think, she worried about me, probably more than her mother.

That did not sit well, but it was how I paid the bills. I eagerly shoved the thoughts aside, and smiled back at my little trooper.

"That's enough," Tisha said firmly as she gently pushed Nina out of the picture. "Come if you can."

"I will try," I said, a little surprised at the sound of slight concern in Tisha's voice.

Since our violent bonding, Tisha had been reasonable when calling and leaving messages. I had to be honest. I thought she was doing it to irritate me more. However, I wouldn't go so far as to say, kind or courteous, but our usual heated arguments were less frequent now.

"Bye," she said, her jewelry sparkling in the flow of the overhead lights in her living room. "Be careful. You look like hell."

I spoke too soon. Was that concern coming from Tisha?

The world must be coming to an end in a mere few minutes.

Okay, so she could do kind when she wanted.

But then so could I.

"Yeah."

We disconnected with my thoughts centered on Nina. Wow, she'd grown in the last two years. Only four or five inches shorter than Tisha, who stood at five feet nine inches, Nina was growing like a weed and well on her way to being a real beauty.

I removed my travel bag out of the living room's closet when the door rang.

The camera showed Jane, packed and dressed, in the door's entranceway. I clicked the open button and she waltzed in her face a stony mask, her sunglasses on.

"Not even dressed!" she said around an unlit cigarette, no doubt her first of the morning. "Hurry up! It's nearly seven."

"All right, I'm going!" I said and went back into my bedroom to load up the travel bag. "Tisha called and I got thrown off track."

"How are they anyway? Both out of therapy?" Jane shouted back.

Jane wasn't trying to be funny.

"No, I think Nina will be in it until she's forty…" I said as I hauled my suitcase onto the bed wincing all the more since it required two hands to do. My right went numb again after I dropped the bag onto the bed. I could purchase an apartment drone, but I hated robots.

With all of the technology and medical advances, why couldn't they come up with something to treat bruises?

I heard the telemonitor click on. Jane was a junkie for the news. If it happened violently and painfully, she wanted to know about it. She continued to speed surf through channels until she found the news. She never missed an opportunity to suck up the filth people did to each other.

"This is the early morning news with Sue Chen," said a narrator.

"Good morning, I'm Sue Chen," said news anchor Sue Chen. "…Today in Markenson Heights located in the East End of D.C. a genetically engineered human was found murdered. This killing brings the death toll for the genetically engineered in D.C. to thirty-three this year alone…"

Hatchling killing?

I stopped packing and like a zombie under a trance, I glided back into the living room.

Sue Chen's perfect black hair and neatly trimmed bangs proved glossy under the lights. Her gray, pinstripe suit, sharp and crisp, made my back hurt for her.

"So what?" Jane asked, disinterested in hatchling news. She didn't like hatchlings anyway. Her dislike had more to do with her father leaving her and her mother for a pretty hatchling named Tara than her own interactions with them.

She had warmed up to Trey though, so there was hope for her yet.

Markenson Heights lay only about forty miles from my apartment. I've passed by on numerous occasions, as it was not far from my place. A small grimy group of houses turned to apartments, Markenson Heights didn't invite people who weren't down on their luck. They were gloomy and dismal, but the underground organization worked tirelessly to make them look that way.

My thoughts turned back to last night and Trey's visit. *My underground escort won't be ready until tomorrow, Trey said.*

After our shower last night, we went to bed and became reacquainted. In the wee hours, I woke up naked and very much alone. The tangled covers smelled strongly of Trey, and were my only evidence he had been there. His problems with the Raymen Cartel and the T.A. were his to solve, and his very life depended on it. Last night, he made love as if it were his last, with unbridled lust, nips and moans.

He did not say goodbye.

Please, don't let that person have been Trey.

"You all right?" Jane asked, her eyes narrowed suspiciously. "You don't look too good."

"Tired," I said back, distractedly, my thoughts still on Trey. Rumor was that Markenson Heights was a gateway to the underground. "I'm going to be in the vehicle with you all day. I'm not up for a chin-wag."

Her worried face broke into a grin. "Ditto."

CHAPTER

11

There's a long-standing joke that goes like this: the two biggest cities in Mississippi are Memphis and New Orleans.

Originally settled by the Chickasaw people, Memphis changed hands many times before being founded by Andrew Jackson and two other, less than memorable partners.

Downtown Memphis, a former mecca for African-Americans in the twentieth century lay deserted at eleven at night. Well known for Beale Street, blues and bar-b-que, this legendary strip of land still captured many visitors each year with its museums such as the Civil Rights Museum, which was built on the site where the great Martin Luther King, Jr. was assassinated.

I sat down my wauto on this historic street in front of Henry's. In the days when my grandmother still lived, she called places like Henry's hotels Rental rooms, as they were called now, no longer ate up the parallel roads next to highways. Few if any in some quadrants existed at all. Travel between territories was difficult, if not flat out dangerous. Most territories' governments were kakistocracies. Dysfunctional sets of politicians running and ruining the lives of its citizens.

Memphis has always been known for its accessibility. Long ago, it was a major transportation hub and a busy river port in addition to the hundreds of railroads that crisscrossed its area back in the days of steam engines and cowboys. It continued to draw so many people because it was one of the safest quadrants in the Southeast Territories. People constantly came and enjoyed themselves. Plus they survived to make it back home in one piece.

Hell that was great publicity in and of itself.

But I wasn't here for pleasure.

Throughout the trip down, Jane spun stories about Amanda. She made Amanda sound like some Girl Scout, saint, and golden girl all wrapped into one. I doubted the young Christensen was free of any wrongdoing and totally innocent. Everyone kept secrets. To err is human, and I bet Amanda Christensen did a lot of erring.

Henry's was a three-story level building decorated in blue awnings and slick metallic doors. It seemed clean enough. The automatic windows lay in shadows. Puddles of streetlight revealed nothing odd or out of the ordinary. I found this strange for the night usually brought out the local baddies, ack-addicts, and prostitutes.

Perhaps the regulators swept this sector often, keeping the riffraff from polluting the areas were tourists might frequent. That alone would give the appearance of a fair and safe quadrant now wouldn't it?

Mayor Christensen cared an awful lot about how things *appeared.*

Nevertheless, strapped to my right ankle was my pug and under my left shoulder was my laser gun 350. Again, I felt somewhat protected and prepared. It did occur to me that Jarold Montano managed to take the 350 off of me and nearly killed me, had I not had the ankle holster.

Next time he'd be ready for the pug.

Surely there wouldn't be a next time, until I went back to D.C. Right now, I had to find this girl.

"Aunt Belle can be pretty tough," Jane said as she lifted the passenger door and climbed out. "She's been horribly scarred by Mandy's disappearance. The publicity alone is making her sick. The media has turned the damn thing into a circus."

Oh, I bet it was. But I kept this thought to myself. I hoisted my travel bag and satchel out of the trunk and came around to Jane, my arm still singing in agony. "Sure, but this will get uglier before it gets better." Thinking the media's darling was still being portrayed as the grieving mother. Her ratings had actually gone up by about forty percent for her chances of becoming governor.

Jane gave me a half shrug, her broad backpack protruding at least seven inches from her back. Despite the load, she carried it with grace.

"I'm serious. You may discover stuff you don't want to know about Amanda, your aunt, maybe your entire family."

She caught my tone. "I know."

I doubted that she truly understood. Objectivity, a P.I. essential, would be lost in a cloud of fog that resembled early morning in the London district.

We went inside and checked in. Once done, we took the creaky old stairs up to our floor. We went to room two-twelve. The keycard opened the room without incident. There wasn't much more security than keycards, which were found most often in older rental rooms like Henry's and apartment buildings like mine. Newer places didn't rely on keycards, but personal pin numbers, robotic guards, DNA, and other technological advances.

As the doors opened to our room, the smashing odor of mothballs, hit us in the face.

"Whew!"

Two double beds, a bathroom and a small sitting table and two chairs filled up the small, square space. Cramped but it would do for our time here. Jane hurried over to open the windows to air out the place.

"At least there aren't any holes in the roof," Jane said as she dropped her pack to the floor with a thud. "Remember that place in Toronto you had us holed up in. Dreadful."

"At least it was free," I said back, dropping my bag to the floor beside my bed with a soft *thud*. "This place is costing us a sizable bit of currency. The exchange rate between SE currents and the district's dollars is hurting us."

My body still bore bruises courtesy of the tango with Jarold and my joints protested my sudden movements. Bluish-green circular spots dotted my right thigh and sections of my calf. If possible, my body felt worse than it had yesterday.

"It's night, let's get some shut eye," Jane suggested and immediately took off her boots. Within minutes, her snores filled the air. Sprawled across her bed, fully clothed, she must have been drained. She did do most of the flying down to the quadrant.

I put on my pjs, made up of yellow satin camisole and short-shorts. I tossed and turned in the new bed, feeling every lump and cavern. Rental rooms always caused the most insomnia in me. It wasn't my bed and it took a few days for my body to come to terms with that.

If I stayed that long.

CHAPTER 12

Friday, the thirteenth, arrived with hurdled splats of fat raindrops against the window, creating a drumming sound that woke me well before my customary time of noon. The glowing time on the clock did not lie.

Two minutes after six o'clock.

Outside the thunderous clouds painted the sky an eerily bluish black. With much effort, I got up, passed Jane, sleeping soundly in the other double bed, her hair scattered across her pillows. In the distance, the doors of a rental room opened and closed. Heavy footsteps echoed down the hallway and vibrated throughout the corridor. The walls must've been made of paper, for I could hear everything clearly as if I was in the neighboring room.

The open window, drenched in rain, offered a watery view of the sidewalks and Beale Street below. Empty, the downpour had chased all indoors. Though I couldn't understand why anyone would be out at this ungodly hour.

Now fully awake, going back to sleep was impossible. Interrupted sleep was unfinished and aborted step in the natural cycle of things. Disturbed slumber left a nasty taste in my mouth, like hot instant cocoa that hadn't been stirred thoroughly, and I drank the grit.

Thoughts of hot chocolate lead to thoughts of steaming hot coffee. Coffee could smooth out the rough edges of being awake way too early. A good cup of java could set my clock right.

The temperature in Memphis was somewhat warmer than

D.C., but not by much. The rain surprised me for March in D.C. came prescribed for snow, ice, and most cases flurries. Not so for Memphis. The rain must be the precursors to spring. Not to be undone, the edge of winter blew about cold, frosty winds. The air from the window turned my breath into smoke.

It wasn't spring quite yet.

I was about to turn from the window when a shadowy figure stepped out from underneath the awnings of the store across the street. The shining red circle of a cigarette drew my attention.

Who would be out in this sloppy, cold weather?

The person wore a hat with a wide brim and rainwater tunneled over its flap. It spilled out and down to the already saturated sidewalk.

Then, he (or she) glanced up at my window. Startled the cigarette fell to the ground and the murky body melted back into the shadows as suddenly as it appeared.

Imagining things?

Nah, someone was watching me.

I hurried back to my bed, ignoring my protesting body, and ripped open my travel bag. Inside were about four days worth of clothes, give or take, and extra shoes. In the unlit room, I hastily dressed in sweats, sneakers, and guns.

Three short steps from the door, Jane called, "Where do you think you're going?"

"Out! No time to explain," I said in puffs as I pressed the open button and fled through the gap.

No time for the elevator, I banged through the hallway's exit doors and took the stairs down in twos, careful not to trip and smash my face into the century old carpet.

I bustled through the lobby and out in the soggy morning. With fluidity I took out the 350 and ran across the street to the spot where I saw the man (or woman).

No one.

I could still smell the burnt tobacco of cigarettes and

something else, like beer, floating around the spot underneath the awning.

I checked the store's front. Lined with litter and bottles of alcohol, the inside room lay in sullen, unlit darkness. It figures, a liquor store directly across from the rental room. Its posted opening time was eleven o'clock. So whoever was out here was definitely watching me, because they weren't coming from the store.

Or any of the stores for that matter. All of them were closed.

Soaked and hyper thanks to my adrenaline surge, I kept my gun out and walked around the area where I had seen the mystery stalker. Briefly, I pondered if I had imagined it. Did I really see someone or was it the overactive imagination of a woman with too little sleep?

The awning protected me from getting wetter, but I couldn't see my rental room's window from here. I took three steps forward. The rain continued to fall, free of the awnings. I could easily see the window to our rental room and the lights were on.

Sighing, I stepped back against the store's doors.

I scanned the front section of Henry's and didn't see anyone coming or going.

Maybe I did dream it up, but I didn't think so. Where had the person vanished too so quickly?

I searched the debris and dust bits floating in the puddles of rainwater on the sidewalk and along the edge of the street. Bobbing in the chilly water was a cigarette butt. I picked it up between my index finger and thumb and then quickly cupped it into my palm, tightening my hand into a fist to protect it from more rain.

This was a clue!

I reholstered the 350. With a small shout of glee, I started to cross the pavement back to Henry's when a wauto, flying lower than necessary, whipped past, nearly taking me with it. I tried to jump back onto the sidewalk, but I tripped on the curb. I fell backward into a puddle of muddy water in time to save myself from becoming road kill.

I snapped up to a sitting position. My arms stretched up in the air in an attempt to protect both the clue and my weapon. Water in the barrel and body of my 350 could ruin it. The wauto's driver zipped away into the Memphis air, leaving a lovely cloud of exhaust fumes and a determination for me to catch him.

With enthusiasm, I ran across the pavement and made it back up to my rental room.

"What the hell happened to you?" Jane barked as soon as the doors opened to reveal my sopping wet attire, her arms akimbo. "Where did you go?"

"There was someone watching us," I said and held out my palm. "He saw me looking at him and seemingly vanished."

Jane's eyebrows crouched down into a frown. "Who tried to run you off the pavement back there?"

So she *was* watching me. Score one for Jane.

I shook my head, tossing water droplets onto the floor. It could've been the person under the awning or it could have been mere coincidence.

"It's raining cats and dogs out there…"

"I saw him, Jane," I said with more confidence than I felt.

"He?" she asked as she sat down on her bed and took out her knife. "I ain't saying you didn't see him, Cyb. I'm wondering who would be following us way down here?"

She had a point.

"No one knows we're here," I said, unsure of the statement as it slid out of my mouth. "Unless you told your aunt, and then everyone knows we're here."

"I didn't tell her," Jane said defensively. "Don't start pointing fingers unless you got evidence to back it up."

Already I wasn't sure of anything or anybody. The case was less than two days old.

Jane chewed her lower lip. Her harsh words hung in the air between us.

"Here, put this in a plastic box," I said as I held out my tight fist where the cigarette was protected from getting any more rain. "We'll have to be extra careful."

Jane picked up the box she normally used to store cotton balls and dumped them out. She brought it over to me and said, "Drop it."

"The mysterious watcher dropped this."

I refused to argue with her about her aunt. My gut told me I was simply delaying the inevitable, but right now all I cared about was finding out who knew we were in Memphis.

I slipped into the bathroom and pealed off my clothes, layer by soppy layer. Briskly, I toweled off, trying in vain to get dry. Memphis's temperature fluctuated between fifty and fifty-five degrees in the afternoon; this morning felt more like forty, too warm for snow and too cold for dancing in the rain.

Jane was quiet before coming to the bathroom's door.

I toweled off and realized I had no clothes that weren't wet in the bathroom with me.

"Uh," I stuttered, suddenly chilly without the towel to distract me.

The door slid back abruptly and Jane held out my clothes to me. Her face turned away from the open door. "Thought you might need these."

Rapidly to stop the chills and to get decent, I yanked on a sweater and jeans. My bare feet ached, but she didn't bring any socks. I walked out to the room. Crouching down beside my bed, I pulled on socks from my travel bag. Thank goodness I brought three other pairs of shoes to wear.

"We have that large bulky scanner that could tell us DNA and fingerprints on this cigarette," Jane said, her voice somewhat muffled as she examined it.

"Yeah, but it's back in D.C. taking up space behind my desk," I said as put my right foot into my black boot. This kind of weather requires boots that repel water and my own boots, complete with compact soles, would work. "Captain Hanson should have several we could use."

Before I could get my foot into my left boot, the telemonitor came to life, buzzing and illuminating the partially lightless rental room.

"Aunt Belle," Jane said, her voice unusually quiet. "Answer it or no?"

"Answer it," I said as I tied a nice bow with my laces. "We're up. Might as well get started."

How'd she know we were here and in this room? We checked in under aliases.

Jane caught the unspoken question and shrugged. She clicked on the telemonitor to receive the mayor's call.

"Good morning," Mayor Christensen said with sharp happiness. "I thought you gals would like to come over to the house for some breakfast before you start your day."

Jane hesitated, but delegated the decision to me with a head toss.

She didn't just call me a *gal.* Ugh!

"I would like to get started on the case as soon as possible, Mayor Christensen. Starting with Captain Hanson this morning. Is he in today?"

She stiffened and her lips pressed into a fine line of annoyance. I could spot that look anywhere. Many people have that reaction to me. I'm sure she had other plans for me. Not to mention, she wasn't used to someone countering her orders.

Her eyes focused on Jane, but she spoke to me. That trick might work when belittling her staff, but not for one whose ego was as large as yours truly.

"I will check with him and give you a call back with his answer. This is such short notice," she said sternly, her smile waning a little.

"No problem," I said, with a broad smile of my own. "Bye."

I reached for the remote and clicked off the telemonitor.

"I could've used some breakfast," Jane said, her voice dejected.

"Let's go get some," I said, as I picked up my satchel.

Her eyes grew wide with surprise. "Aunt Belle asked us to-"

"I know," I said slowly, making sure to highlight each word as I spoke. "We do *not* have time to get chummy with our client or anyone. We don't know who's responsible for Amanda's disappearance."

"Everyone is a suspect. Even Aunt Belle," Jane said, nodding her head, her eyes brightening with that hungry, raw look inspectors get on a case. "Inspector Rule number two."

"Excellent, you score a one hundred for today," I said, playfully slapping her on the back as she exited the room.

She may make a good inspector yet.

CHAPTER 13

Henry's provided a full service restaurant, but only half of it was actually used. Restaurants went the way of other luxury items liked butter and dairy. Creamer was a powdery substance that was non-dairy and made from soybeans. The tables and booths bore cotton tablecloths, but none of the dinnerware was real or valuable.

We weren't surprised that we were the only two people in the place at seven-thirty in the morning.

A robotic waiter floated over to us. The oval, silvery thing wore an airbrushed gray suit. His head contained a brunette wig and a fake, painted on smile complete with white rectangular boxes as teeth.

We sat down in a pale pink booth and he extended his waxy hands to each of us, providing a breakfast menu. The boxy handheld menus weighed more than my PDA, and appeared to do less. The monitor was some monochrome color and the menu choices were slim at best.

The choices didn't inspire my hunger, or make me feel like eating.

"Coffee, black," I said, my mind on the cigarette in the small, plastic travel box in my satchel. Whose was it? A regulator spy for Mayor Christensen? How else did she know where we were? There had to be a least a dozen or so rental rooms in the quad.

The robot's hand retracted from the table, taking the pathetic three-item menu with him.

"For you miss?" it asked in a stuffy, British accent.

Why programmers consistently gave robots accents, I'll never know. Must be some private internal programmer joke.

"Coffee, black and toast," Jane said around the still unlit cigarette in the mouth. Her first one of the day. It dangled from her lips as if disappointed it hadn't been lighted.

It didn't wait long. As soon as the robot moved away, she lit it, her hazel eyes squinting against the smoke. She reached for the foghog. With her index finger she pressed the side button and it hungrily sucked the cigarette smoke into its round belly.

"Let's start with the boyfriend, Nathan."

"You handle that. I'm going to see the Memphis regs," I said, my eyes glued to the robotic waiter. I didn't like or trust robots. You never knew when one of them would flip and go berserk.

Once a robot that cleaned house for a wealthy family in some affluent neighborhood in the Midwestern Territories caught a bad virus and killed everyone in the house with a vacuum cleaner. Bashed in their brains and then tried to clean up the mess with the murder weapon.

Nasty thing.

As if sensing my displeasure, the robot glided back over with two cups of coffee clasped in its hands. Jane took one look into her ceramic cup and decided against eating at Henry's restaurant anymore.

"What is this?" Jane asked as she lifted a hunk of burnt toast from her coffee cup. Drenched in coffee, it was blackened nearly to dust.

"Will this be all?" it asked and the door opened on his stomach, providing a keypad to enter a room number. The total cost was six SE currents.

I punched in our rental room number and said, "End service."

"Thank you madams," it said and drifted away.

Jane shuddered and pushed the cup away from her. "I'm

outta here. Going to see the boyfriend. I got his address from the files."

"I'll be at the Memphis regs main office," I said as I climbed out of the booth. "Meet you back here at, say three or four o'clock?"

She shrugged. "I've got to get an aerocycle."

"Rent one?" I asked, thinking of the cost involved. “I'd assumed we fly my wauto.”

"No, Aunt Belle has one I can borrow," she said. She stood up too. In her boots she was still shorter, but not by much. "Okay with you?"

"Fine," I said, not at all worried about her using her aunt's craft. Free was good. "Later."

She headed back to the rental room to contact her aunt. I walked outside to reclaim my blue wauto.

I thought about the moon colonies and Amanda's supposed extracurricular activities. She might be on the moon, hanging out, to get away from her parents or to annoy them. Teenagers did stuff like that.

Or so I was told. I felt too old to remember my teenage years, although I'm only thirty-two.

Thirty-two is an old age in some circles.

Especially the young.

CHAPTER 14

Outside, the sky clotted up with intensity and prepared for another rainsquall. I steered the wauto toward the downtown Memphis regulator headquarters according to coordinates supplied by the local internet website. It wasn't far from Henry's and I hadn't heard from the mayor. Not that I was going to wait until she had time to brief Captain Hanson on what to say and what not to say.

It still bugged me that she knew where we stayed the night. Our arrival was supposed to be a surprise, something to keep everyone guessing. Yet Christensen knew, even down to the room number. I wondered if Jane *had* told her.

But Jane said she hadn't told her and for now I'd have to believe that.

The Memphis Regulator headquarters occupied a square section of the street. Only two stories high, it was wider than it was high. Built from brick and century old windows, it seemed more ready for a historical christening than it did a place of violation fighting.

A paved lot held designated spaces for visitors and I set down the craft there and got out.

The 350 remained locked in the glovebox and my pug was shoved under the front driver's seat. I didn't want them to know I'd come to Memphis armed. Entering regulator headquarters with weapons wouldn't put them in the best of moods, so I checked my internal honey balance. I could get through a little session of Q and A with the captain.

Wearing my best it's-your-lucky-day-smile I passed

through the two metal detectors and the security regulators, right on up to the desk clerk.

The desk clerk's name was Herman and he appeared to be really bored.

"Yeah?" he asked, his eyes trailing the latest ring of prostitutes back to the booking desks.

I could almost see the drool dripping out of his mouth.

"I'm here to see Captain Hanson," I said, my eyes not following the prostitutes, but trying to get the desk clerk's attention. I increased the wattage of my smile to it's your-incredibly-lucky-day smile. I wore my sky blue sweater and jeans with boots. Nothing screamed private inspector, but still I was a citizen, even a second rate one. He wasn't even interested in the streaks of crusty scabs that streaked across my face, nor the now greenish bruise smeared on my cheek.

The place bustled with activity. Regs shoved people through crowded hallways to destinations unknown and to discuss situations that many would later regret.

"Who's askin'?" the pale, scrawny desk clerk asked lazily. His brow furrowed as he caught a male, about fifteen years old sprint through the metal detectors toward the exit—and freedom. "Hey! Stop!"

He rose out of his chair quite slowly to scream at the escaping youth, but the security regs apprehended the boy before he escaped. The youngster moved with such speed and agility, even I was impressed. Immediately, the boy was cuffed, shackled and led back down the hallway from which he'd come. Except this time he had an escort.

"Keep an eye on him this time!" shouted the desk clerk, as he lowered himself back into his seat.

The escorting reg flipped him off and snatched the boy along.

The desk clerk's eyes moved back to me and he said, "What you want?"

"Captain Hanson," I replied coolly. Obviously this clerk

had attention deficit disorder for everything that moved, shouted or groaned in the lobby caught his attention. No other part of his body moved except his eyes and they were everywhere and on everything.

Honey supply was now at seventy-five percent, my internal censor warned.

"The captain is busy," he said effortlessly, not even bothering to pretend to check with Captain Hanson. The large telemonitor screen to his right showed row after row of logged arrests. It flickered and updated itself every few minutes.

I gave him my smile again, but his attention waned.

Honey supply at fifty percent and dropping.

Clearing my throat, I said, "I am here about Amanda Christensen."

The desk clerk's mouth opened into a wide yawn and he said, "Sure you are. Reporters have to wait for an official press conference..."

Honey supply at twenty-five percent and definitely in the red. Future outburst and curse words, possibly violence were on the horizon.

Mr. Personality here was ruining my chance to get through this without resorting to anti-social and disruptive behavior.

I wanted to see Hanson and soon. To do that, I would have to get past Herman.

"Okay, fine. Here's the deal. You have about three seconds to take me back to Captain Hanson or I'll break your face," I said calmly. I didn't raise my voice, but my irritation seeped into my message and the undercurrent of anger at last caught Mr. Personality's attention.

"Are you threatening a regulator, lady?" he spat and then released a huge guffaw. "Ain't that right pretty? Silly woman...break my face...sure...Looks like somebody already put ya in ya place once..."

"One," I said, counting mustn't be his forte. "Two."

That wiped the smile off his face and he looked me in the

eyes. Something there must have startled him because he said, "I'll see if he's in."

"Thank you," I said as I swallowed the word, *three*.

He picked up his ear piece and slung it over his ear. The microphone jutted out and down along his jaw line. I knew the range between mouth and eyes didn't matter so much because the microphone was super sensitive.

"Captain Hanson."

His telemonitor flashed, but never showed the captain's face.

"There's a woman here named," he stopped and turned back to me. "Your name?"

"Cybil Lewis," I said slowly, my hands still folded in front of me as I leaned my elbows on the counter. I hadn't raised any suspicious glances from the surrounding regulators. My body language conveyed civility. Inside my irritation pressed against my fabric of restraint.

"Cybil Lewis. Says she knows something about the mayor's missing brat, uh, kid," the desk clerk whispered, but it didn't sound anything like a whisper. I'm sure folks down all three hallways heard. A model of discretion, this one.

He kept his head diverted away from me and when he ended the call, he swiveled around and said, "He will see you now."

I nodded. "Where is his office?"

He pointed in the direction of the stairs. "Go up to the second floor, make a left at the top and head down until you see his nameplate," the desk clerk said, his voice shaky, his eyes still not focused on me. "Here's a visitor's badge."

He handed me a plastic badge with the word "visitor" on it. The frayed edges and scratched surface testified to its use. It must be the only one they had.

I slipped it into my pocket and elbowed my way through the throng of people to the stairs. Taking them one at a time, for there was no room to move faster, I thought about what I would say to the captain. How would he feel about the mayor bringing in a private inspector to do what he had apparently failed to do? My toes would be more than a little sore if the situation was reversed. Not to mention, I had dealings with regulators in the past. They always seemed to have an overdeveloped sense of right and wrong. For them, the world came down to black and white. Right and wrong.

For me, the world came down to multiple shades of gray.

That kind of ethic is what got me kicked out of the army in the first place.

But that's another story.

The doors labeled as Captain Hanson's were broad and wide indicating a large office indeed. I took in a deep breath, still unsure of what kind of jerk resided on the other side. If his desk clerk was any indication of the type of people he hired as regulators, than he must be a complete idiot.

The doors slid back and I stepped into a polished office of silver-tone and black. Wall to wall gray carpet, shiny silver-tone desk and gleaming black desk accessories and computer, gave the office a clinical, cold feel. His decorator must have been into contrast.

From behind the long, but slim desk, a man rose from his chair like a king rising up from a throne with the knowledge that he alone ruled with absolute power.

"Ms. Lewis, I presume," he said, his voice strong and soothing at the same time.

"Yes," I said, struck nearly speechless by his handsome face. I expected a red-faced bubba with an overlapping stomach, limited education, and dirty fingernails.

"I'm Captain Hanson," he announced, his smile wide and his handshake solid. Manicured nails and soft fingers brushed mine as he let go. "Sorry about the incident down at the desk clerk's station. Herman is, can I say, slow."

I nodded and glanced around the capacious office decorated with minimalist in mind. The room contained his desk, a lamp and a telemonitor. Captain Hanson did not appear to be a pack rat or a collector of things. Except his left wall bore plaques and awards he'd been granted on one side, but the adjacent wall contained pressed leaves in wax paper that had been framed. The collection covered more wall space than did his awards.

Obviously a man of substance and knowledge or one who wanted others to think so. What a bold statement of vegetation in a regulator captain's office...it was quite peaceful, the opposite of the violence involved in tracking down and arresting violators. No press releases or electronic clippings of current or solved cases, nothing that would distinguish his office from say a lawyer or an accountant.

Off to the right of his desk, beneath the collection of leaves, were a table and two wrought iron chairs with black cushions. The set would be better suited for an outdoor café, not the meeting table in a regulator office. Perhaps his decorator was female.

His eyes lingered on my damaged face, but he didn't comment.

I did say he was smart, right?

"Please, sit, Ms. Lewis," he said as he invited me over to the table. His voice conjured goose bumps across my skin and my hand tingled where his had covered mine. Definitely not a good sign. The tingling indicated my attraction level. I must keep focused on the task of questioning him, not of bedding him. *Come on, Cybil, hold it together for five seconds!*

Captain Hanson stepped over to the table with such grace that it made Mayor Christensen's movement look like a bull thrashing around in a glass shop. His shoes were standard regulator issued and he was clean-shaven. The aftershave was spicy and still somewhat refreshing. He wore a turquoise sweater and black dress pants. The blue in his sweater highlighted his crisp, cerulean eyes. Turquoise must be the Memphis Regulators' official color. I thought back to Mayor

Christensen's visit to D.C. and her entourage of well-dressed thugs.

Like a true southern gentleman, he stood until I sat and then took the seat across from me at the circular bistro set.

"Okay, now I know who you are. Your face was plastered all over the news files some two years ago. When Mayor Christensen mentioned your name, it had a funny familiarity, yet I couldn't connect your face to your name."

I blushed! Me, the usually boastful and rightly so, was stunned into blushing.

"Well, yeah, but I had lots of help," I said quietly.

He shook his head, his salt and pepper hair not losing its style. Cut short and feathered back, the style wasn't new, but it framed his face well and brought out his strong chin. "Don't be modest. You caught Governor Price. Never really cared for him, personally, but he was the boss."

I laughed.

Not only was he not a dim-witted, bumbling regulator, he was charming and likeable.

He grinned and the bastard had two dimples.

You know my affinity for dimples.

"You obviously got my files on Amanda Christensen," he said. "What do you think?"

"I still don't feel like I know her," I said, as I willed myself to stay on track. Yes, I was aware that he was picking my brain, but if this was going to work at all, I had to pretend to give him information first. Or else he'd never recipercate…quid pro quo in action.

"What can you tell me about her that wasn't in the files you sent to me?"

His blue eyes carefully watched me. His manicured fingers drummed on the table and he ran his hand through his hair. It fell right back into place as if it had never been disturbed. In thought he folded his large, blunt fingers on his desk as if the drumming hadn't solved his dilemma.

Older than me by at least fifteen years, I easily found him good-looking, which I usually didn't do with men nearly two decades older than me. Slight muscular build, small waist, and large hands, he must workout despite his age. Perhaps he was overtly vain and spent every waking hour when not at work, trying to starve off the aging process, like the leaves that still looked fresh, green, alive—youthful.

"Amanda Christensen's file, the real file, takes more memory than I had to send to you," he said, his voice suddenly somber, but still pleasant. "She was a wild child. We brought her home many times and I'll be honest here, we didn't take her disappearance too seriously because she had run off before."

"She had?" I said, more than a little shocked by this tidbit, though not floored. I had suspected that the Memphis Regs didn't take the girl's disappearance as well seriously as they should have. Regulators. And Trey wondered why I despised them so. Their work was careless, sloppy and in most cases, totally ineffective.

"Where she'd go the last time you guys brought her home?"

"To her boyfriend's house where she'd stay for days while his parents were away," Captain Hanson said, his voice grave "The mayor would call us, all in an uproar. We'd go there, tell Amanda to go home, and, if need be, cuff and drag her back to the mayor's mansion."

"She isn't with the boyfriend this time," I said as I watched Captain Hanson's eyes.

"Unfortunately, no, Miss Lewis," he said, his eyes clicked with mine. "I have no idea where she is. I've had men all over this once they checked with the boyfriend's house and discovered she wasn't there."

"Ransom?" I asked, already knowing the answer. No, Amanda's disappearance had been going on for too long to be ransom. Usually kidnappers wanted their money fast. Four weeks was too long to wait.

He shook his head no.

"Tell me more about the boyfriend," I said, my mind wandering back to what I recalled from the file, which wasn't much. I'd been given a sketch of him...birthday, age, race, nothing more.

Picking Captain Hanson's brain wasn't the purpose of my visit. But, sometimes you had to eat humble pie to get what you wanted. The cigarette in my satchel belonged to someone and I needed to know whom. But not before I stroked a little ego.

"Ah, Nathan Martindale," he said, now a smile on his face. It exposed teeth, but it was hardly kind. "I don't know much about him... know his parents were a creepy lot..."

Something in the captain's tone gave me pause. It was a slight hesitation as if he didn't quite know what he was going to tell me. Almost a stutter, like the lie was on the tip of his tongue and he didn't want to say it.

"You never thought to check him out, since, uh, your regs were at his home a lot?" I said, watching the captain's face. A thin layer of sweat had emerged onto his brow, but he still seemed collected and cool. The perspiration could've been a trick of the overhead lights.

"Well, his parents weren't worth the money paid to the hospitals for their births," he said slowly, and oh, so carefully. "They were constantly in and out of the cradle..."

"I see," I said and I really did see. The Memphis regs didn't take Amanda's disappearance seriously and despite what he said, he still didn't. Not really. His eyes kept scanning the table, except when he spoke to me, and then his eyes burrowed into mine.

Captain Hanson was lying to me.

But why?

"Anyway, tell me what you need, Ms. Lewis," he said, calmly switching back to me with a small grin of relief. "The mayor said you'd be contacting me, but I had no idea it would be in person. Not that I'm not glad to having met you in the living, breathing, lovely flesh."

Somehow his words didn't quite ring true to me, this last part. The earlier stuff seemed like half-truths, but this last sentence was directly bogus—except for his flattery. He knew I'd come and he knew what to tell me when I did arrived.

Or it could be that I was naturally suspicious of everyone?

"There is one thing. I wanted to ask if I could have the full support of the Memphis regulators," I said, using my poor-woman-in-distress act. "While here in the quad working my case. This should be a partnership between us."

"Sure," he said, a tiny bit of twang slipping into his speech. Up until now, he'd succeeded in keeping it out. "What can we do for you?"

"I need this scanned," I said, taking out the discarded cigarette.

It was my only clue, but I couldn't think of a better way to get to the regulators' scanners except to ask. Although Captain Hanson wasn't showing all his face cards, I had only one and I had to play it.

"Not a problem, Miss Lewis. Any of my staff will assist you in whatever you need while here in Memphis. With any luck, we will bring Amanda home."

With that he stood and we shook hands again. He waltzed back to his desk and made an announcement over the complex's audio system that I was assisting with an important case and every regulator was to give me aid if I needed it.

"Now, to get down to the lab, go back past Herman and around to the far right hallway. Follow the signs down into the basement where the violation scene techs are located," he said, his eyes looking right through me. He seemed anxious for me to go.

I took the stairs back down to the first floor, passed the desk clerk and around to the far right hallway, which was painted a pale yellow. As I walked, I recalled my days as a private in the army. The men in my division often referred to me as "nut buster" because of my inability to follow directions barked at me by a higher ranking official. Even back then, I had a tendancy to question. Once the drill sergeant and others realized that I could take any punishment they dished out, they started to punish the troops in my platoon, thus the busting of other privates' nuts.

I rose haphazardly up the ranks and the further I got, the more bullshit I had to wade through. Some of it came from women, other times it came from men, but all of it wasn't worth the tag line printed on tee shirts.

After a nice, casual workout a la bedroom with the commanding officer after breakfast, which later became a sexual harassment charge, I resigned from the district's army with an honorable discharge. I had to wrangle the honorable part by showing digital pictures of the commanding officer sexually harassing *me*.

Amazing the things one thinks about when around a bunch of people in uniforms.

I reached the lab section of headquarters nestled down in the basement, a long, rectangular room that ran the width of the building. Here, scientists tried to help regulators solve violation efforts and piece together evidence to convict the guilty and to exonerate the victims of wrong place wrong time.

I approached a bubbly blonde whose name tag read Buffy. Great and I couldn't keep the bad blonde jokes out of my brain. No other scientists appeared to be in yet. She wore a white lab coat and her shiny ringlets up in a bun. A few curls escaped to surround her face like baby'sbreath and she smiled as soon as I approached.

But the smile could've been for the regulator beside her. I couldn't really tell.

Standing a little ways behind her was a standard issued regulator. He stood erect, his eyes directed ahead at Buffy's computer screen. He wore a turquoise shirt and black slacks and hiking boots. His skinny arms folded across his chest and his legs stood apart. His starched, straight, uniform made my back hurt it was so damn *perfect*.

"Buffy, can you scan this and tell me whose prints are on it?" he asked, his voice full of the commanding tone that reminded me of nails on chalkboards.

"Yes, Derrick, but--"

"Regulator Jameson," he said, his tanned face a blank visage of stone, "Surely you can remember that."

"...give me a few hours. I've got other cases to do first," she said with a smile, ignoring his interruption and his harsh tone. She shot the same sincere smile as if he had proposed.

Regulator Jameson reeked of that fresh-from-the-academy-hard-as-nails attitude that I absolutely detested in regulators, especially rookies. It's what most often got them killed in the line of duty, but it could also help them fly up through the ranks...all the way to captain. Hanson had some residual of this on his personality; over time it had probably been honed to be less intrusive.

This wasn't a good sign for me. I wanted to get the scan and get out of there.

"I want it in an hour," he demanded, his voice amazingly militant. His tanned face stood out against his uniform.

Where would you get a tan like that in the middle of March? Tanning bed? Fake tan in a can? Miami?

Buffy stared back at him and then moved her bright green eyes to me. "Not until you tell me who this is," she snapped back at him. It wasn't malicious, but friendly, like a polite tap, not a hard whipping.

Startled, Jameson blinked and glanced over at me. "Who are you?"

"I'm Cybil Lewis," I said as I extended my hand, brushing past Jameson and forcing him to step back out of the limelight. Now that I was in Memphis, I felt free to toss the mayor's name around. It could open doors, sure, but I knew that it could also close some as well. I was guessing that here at regulator headquarters, it would open them.

"I'm here on behalf of Mayor Christensen."

"Oh yeah. You're the one Captain Hanson said to assist with whatever you need," he said, his eyes gleaming with entertainment or malice. He turned to Buffy and said in a snide voice, "She is here on behalf of Mayor Christensen."

I could see the urge to smile. The corners of his mouth moved in the direction of a grin, but not completely.

Warning bells sounded in my head, but I ignored them. I focused only on getting the prints and possible DNA from this cigarette. So what the guy was an ass? I met several of those a day.

Buffy's eyes widened in awe. "You're Cybil Lewis!" She squealed like a teenager at a concert and I smirked.

I didn't get that from females too often.

"You-you ousted Governor Price not too long ago with that excellent detecting of his plans to take over the Southwest Territories," Buffy rambled on, drawing a long, hard stare from Regulator Jameson. He went so far as to shush her, but she ignored him.

"Yeah, but it happened a while ago. That's not what brings me down here today. Could you run this through the scanner?" I asked, trying to steer her back to the task at hand. Celebrity didn't really work for me. My ego was large enough as it was.

"Absolutely!" she said and took the plastic container from my hand. With her latex covered hands, she lifted the lid. Next, she took a pair of tweezers and lifted the cigarette from its case and sniffed. "Smells like rain."

I nodded, not wanting to give anything away and very aware of Jameson hovering over my shoulder. He didn't seem to be familiar with the Change case or my involvement in the violation charges against former Governor Price, but then he was really young.

And he wasn't happy that Buffy was dropping everything, including his prints, to look at my cigarette.

Jameson wasn't busy on the street or doing any investigation work because he stood at Buffy's station for a good twenty minutes, watching her work. Perhaps he didn't trust her to do a good job. I had the feeling that he was hanging around to see my results. I didn't know why I felt this way. Just my gut speaking.

Buffy placed the cigarette onto a sleek scanner behind her after she had separated the outer edge where the person's lip sucked nicotine. The scanner rested along the edge of her desk, surrounded by framed photographs and clocks. A baby blue butterfly clock that read the time as nine-thirty with its mechanical hands, while another square butterfly clock the color of taupe gave the time as ten o'clock.

The flash of red light drew my attention back to the scanner as the laser beam drifted over the cigarette.

I waited.

Jameson waited with his arms folded across his chest.

Buffy hummed a tune to herself.

Finally, her computer screen flickered.

"Well, here's the good news," Buffy said around a wad of bright pink gum. "There are fingerprints on the cigarette."

"The bad news?" I asked, already not liking this.

"They're classified," she said with a sigh. "Somebody doesn't want us to know who this guy or gal is. It could be anyone. At this point, there's no way for me to tell."

"DNA from the saliva? Male or female, can you at least give me that?"

Something, I needed something. Wonderful. Although the prints were classified, I knew that meant only one thing. Territories Alliance or regulator. It could be a T.A. agent was following me. No doubt in hopes that I would lead him to Trey. Or it could be the Memphis regulators spying on me for Mayor Christensen.

Buffy swerved partially around in her chair, allowing to me get a good look at her profile.

"Here, one second." She clicked a few buttons on her touch screen, nails causing the plasma to ripple as she skipped across message windows, and then waited.

The computer bell rang and Buffy clicked on the highlighted box. It enlarged to fill the screen with a report. "The person is definitely male, but I can't give you any more than that. It's red flagged and tapped up tight—classified."

I stood there staring at the file as if willing it to give me more.

"Listen, I've got work to do. Anything else?" Buffy asked.

As before it didn't sound rude or crass. Something about her voice made it amusing, even nice. Perhaps it was her smiling face that took the edge off her words.

"Thank you," I said as I turned to leave. I walked a few paces and looked back to the pair.

Jameson lingered around to discuss something with Buffy. He had his hand wrapped around her wrist and appeared to be jerking her arm as if to emphasize a point. Her clear complexion grew slightly pink, but she shook her head no to whatever he was saying to her.

I thought to go back and set Regulator Jameson straight about putting his hands on women, but instead I found my way back to the front. I'd gotten what I came here for.

"Ms. Lewis!" someone shouted as I passed the desk clerk.

Hearing my name bellowed out across the room made my stomach tighten. It couldn't be good, that much was for sure. This day, like the ones before, was sinking into bad luck like a person who'd broken a mirror.

"Yeah," I said as I stopped before the security trunks

Herman, the desk clerk, gestured for me to come over to him. Half an hour ago, he didn't even look me in the face or acknowledge my presence except for grunts.

Now he wanted to talk?

I shoved my way through the packed intersection of the lobby up to his desk.

"Yeah."

"Call came in for you," he said as he handed me the earpiece and turned the telemonitor around for me to watch the picture. He clicked on the message and turned his attention to watching the prostitutes waiting outside the booking room. Must have been a raid or something where so many were scooped up at once. Why stay and peddle your wares here when they could do it freely in the Northwest Territories?

Jane's face popped on screen. "This call is for Cybil Lewis. Meet me at the rental room by eleven; I've got something you should see. End call."

Straight to the point. I glanced down at my watch, ten minutes after ten.

"Thanks," I said as I handed back the earpiece to Herman, the bored watcher.

He mumbled something I couldn't quite catch.

I wandered out of headquarters knowing only a little more than I did before.

Perhaps Jane had better luck with the boyfriend.

CHAPTER 15

"Tell me again why we're here?" I said fighting to keep my voice pleasant in light of the bold wind blowing and slicing through my coat. The noonday sun had been erased from the welkin by a hoard of dark clouds.

"Because," Jane said as she squatted down next to a midnight-black aerocycle, her reflection gliding across the polished finish, "Aunt Belle paid us and because my cousin vanished."

"It is molecularly impossible for a human being to vanish," I said against the wind's fierce howl and suppressed the urge to squeal. The cold slipped in and poked my skin. "Ugh!"

Jane raised an eyebrow and a queer look appeared on her face, before focusing her attention back on the muddy footprints that circled past her aunt's aerocycle, a slick, two-blaster vehicle with lots of chrome and leather, and on to the river's edge.

"You sure this is the spot?" I asked, irritated and a little bit cold. My toes were numb and I hopped from foot to foot trying to keep the blood flowing. Jane was doing more detecting than I was at the moment. The cold winds seemed to slip under my scabs and made them squirm and itch.

I followed Jane carefully as she stepped over the frozen, muddy tracks into the brittle yellow grass. She squatted down and the blades were mashed under her black combat boots. She ran her fingers through the surrounding stiff stalks.

Her sunglasses hid her eyes from me. "She was here. The boyfriend said this was her favorite spot to be when pissed off at her mom. He even said that she'd worn high heels when he last saw her. Look, there are holes in the mud."

I stared into the blackness of her sunglasses.

"Okay, led on."

I saw the tiny, nearly nickel size holes in the mud. They weren't the only tracks here, which meant our girl hadn't been alone…if the marks belonged to our missing person at all. This could be many people's favorite spot.

"It poured last night," I said. "How can there still be prints here?"

"Because it only rained in our section of town and further east. Not over here on the west bank," Jane explained. "The meteorologist called them scattered rain showers."

"But this could be anyone's hang out," I said back, playing devil's advocate because Jane didn't need to get her hopes up too high. Too much time had passed to think Amanda was still alive, but I too clung to hope anyway with the whispers of reality cutting through every now and again.

"Mud, lipstick, and high heels," Jane was saying as I focused through the frigid day. "She was here."

I nodded, relenting to her assumption. "The big question is: where is she *now*?"

The Mississippi River, dark, dirty and draining, licked at the embankment like a lover with patience and gentleness. In slow, southern leisurely fashion, it made its way through the divided states, and on to the Gulf of Mexico, taking the deep, dreadful environmental garbage (literally) to a watery grave.

Jane and I continued to scour the area with my mood plummeting further and further into the black. In this cold spell, I only wanted one thing. A warm bed and a hot cup of cocoa.

Okay two things.

We scanned the area in a one hundred-foot radius from the tracks.

We found nothing, nothing that would point us in the

direction of Amanda Christensen. Where did she go after she came here?

If she came here at all.

"Can we go now?" I didn't like the way it sounded, like a whine. I don't whine, but damn if the horrid weather wasn't making me behave in the worst manner possible.

Jane was still in training and I was a seasoned as a Cajun fish fry. This cursed personal case spurred her on like an enraged lion. One that may attack its trainer.

She shot me a brief smile that disappeared as soon as it began, barely lifting her cheeks and nowhere near finding its way up to her eyes.

"You're pouting," she said, her voice flat and without emotion. Digging around in the hard dirt could do that to you.

"No I'm not," I said back defensively, huddling deeper into my coat. "I'm complaining and there is a difference."

"We've got company," she muttered as she stood up.

I looked over my shoulder in the direction of the humming noise of a blue wauto. It set down a few feet away, blowing loose dirt, dust, and debris across the area.

"Cybil Lewis," a male and annoyed voice called from the wauto's roof-mounted speaker. The driver side door opened before the craft had time to completely set down.

"Who wants to know?" I asked, my voice steady and firm.

Through the raised door, Regulator Jameson stepped out. He didn't wear a coat, but he did wear a toboggan hat that matched his uniform. Twice in one day. How lucky I must be…

"Mayor Christensen sent this," he said, his voice matter-of-fact as he held out a dirt-brown satchel. "In it are a few containers of coffee, sandwiches, and napkins. Wouldn't want you two ladies getting messy out here."

How did he know we were out here to begin with? How did the mayor know?

The mayor had to have us followed. It wasn't a wauto or

I'd picked up on it. It was more than likely a tiny tracking device or something similar. Regs used them all the time. GPS too.

Not for the first time did I think that Jane and I were being followed. Jane hadn't left it on the telemonitor as to where we'd be going. She was too smart for that and to the best of my knowledge no regulator followed us from Henry's to here.

Jane stepped over to Jameson and took the satchel. She held it distastefully away from her as if it was filled with feces instead of food.

Then again, the look could have been because Regulator Jameson had called us *ladies*.

"Thanks," I said to him. The sooner he was gone, the sooner we could leave too. I didn't quite trust him, but again, I rarely trusted anyone.

He bolted to his heated wauto without further comment so quickly that I didn't see the door open fully to allow him entry.

In moments, he was gone.

"Hungry?" Jane asked, a tight smile on her face. It looked like it hurt…a lot.

"Don't test me today, Jane. I'm freezing and tired."

I only wanted to be warm and to solve this case so that I could go back home. I missed my bed and my apartment. Familiar things—smells, sights, and sounds. My body still ached from Jarold's punches and the sooner I could relax in a tub of hot water, the better.

"Fine, I'll let it sit. But when Aunt Belle asks about…"

I heard the plop and clank of something against the embankment.

I took several steps back to the edge of the river and glanced down.

Suddenly, I lost all desire for food.

Drifting amongst the debris and ice chunks of the Mississippi River and snared to a piece of wood, was a body.

CHAPTER 16

It wasn't pretty, but rarely is death as glamorous as we've been lead to believe by movies. Death, up close, isn't beautiful. It is gritty. Death pushes its way into life, snatching loved ones at inopportune times, taking hearts with it and leaving in their place a cold box of grief.

Death hurt. It stank. And it was permanent.

Jane crouched down closer to the body. Her sunglasses still kept her feelings from me, but I could tell this stab went deep, deeper than Marsha's death had been, deeper even than her father's abandonment.

"Damn, Cyb. The regs were just here," she said, her voice strained and trembling although she ignored it. "I didn't see or hear anything."

"By the looks of it, it's been in the water about three, maybe four, weeks," I said calmly. My braids held back by a thinning rubber band, suddenly felt too tight.

She wasn't Amanda Christensen anymore, not a person, not a daughter, not an honor roll student and definitely not Jane's cousin. Now, she was only "the body" or better, "it."

Jane and I hated losing, but we lost this one. We didn't find Amanda in time. From the looks of it, we didn't have a chance anyway. She'd been killed almost immediately after disappearing some three to four week ago.

Hopefully the forensic team for the Memphis Regulators could come up with an exact time, but I'd bet my last bit of district dollars she was killed if not as soon as she disappeared, but shortly there after.

Jane stood up fast. "I've got to get some air and call Aunt Belle."

She stalked past me, still careful of preserving the muddy tracks, because now this was a violation scene. The regulators would be swarming all over this area, mucking up the case and ruining evidence.

But hey, it was their case and I didn't want us catching the blame for missing evidence, and such.

With one glance downward to Amanda's floating corpse, I asked myself, not for the first time, why I did this job.

Oh, yeah, because I earned a paycheck and the army didn't want me anymore. I'm not good with authority. But cases like this, made my chosen profession difficult to stomach.

Jane's laptop was out and soon the screen was filled with the face of Mayor Christensen. "Aunt Belle, I've got something to tell you..."

I turned away to crouch down by the edge. This river once held entertainment; its purpose as a port and host to showboats was now legendary. Today it carried death. I took out a pair of latex gloves from my pants pocket. Technically, I could not remove evidence and I definitely wasn't supposed to touch anything at the vio scene. As a private inspector, I was a second rate citizen when it came to the regulators. Citizens could do citizen arrests, but private inspectors couldn't. The i.d. chip placed beneath my skin told everyone with a scanner my identity and profession.

Deep down I had the feeling Captain Hanson didn't want me snooping around any more than I wanted to be here, despite his forthcoming personality. The suspicion that he was hiding something nagged at me.

Jealousy was at the heart of anti-p.i. rules, I'm sure. Regulators were trained and paid to regulate the laws, but rarely did they do that. Some regulators were the most dangerous violators on the planet.

I stopped thinking about that as I stared at the partially frozen body.

Amanda Christensen's chocolate-brown hair melted into the soiled ice and shot out of the Mississippi water like whiskers on a cat. Bloated due to being in the water for so long, her facial features, distorted and grotesque, loomed out from beneath the water's top layer, almost like a film. Difficult to really make out her face, I was certain it was Amanda.

The necklace around her neck identified her as such. That present came from her father and she liked it most according to her mother. It spelled princess in ancient Egyptian hieroglyphs and it was specially made for her during a recent trip to see the pyramids.

Memphis was in fact named from the real city of Memphis in ancient Egypt and it was this reason that Amanda first became interested in Egyptology. When she grew up, she wanted to be an archeologist.

That wouldn't happen now.

I couldn't see a lot from my spot by the water's edge without waddling in or taking her out.

I knew the cause of death wasn't drowning.

It was a laser gun blast to the left temple.

CHAPTER

17

The mayor's usual warm, rosy face held very little color and looked like watered down coffee. Her mouth drawn into a little wrinkled *o* did not ask any questions and her shoulders slacked. Her posture was normally so correct that I could hang pictures with it.

"Mayor?" I could feel her shock at the news. The expression on her face was one of internal debate, a process I knew very well.

The three steps of grief, to which I am so familiar, would commence at any moment. In fact, I bet the mayor was agonizing over all the things she would have, could have done, and what she could and did not say to her only offspring.

I am an un-certified expert in grief management having lost my mother, my father, my secretary and an extremely-too-long list of loved ones to violent ends.

Death and I were on a first name basis.

"Are you sure it's Mandy?" she asked, her voice croaking on the name. It was so soft it reminded me of crushed rose petals in a fist. "Janey, are you one hundred percent?"

Mayor Christensen's internal debate had spilled out to us. Phase two of the grief cycle. Blame. In order for her to make sense of this, she needed to assign blame. This definitely didn't make any sense. Children weren't supposed to die before their parents. It was out of sync and definitely *wrong*.

"If only the damn regulators hadn't taken so long to get started..." she trailed off, her voice small and shaky. Plenty of blame to go around this time.

"I'm certain Aunt Belle, but of course, someone in the family will need to make a positive id," Jane whispered back, her voice level and firm. She was family of course, but someone other than the people hired to investigate Amanda's disappearance, needed to come down and make a positive match. "I'm sorry, Aunt Belle, I'm so sorry…"

Mayor Christensen's hazel eyes watered, but no tears fell. Her mouth was a grim line and for once, I actually felt sorry for her.

"Yes, of course. Janey, get out of there and I will send the regulators immediately. This is not your fault. You did the best you could."

Phase three, pretend everything is all right and get back to business. The three phases would be repeated over and over again for days, maybe even years until at some point the mayor stopped it and faced death head on. Grief knew no end, and that was a tough lesson to learn.

Hell on some days, I find myself back in the grief cycle again. Mother's day was a biggie. Maybe you never get out of the cycles.

"We'll give statements to the regs," Jane said. "I'm so sorry."

"I'm sorry for your loss," I said gently over Jane's shoulder, though at the sound of my voice I thought the mayor actually scowled.

She nodded numbly and disconnected the feed.

We've been paid up front and agreed to find the mayor's daughter. We had done the job in remarkable time, but somehow it felt unfinished. We didn't actually find her alive, but we did twist her boyfriend's arm hard enough to find out where he'd last seen her. So hard in fact, Jane thought she broke it, but that was his word against hers.

So why did I still feel like worms were crawling around in my stomach?

CHAPTER 18

The return ride to our rental room at Henry's resembled a mime convention...no talking. Jane maneuvered the aerocycle as it zipped so that it dipped and skipped across other lanes and wautos. In her wake, drivers honked, cursed and tried to cut her off in road rage protests and life endangering retaliation.

I held on for dear life, tightly gripping Jane's black leather bomber.

But she seemed oblivious to all the chaos that sprang up in her wake as she raced across town. Lost in thoughts and no doubt memories of her cousin, her driving made me wonder if Jane wasn't eager to join Amanda in the morgue.

If there would even be enough of us left to scoop up and put into a jar. Mid-air collisions were often fatal and pieces of humans, wautos and whatever else floated down to the earth with such speed and force that very little remained of the individual or people in the crafts.

Have I mentioned I *hated* aerocycles?

Enclosed in a shell of reinforced fiberglass and metal, I feel safer. Although a collision at this height either in a wauto or aerocycle would probably kill me, I still liked being in a wauto.

Jane jetted along.

Not all cases ended with a happily ever after.

All right. *None* of my cases end up with a happily ever after.

Honesty. My best policy.

Yeah right.

The elevated lanes were miles up in the air. Down below us rested a quiet, rain-drenched Memphis. The afternoon sun, cutting through a tiny section of sky, spotlighted a section of the partially wet city as we zoomed above in lighted lanes. We passed over a small pond and from this distance it resembled a sullen gray coin.

The air whipped across my throat where my helmet stopped. So cold that I envisioned it stripping away flesh and forcing my eyes to tear up. It made my wounds itch and beg to be scratched.

I knew we were in for a little more rain. The air was damp with promise that a downpour was on tap for later. In the distance, the lowering sun turned the clouds a mustard color. Thick with moisture, the air smelled like rain.

And I thought of Buffy, the VSI girl.

"Looks like rain is coming," Jane said into her microphone.

The aerocycle's X blasters roared so loud that there was no way for me to hear her speak. So we both wore helmets with little microphones so we could talk to each other.

"It may turn into snow," I said. "Or ice if the temperature dips down enough tonight."

"Yeah," she said. Her voice had that quietness that came with immense sadness.

As if hearing our conversation, icy rain leaked from the sky, spraying us with tiny ice pebbles. The sun still peeked out from rends in the clouds.

It wasn't the first time today that I'd been caught out in the rain. Despite that knowledge, it still didn't put me in a better mood.

Finding Amanda dead didn't help either.

After Marsha's death, Jane continued to work. As did I. We were smack in the middle of a case that wouldn't, no, let me correct that, couldn't be dropped. Some people wanted us, and the rest of humanity that wasn't a hatchling, dead.

Jane took the left lane and we headed downward toward

the city. Overhead clouds rippled as if a giant finger poked the sky creating a mass of crinkles.

Fate was like that too.

A huge finger that jerked everybody's chain.

CHAPTER

19

When we arrived at the rental room, Jane immediately packed herself an overnight bag and disappeared into the hallway, heading toward her aunt's house. I logged onto to my handheld and booked an eleven p.m. flight out to the moon colonies. Although I knew that Amanda was dead and not playing hooky on the moon, I wanted to talk to the people at the places she frequented there. Perhaps, someone knew something about the mayor's only child.

I didn't admit it to myself, but I had a bad case of restlessness. Not that the mayor was paying to find out who killed her daughter—she wasn't. Despite my own hunger to get home, I couldn't sit in the rental room as if nothing had happened at all. Every time I closed my eyes, Amanda's bloated and laser beam blasted face drifted up to greet me.

A ghost, unable to sit still at the morgue, Amanda was reaching out to me. Yeah, I didn't believe that any more than you, but I l wanted the creep who killed her captured.

I stuffed clothes and other necessities into my satchel, spilling out the non-necessary contents onto my bed. I didn't plan to stay overnight on the moon. The trip took about a day and half, but going up and turning around and coming right back gave me something to do. Warfare streaked across the gravity fields and people lay dead up there. The moon wasn't exactly a vacation spot. I read in a recent article in the *D.C. Mirror* that there were so many deceased soldiers, dozens of open cargo trucks had become mass gravesites.

What people wouldn't do to become citizens of certain territories.

For the next several hours, I slept. I woke up around five and had an early dinner of peanut butter and jelly. I drank some pretty decent coffee. Both the sandwich and the coffee came from a small deli across the street from Henry's and two doors down from the liquor store. The deli, a place called Little HoFi's Deli, had an extensive selection of something I couldn't get in the D.C. District—cheese. Cheese required milk, but the owner, Henry Williams, said that his father managed to thread out any mutations from four of his cows. The cows had bred other cattle, which were no longer prone to mutations. Those claims were difficult to prove, for threading out mutations wasn't as easy as Henry made it sound. It took years, hell, from what I've read on it, it could take centuries to do. Needless to say I was sorely tempted, but I erred on the side of caution and ordered peanut butter and jelly instead.

I'd only had cheese once in my life and that was with my grandmother, a long time ago when I couldn't have been more than two or three. I remembered the day because it was my birthday and I got to wear my favorite skirt, a denim one with rhinestones along the pockets. They made an arc of glittering stars along each pocket mouth—gleaming like teeth, at least to me. I used the deep pockets for my toys. My grandmother and parents, along with Tisha, had chosen to go out for my special day and I was lucky enough to get to pick the place.

I chose Manny's Pizza. The place was only down the block from our house, and served big, gooey slices of heaven. Grandmother loved the idea, but the cost, well, was high for our family. Only special occasions could warrant pizza with cheese—real dairy cheese.

The memory called up ghosts of birthdays past and riding the recall's current were emotions of longing…to be a family again, to hear them speak, and to be embraced by unconditional love.

Shuddering at the thought, I ate my dinner in record time,

savoring the coffee and its warmth before I headed out in the Memphis chill. I rechecked the traveling bag, shoved in an extra pair of jeans and a long-sleeved tee-shirt in case I got stuck there unexpectedly. I picked up my jacket, checked my weapons in my bag, separating the batteries from the guns, and left the rental room.

Back in the safety of my own wauto, I wondered what Jane would do as I headed for the Memphis Launcher. She didn't speak to me, but her jerky actions told me that she was hurting ...badly. Without waiting for my comments, she fled to her family. They would need her of course to lean on, to help out with notifying others and putting together the arrangements. I had no real clue as to how Christensen was taking it. Every time I'd seen the mayor on webcast programs, interviews, etc. she presented such a well put together front that my attempts to imagine her as anything else, met with mental blank gaps in my mind.

At the Memphis Launcher, I made it through security only because I left my weapons in my vehicle. My luggage only carried clothes and toiletries enough for one night. They didn't question me about it. I had to carry something. Showing up without luggage to any Launcher set off warning bells to the security crew that you may indeed be about to blow something up. Everyone had overnight clothes or else you wouldn't be flying...rather that be to the moon colonies or to the other territories.

Even in this less than stellar time, people didn't want to die while on the way to vacation, business, or relocation. Hope was launched with each take off to the moon. A bomb, or worse, a hijacking had a tendency to stamp out any balloons of hope floating around the passengers and their currency.

After going the wrong direction to the wrong gate, I finally made it to gate MC3601 on the twelfth floor. Not many people were headed to the moon at eleven at night. I counted five in total, not including the flight crew.

Only morons seeking murderers.

Brownie points for me.

CHAPTER

20

Juan, the owner of the Joker's Pun, held the blaster, a a gun much bigger and longer than my 350 to the soldier's chest. He fired without even blinking and the young man was blown backward to the wall, smacking it with a sickening *crack* before smashing forward to the floor. The wound at his back was the size of well-rounded pizza, complete with lots of sauce and tossed toppings from his uniform.

"Ain't skipping out now, are ya?" Juan muttered and tipped his hat back off of his head. A double helix tattoo decorated the right side of his meaty neck, and other tattoos covered the area of his forearms and biceps. There didn't appear to be any theme or pattern to the inked art, random images... Very much like what traveled in and out the Joker's Pun.

He searched the faces around him, but I didn't want our eyes to meet. "Anybody else wanna skip out on ya bill?"
His mechanical eyes, an extra set above his other pair, slept in rotatin shifts.

The bartender muttered earlier that Juan was an alien—the tattoo a fake; others said he was a hatchling gone array and the geneticists sent him here to keep out of the public's, uh-hem, eye.

I watched this from my spot at a rear table at the Joker's Pun. The information came about in the last two hours of me sitting and floating amongst the regulars.

And I wasn't alone as a couple of guys picked up the now dead soldier and carried the body out, blood droplets dripping to the floor, creating a ghastly trail. I didn't doubt they'd toss the guy into one of those cargo craft mass graves, like common garbage. No one sorted through the dead to determine what an actual fatal blast in battle or murder was The soldiers were identified by the barcode on their wrists, packaged into a coffin, sealed up like a piece of meat, and shipped home in dry ice to their families. It was like packaging frozen chicken fingers.

A greasy guy by the name of Martin sat beside me, reeking of sour beer and sweat.

“You got my bill, right?” Martin said with a smile that was amazingly white in such a dreary place.

Up at the stools that encircled the bar, several of the regular patrons kept their gaze on their drinks, not at Juan, who still stood in the spot, waiting for someone to clean up the bloody mess. Several of the woring girls flinted around him, buzzing like bees and trying their best to appease the raging beast-Juan.

"Must have been new around here," Raker, a fellow drinker, cackled and sipped the fallen soldier's beer as the music started up again. "He won't be needing this."

"Cheers," Martin said and lifted his glass, as Raker about drained his. The smoke infested room held many shadows amongst the dust, drab and stank of spilled beer, dead corpses, and sex.

For the last hour, all Martin did was drink. Fatigued weighed on my shoulders. I’d been here three hours too long already—not counting the eighteen hours to get here. I’d learned more about Juan than I ever wanted to know, and honestly, most of his patrons sold him out pretty cheap. No money ever changed hands—only booze purchased on my ticket.

"Back in here again, I see, Martin," Shea, one of the three waitresses, cooed as she wrapped her arm around Martin’s shoulders and pulled herself closer. "You don't need company tonight, I see."

It wasn’t a question, and it had all the ring of an accusation.

"Not your kind of company, Shea, " Martin said, soberly,

pulling away from her embrace. "I'm not accepting services, sweetheart!"

This last he shouted in case Juan thought he was touching the girl without paying. Martin had been around the *Pun* long enough to know better.

She pouted, making sure that her glued-on whiskers were intact. "Suit yourself. You're the one missing out."

"Can you excuse us?" I said turning my voice to ice. "We are conducting business here."

Shea frowned as she gave me the once over. For a second I thought she was going to give me shit, but she thought better of it and scooted on toward the back room where the dance hall thrived despite the early hour.

"Martin, about the girl you said you saw here a few times," I started, but then the front door of the Joker's Pun opened, taking Martin's attention with it.

The doors swung open as three more soldiers dressed in the flat gunmetal gray trousers and shirts spilled in. Fresh cuts, scraps and bandages littered their face and hands. They wore that same look that all soldiers had…horror etched faces and wide eyes filled to the brim with violence, atrocities, and death.

"They don't look older than snot," Raker yelled as the soldiers passed. "Eh, see Martin, they're sending up toddlers."

"Yeah," he muttered and singled the bartender for another.

Martin turned to me, bleary eyed and said, "You from Europe?"

"No," I said. "About the girl…"

"Excuse me. Gotta go to the little boy's room," Martin said, as if he didn't hear me and got up from the table. The desire to kick him swelled up inside me, but one look at Juan's gun squashed it.

Martin must've spent his entire pay here, and I don't think Juan would take too kindly to me eliminating or injuring one of his regular, steady sources of colony credits.

On the wire were transmitted games of soccer from Canada. Static and several wavy lines rolled through the screen, but the Joker's Pun had to be one of the few places on the entire moon that picked up the games at all.

The moon, dark, gray and pretty much dull, had been home to fighting amongst the two Earth colonies that had decided to park here. The divided territories that were once the United States fought it out about every other day, with a stalemate arriving at the day's end. Then sometimes, I'd hear word that the Southeast Territories won; the next day, the Midwest.

It was all the same to me.

Death, death, and oh, did I mention, death?

Someone down closer to the door lit another cigarette. The pungent fumes filtered across the patrons' heads to the opposite end of the bar where I sat in a booth with Martin. I could see the fine, red glow of the cigarette. I thought of Jane and wondered how she was doing. Here any age could smoke, drink, or sell themselves for sex. Regulators, Territory Alliance Agents, and generals didn't come here. Anarchy ruled.

Enter at your own risk.

Suddenly my eyes caught a blur of pasty white flesh and blue jeans as Martin raced to the door. I slapped down some coins on the table and followed him out to the parking lot.

About three steps into the parking lot, he fell to his knees, held his stomach and lost all the great beer he'd had consumed and I had paid for.

"That's nasty," I said. "Have you no manners? Skipping out on me."

As Martin wiped his mouth with the back of his ratty sweatshirt, I caught a whiff of the odor, sour for sure, and rocked backwards. I nearly ran into a person who was passing by.

"Watch it!" the female voice barked before I almost fell onto her.

With determination I caught myself and whirled around to face the woman..

"Excuse me," I said, trying to show I still had a decent upbringing buried somewhere…deep.

"Whatever."

The girl huffed, sidestepped me and planted her foot directly into Martin's pile of bile and sour beer vomit.

"Ugh!" she cringed and swiftly removed her foot.

She had long, curly brown hair that had hints of blonde throughout, and a narrow nose that stopped short above her full, thick mouth. She wore close to nothing at all, and her rail-thin legs stuck out from her incredibly short skirt like chop sticks.

"Listen, I'm looking for information on a girl. How about I buy you a drink?" I offered.

Martin had already passed out in the yellowish mess. He'd awake in the morning with a large hangover and a nose full of puke. Served him right.

She frowned all the more. Young, nor older than twenty, the scanty outfit she wore with high heels seemed ridiculous. The girl had a starved look to her. "There are a lot of girls here."

"And I only need information about one," I said, gesturing toward the Joker's Pun doors.

"You're new here," she said as she tried to get the last of the substance from the side of her shoe. "Ugh!" She rolled her eyes, a brilliant green even for this dreary place. Then hesitantly, she said, "Yeah, I'll talk to you. You payin'?"

"Every day of my natural life."

I followed her inside and she passed the bar, waving at Tony, on back to the thumping beat of the dance hall.

"Well. Let me be the first to welcome you to the moon," she said with a smile, revealing a gap between her two front teeth.

She stopped at a small area, no larger than a closet, stuffed with chairs. She sat down in one and I took the one beside her. The music was loud, but muffled by the closed door.

"Okay." She shrugged making her slender shoulders beneath the gauzy blouse rise. "What do you want?"

I showed her a jpeg of Amanda on my PDA. "Have you seen this girl before?"

The girl shrugged again. Her eyes stared at the door. From beneath slivers of music slipped in and the girl tapped her foot along to the beat.

"I buy you a beer, you answer the questions, that was the deal," I said, my patience with the moon colonies inhabitants wearing down.

She sighed again and looked at the picture. "Yeah, that's Stacy."

"Stacy?"

"Yeah," the girl clucked her tongue. "She dances on the weekends, here. Well, she used to, but I don't know. I ain't seen her in a long while."

"By dance, you mean…" I didn't want to hear the answer, but I had to ask.

"Not naked or nuthin'. Stacy wasn't like that," the girl chewed her gum, looking younger than a few minutes before. "Now, if you lookin' for a show. Stick around another ten minutes. I dance like a goddess."

I cleared my throat, thought of all the leery, creepy men here, and asked, "Have you ever seen her with anyone?"

The girl nodded. "Some older man. Sugah daddy I guessed, but Stacy wouldn't tell anybody his name. He like, came here only once, and all the other times, it was her."

"Thanks," I said to her and dropped beer money into her hand. She simpered off to the main dance room.

I waited about ten minutes and walked across the hallway to the dance room. I opened the door and stepped inside. The smoke thinned as I crossed the hall. The whining music proceeded to get louder and by the time I entered the crowded space, the level was at full blast. I could barely hear myself think. The pounding base felt like my heart, *boom-boom-boom.*

The bar area smelled mostly of smoke and beer, but this place had another scent all together.

It was the stale, sweat-stained aroma of sex.

Dim and unlit except for a few candles and illumination devices scattered throughout, no one smoked back here. The smoke might interfere with what they're actually looking at.

A sparse crowd of men sat across the room at makeshift tables. On the stage, the girl I had interviewed raised her hand and the guy in the bright yellow suit raised his glass in an offer of thanks. Or an invitation for later, I wasn't sure.

Alone on the rug, nestled beneath a solo lamp, she shook her long lustrous hair in conjunction with her round, full breasts. She seemed to not be aware of the pack of men below the stage who slobbered and panted for her. The music blared on and she seemed oblivious to the rhythm. She danced, but coordination wasn't high amongst her list of talents.

If she danced like a *goddess,* then divinity had taken a nosedive.

The men howled and whistled in encouragement, but she didn't need it. She was too busy riding high on the act of exhibiting her skinny body. The music blared as she performed to the beat, dancing with the song and losing herself in the bass. Showing off her ribs and too small stomach, caved in upon itself.

I fought down the urge to run onto the stage, cast my clean shirt over her nakedness, throw her over my shoulder, and run for my life, hell for *her* life. This girl needed to be fed, not displayed like a starved sex kitten.

Mesmerized by what I saw, I could not look away nor could I really look.

The girl was barely legal if that. Finally disgusted, I made my way out of the hall, and down the cramped corridor to the bar. I noticed that some of the backroom spectators had trickled out to the bar area in favor of more entertaining programming.

Soccer.

I called for a cab to take me back to the launcher to wait for my flight back to Memphis. I had learned absolutely nothing, except that Amanda danced on the weekends at the Joker's Pun. Nice, well-put-together women did not go to the Joker's Pun for fun or social parties. The Joker's Pun was a thinly veiled street corner for prostitutes.

On the flight up to the moon, I met a woman who was looking for her daughter. I asked her why girls flocked to there. She told me that she believed it was the same drive for freedom, for exploring the unknown that had forced Columbus across the Atlantic as mixed up as he was. What they found, the woman said, was a ghetto—the same thing they could've found on Earth. She recounted how her daughter and many, many others begged for food and in return were often beaten, raped or otherwise abused.

I couldn't figure out why Amanda would run to such a place. The quad had many of places to slum it.

Outside my window glittering fireworks were being set off in the north. The war was moving closer; soon this block of apartments and churches would be a battleground. My cabbie seemed not to notice. A robot guided the wauto without conversation or pretense.

No human in his or her right mind would fly a cab in this shithole.

For once I was glad a robot was behind the flight console, although, my hands were gripping the rear seatbelt in case I needed to unhook it and make a jump out of the door in mid-flight. Robots were not safe, but in this case, safer than a human being.

I passed gates and high-level security compounds in various apartment buildings and rented rooms to the northeast, where the government military officials of both sides lived protected. Their lights burned brightly against the ink-black sky.

"Coffee," I said and the small, boxy metal coffeemaker shot coffee into a recycled paper cup. When done it beeped. I thought more about why Amanda and girls like her were here. All the females at the Joker's Pun were here for one thing.

And it wasn't milk and cookies.

Colony credits.

Amanda didn't need it so why dance at a dump on the moon when all she had to do was ask her mother?

Not that Amanda would be the first to go out and slum it with the common folk. Juan definitely was a killer and could've killed Amanda, but what for? Because she wouldn't dance naked? I didn't get the impression that girls who did strip were hard to come by. Amanda could've been coming to the moon to score Zenith or some other drug, but why so far from home?

Unless, she wanted to keep her new boyfriend secret. She couldn't go anywhere in the quad because she was known as the mayor's daughter. But here amongst death and destruction, no one cared who she was. Hell, most people didn't even know who they were on most days.

I quickly ruled out the cast of characters from the club. No, none of the people at the Joker's Pun had the means and money to get to Earth, kill Amanda, and then get back to the moon colonies. Time—yes. Currency—no.

My gut complained to the strong, bitter coffee. Surreal and light-headed, my body craved sleep, but I couldn't. Not until I was back in Memphis. I'd been awake for over twenty-four hours.

I needed to know more about Amanda, who came to the colonies as Stacy to dance away her nights with an older man. There was still so much I didn't know.

But one thing was for certain.

Jane was not going to like this.

CHAPTER

21

The Methodist Church of Southern Memphis sat at the end of a long stretch of paved road. Back when people used automobiles, the road must have been a terror for traffic, because it had only one lane each way. Yet the church sat about six hundred people. The parking lot wrapped around the church in a "u" pattern, providing enough space for people to park, even though the road didn't give enough lanes for the herd of people who arrived.

Sunday morning's sun rose to a sky clear of clouds. Solo on such a grand stage, the beautiful sunlight illuminated the ugliness man continued to wrought. It was a precise crystal blue. Even though the day outside was gorgeous, inside the church was horrid. People plowed into the double set of doors beneath the overhanging cross with all the rudeness and outright crassness of those panicked, grief stricken, and nosy. In low, hushed voices, they whispered and some even had the grace to cry, but most were there to watch the spectacle unfold.

Even the press came out, respectfully dressed in funeral black, but I was still pretty disgusted. The family should have been be able to suffer in private, without the teardrop count of Mayor Christensen making the front page webpage of all the e-news pages.

I sat towards the back of the church, trying to get a good view of the people coming to pay their respects and trying to hide my own extreme exhaustion. Somehow I managed to snag about ten hours of rest on the trip home. From my position, close to the doors, I could see Mayor Christensen at the very front pew. Dressed in an all black turtleneck dress and black, sleek boots she was the perfect picture of grief chic. Her purple painted nails fingered the pearl necklace around her neck. She sat rigidly in her seat. People walked up to her, said a few words of consolation and patted her on the back. Some even hugged her, but she was unbending.

Jane tumbled into the church from the side restrooms, clad in all black. Her face blank and devoid of expression, she went directly to the front pew. She collapsed in the seat beside her aunt. I saw several other men and women seat themselves alongside Jane on the bench, but I didn't know any of them. Family had arrived from all across the quadrant, and some from as far away as the Floridian Territory.

Around eleven, the funeral service began and the minister came out to discuss ashes and dust. I looked around the packed church, studying faces, when my eyes landed on Captain Hanson.

He got up from his seat and in haste hurried to the restroom. When he reached me in the last pew, he stopped abruptly, startled, but forced a smile in my direction. He continued on to the restroom. His eyes were bloodshot and he definitely looked as if he'd been crying despite his charming, on-demand smile.

Nathan Martindale, the love of Amanda's life, did not show up at all. Could it be the service was too much? Or had Mayor Christensen stepped in and forbid him from coming?

Nevertheless, the service went on with cries, eulogies and Amens.

My mind kept going back to Amanda. To have the pastor tell it, she was a callow young girl. She had a future, a mother in politics, and a cousin who could spit nails and fight the gods for her. Yet, that had been taken away from her. Snatched, stolen out of her grip, and shoved under water.

Who wanted Amanda dead? Was it kidnappers who failed to ask for ransom? Or had she died before they could? Did she run off, like she had done so many times before, only to meet up with a dangerous drifter who liked little teenage girls?

So many questions.

Finally the funeral was over, reporters tried to get pictures of the casket, a nice girlish pink with ruffles and lace. They were kicked out, but not before Mayor Christensen gave a statement on the church's steps. Mr. Christensen was nowhere to be found, and I made a mental note to ask Jane about Amanda's father. A father wouldn't miss his own daughter's funeral unless something extremely important came up—like his own death, critical injury, or incarceration.

Come to think of it, I'd never met Mr. Christensen, nor had I read or seen anything in electronic print about him. Some celebrities like to keep their personal lives private, but Mayor Christensen shared hers with the media. Yet, there hadn't been anything at all about her spouse. The man was like a ghost.

I didn't leave at first, but rather watched everyone file out of the church.

An hour passed before the place thinned out completely. Bored and itching to leave, it was then that I saw him.

Derrick Jameson.

He wore a baseball cap and sunglasses and was heading out a side exit when I spied him making his escape. His tanned face caught my attention because no one had a tan that good in March.

How did *he* know Amanda Christensen? Better yet, where was Nathan?

It was worth investigating and I was thinking about this when Jane appeared at the front doors beside me. We strolled out onto the church's porch as the backlog of wautos, luxury vehicles, and stretched cargo crafts huddled in stalled traffic.

"What are you doing?" she asked, her voice tense. "You didn't have to come. You didn't even know her."

"People watching mostly. No one's here now. So I'm getting ready to head on out," I said, fighting the urge to slap her for those soured comments about me not knowing her.

"We've got to get this bastard," she said through clenched teeth. "We can't go home until we find who did this. I'm not going—you hear me? I'm going to catch the bastard who did this."

"Yes," I said back, with a soft smile. "But not for revenge, for justice."

I felt the tiniest bit of guilt. Who was I kidding? Though I'd never killed anyone in revenge, I had done, ah, other things to get back at those who hurt me. The Change case, for example, was pure, unadulterated revenge, but I wanted to capture the thing, not end its life.

Only if it hadn't fought back, it would still be around, caged up in glass at some research facility.

She looked over at me and smiled, a little one. "A thin line, but I'll take whatever, so long as he pays. You with me?"

"'Til the end, Jane. 'Til the end."

We stepped down off the porch and on to my wauto. We made a left toward the parking lot. Amanda would be laid to rest on Monday in a private, family-only ceremony. Today's antics had forced Mayor Christensen to make it private.

"How come you're not with your family?" I asked, as I unlocked the doors.

"Aunt Belle said she wanted to be alone," she mumbled. "Plus I can't sit somewhere listening to people cry and talk about how great Mandy was. I need to work."

I tossed my satchel into the rear seats. "Went to the moon colonies. Rumor has it Amanda frequented a few dance clubs there."

She raised her eyebrows in question, but she didn't ask me a question.

"Amanda never went to the moon colonies."

"Jane, I have a reliable tip from a source I've used hundreds of times. I went there. I got proof."

I knew she wasn't going to like it, but damn it, she was

going to have to face the truth sooner or later. I shouldn't have to explain it to her. She should trust my judgments as she had done before.

"This isn't my first case, so don't scrutinize every move I make. I went there and people knew her. Passed her picture around and people identified her."

It came out harsher than I intended. Jane's mouth flopped open and then she shut it. She plopped down into the passenger seat and said, "Of course folks knew her! She's the daughter of a famous mayor! It doesn't mean anything!"

"Jane, I know this is hard for you, but she went to this bar and danced there. Nothing lewd, but she did frequent the place. I went myself, in person, and spoke to the people there. They didn't even know her by her name, but an alias."

"That doesn't mean anything. They could be confusing her with someone else!" Jane spat, her posture rigid with anger. "I want this guy so badly…"

"I know, which is why personal cases are so hard to work," I said, making sure to keep the attitude out of it. Telling her I-told-you-so wasn't necessary. She knew that already. Lost in grief and rage, Jane couldn't hear my words of logic, of proof, and for that I wanted to dunk her head in a bucket of ice water.

She caught the look on my face and took in a long, slow breath. She let it out and clapped her hands together. "Sorry, Cyb., I know…you said we might find out stuff about her that I wouldn't like."

"This is one of those things." I locked the doors and started the flight sequence.

"Yeah, okay, I'll keep snooping around here," she muttered. "Where do we go next?"

"Tell me something. How's your uncle taking this?"

I could have asked her outright where her uncle was, but that might put her on the defensive. Not that she required any reason to get back on the opposite end of the court to defend her family's honor. She didn't.

You never wanted to be opposite Jane when she was on the defensive.

"He's taking it badly as we all are," she said, her head bowed. "Badly, I'm sure."

"Was he Amanda's real father?" I asked, knowing I was slicing close to the bone. But I had to know and Jane could tell me.

"Yeah," she snapped, her head whipped up. She glared at me. "Why did you ask that?"

"Jane, *again,* this is stuff that I'm going to find out. Someone murdered her," I said, my patience slipping through my hands. "You know how this works! You find out all you can about the victim so you can nail the person who killed her."

"Fine!" she shouted back at me. Her body was half turned away from me—as much as possible and still be in the vehicle. "Trash my family! Call my dead cousin a stripper! Go ahead! It don't make any of it true!"

"This isn't about trashing them," I said, feeling my muscles itching to grab her and shake her. "Inspector rule number two, everyone is a suspect. Everyone!"

She looked out the window, her whole body hunched in upon itself as if she meant to fold into nothing. "Even your precious Trey?"

"Yes, even him," I said hotly. "Your aunt! Hell, Jane, you! But thankfully you have an alibi—me."

Jane shook her head no, but didn't scream back at me. Her hands were tangled inside her lap.

I lifted off into the air and hovered behind the scores of others in front of me.

" I'm going to find who murdered your cousin, but you better be ready, Jane for how ugly this might get. Lying to yourself can get us both killed."

She twisted around to me, tears rolling down her cheeks. "I know."

CHAPTER

On Monday, Captain Hanson emailed Amanda's official autopsy report to me. The coroner concluded she died before she was dumped into the Mississippi.

That much I knew already. Cybil one, the Memphis Regulators, zip.

But the report did hold a few surprises.

Amanda had a lack of defensive wounds, indicating that either she was with someone she trusted or was drugged. She had also been raped and what had appeared to be bite marks were on both of her breasts. There was no semen. Most of the physical evidence was lost I guess in the sludge of the Mississippi.

Someone out there raped and killed a sixteen and half year old girl.

I've seen many dead bodies in my somewhat illustrious career. Ripped and mangled, bloated and butchered, but Amanda's haunted me. Children's deaths bothered me.

They should bother everyone.

I sat Indian fashion on my bed in our rental room, dumping this information into my handheld. Jane's cigarette smoke draped the room in a hazy fog. We lacked a foghog inside the room itself. She scanned the telemonitor, listening to news coverage of the funeral and Amanda's death.

I re-read my notes prior to leaving D.C. for Memphis and a few things nagged at me. I wrote them down.

- I needed to gather unbiased information on Mayor Christensen.
- Captain Hanson and Malcolm said that Amanda was rumored to be a wild child.
- M. C. and Jane say she was an angel.
- Malcolm mentioned an older man.
- Who is Nathan Martindale?
- Derrick Jameson?

No answers. Nothing.

Frustrated, I went to the window to look out across the dreary day.

Memphis skies were again muddled with clouds except a patch of crisp blue where the sun shined through the smoky gray. Overhead crafts and wautos zipped about at speeds too fast for this lousy weather.

Yesterdays, and this morning's, newspapers blared headline after headline about Amanda's death. I scanned the files, but didn't come away with stuff I didn't know before about her.

I glanced down again, my eyes drawn to the store where the T.A. agent stalked us several days ago.

There was no one now. But I briefly pondered who it could have been.

I shrugged as I turned away and went back to my bed.

For the better part of an hour, I typed out my thoughts into my handheld. Jane left to go get something to eat

I sighed.

The picture, hell the outline of this puzzle escaped me.

Nothing added up. Could it be because I had nothing to do addition with?

The rental room suddenly became too small and restricting. I escaped down to the lobby for an afternoon snack. Dusk approached and the lobby lay cloaked in shadows. Lit candles licked at the air and the robotic staff hovered on energy saver for there were no new customers checking in. I reached the bottom of the stairs and circled around to the right, past the front desk and on back to the area where the restaurant was located.

Not that I was ever going to eat there again. Vending machines and an ice machine sat in a tiny alcove a short distance before the restaurant's entrance as if a warning to those approaching. *Eat here before going in there.*

Several vending machines sold everything from Peck beer to chewing gum. I only wanted a pack of peanuts. Nothing fancy and definitely not alcoholic. Never buy booze from a vending machine. By the time you pay for it, it may be expired.

I pressed in my room number and then slipped my keycard through the pay slide. The nuts landed inside the machine with a *smack*. I bent down to retrieve them and stood when I heard...

"Oh, there you are Cybil," said Mayor Christensen sweetly like sugar laced with cyanide. "I've been looking all over for you."

She blocked the exit from the vending machine's alcove. Today she wore an entirely navy pantsuit with a string of pearls, matching pumps, and smelled of honeysuckles.

She *couldn't* have been looking all over for me since she was having me followed or tracked now could she? She knew exactly where I was, so I wondered why she didn't get right to the point.

If she wouldn't, I would.

"What do you want?"

"Why, I've wanted to know how well the search for Mandy's killer was going?" she purred and I felt like vomiting.

"I'm working on it," I snapped. "No thanks to you!"

I threw the bag of peanuts down for emphasis.

"Whatever do you mean?" Mayor Christensen stiffened, her hand gripping the pearl necklace. "Explain yourself."

"You know exactly what I mean." I shoved past her and

stalked down the hallway toward the lobby and the front desk. I could almost feel the steam trailing from my head. How dare she come and demand I give her an update when no one gave me any information to solve the case?

"Miss Lewis," Mayor Christensen called, walking quickly behind me. The air was laced with her scent of southern honeysuckles and mint.

"What?" I spun around, my hands in fists.

"Do not make the mistake of angering me," she said softly, her voice warm with threat. Her eyes drifted past me and around the lobby area as if making sure that no one else overheard her. "I am paying you for this…"

“Since when?” I barked, my eyes narrowing, my heart pounding in anger.

“Of course I paid,” she purred again, though her smile seemed stretched to the point of snapping off. “When I asked you to find Mandy. Pity you don’t remember…”

“You’re lying,” I said, heatedly. I actually folded my arms to keep from smacking her.

“You didn’t tell Jane, just yesterday, you would find out who killed my daughter?” Mayor Christensen asked, cool and sneaky. “I consider your statements, binding, Lewis, so get off your ass and find out who murdered my daughter.”

“And I expect a second retainer deposited into my checking account in the next hour.”

“Fine.”

I stared back at her and she smiled that media perfect smile, white teeth, and curvy lips painted the right shade of burgundy. It all seemed to fake, so picture ready that it was unreal.

So much for the grieving mother.

"Good. I will find the person who killed your daughter," I muttered between clenched teeth. “Not for you, but for Jane, someone who really cared about Amanda.”

Without another word, I took the stairs down to the garage

two at a time. My back tingled as if someone had dropped an ice cube down my shirt, and I knew it was because Mayor Christensen stared at me as I fled.

Once I reached my craft, I didn't even bother looking to see if the woman had followed me. I hopped inside and lifted up into the air. Carefully, I flew through the underground garage and out into the fading light of day.

Jane had told her I said I'd find Mandy's killer. How could she do it without first talking to me? We were going to have to sit and have a very serious talk.

I typed in the coordinates for Nathan Martindale house. While on the moon colonies, I had the airport 24 mechanic repair my autopilot. The automatic pilot took over as I answered my buzzing telemonitor. Don't fly and talk on the telemonitor at the same time. Too many mid-air collisions resulted from people trying to do both instead of setting their autopilot.

Trey's face, partially hidden by shadows, appeared to my surprise.

"Cybil, listen, there's something you should know about Amanda Christensen." His voice was rough, almost hoarse. With wide eyes, he leaned into the camera, nearly filling the telemonitor's screen. My body awoke at the mere sight of him, tingling with desire.

"What are you doing contacting me? You're supposed to be in hiding!" I said, my heart racing to its own rhythm. Trey had that affect on me.

He waved me off with his hand.

"I don't have the time to sit on my ass about this! I heard you're in Memphis working the Christensen case. Listen, very carefully to me, Cybil. Amanda wasn't all the efiles are painting her out to be. The cookie-cutter angel is all propaganda."

He kept looking over his shoulders and his voice was barely above a whisper. "She was a Zenith addict."

My flabber was gasted. Sure, I suspected a little reckless behavior like drinking, and a couple of cigarettes, but Zenith?

"How do you know?" I asked, my eyes narrowing. There wasn't any other indication of Amanda's drug use except from him. Why would he make it up? I didn't think he did. He had worked undercover for the Raymen Cartel.

"I-I busted her when I worked for the T.A.," he said rapidly as if he hurried to get it out it wouldn't be so horrible. "I suspect the mayor, her mother, was one of the people who sent in complaints against me and got me fired from the T.A. You're in hot water down there, sugar—enough to boil your perfect, luscious ass. Do me the favor and protect it for me."

Tell me something I didn't already know.

"Zenith usage? Why do I have the feeling you're not telling me everything," I said as the wauto dipped closer to the ground. I was nearing Nathan's house.

"Please, Cyb, be careful. I don't want to see you hurt," he said, his eyes pleading.

"Don't you dare hang up on me! I want an explanation, Trey!"

He gave me one of his sorry grins, and said, "I've got go. Love you."

He was gone as quickly and as unexpectedly as he had appeared.

I sat stunned, both by Trey's revelation about Amanda and by his knowledge that I was in fact in Memphis, and working the Christensen case. If he knew and he was deep underground, then surely others knew too.

Like Schumuckler.

I shrugged off the thought and tried to focus more on the case at hand. Amanda.

The wauto gently touched the ground in front of a one level house on a street with duel personalities. Nathan Martindale resided in a world of trailer parks, prefab homes and broken dreams. The house sagged in the middle, and the edges were caked with muddy dirt. The yard lay littered with broken bottles, busted bags, and other objects of undetermined origins.

I crossed the threshold through the rickety gate and suddenly felt depressed too. The air swayed with sadness as if the home itself was unhappy. Surely hope breathed its last breath inside this home.

The doors opened as soon as I stepped onto the decrepit, paint-peeling porch.

"Who you?" demanded a hulk of a man. His mop of tangled curls hid most of his forehead, but his dirt-brown eyes sliced through the knots directly to me. "You the reg?"

"No, sir," I said gently, trying not to inhale the odor of filth and sweat seeping out from him. "I'm here to see Nathan."

His unshaven face grinned, exposing yellowish teeth in his sagging mouth. "Everybody been wantin' to see Nathan…How much-"

The roar of an aerocycle drowned out the rest of his offer. I turned around to see a crimson aerocycle float into the driveway. At the helm, sat a tall, thin boy without a helmet. Brownish curls stuck out in all angles, as he awkwardly got off. His arm was in a cast.

As soon as he eyes met mine, his features construed into fury.

"Get away from here!" he shouted. He pointed at the man in the doorway with the finger from his cast. "Shut up!"

"Nathan, my name is-"

"I don't care!" he said as he marched up to me. "I already know who you are, Miss Lewis."

His nose was inches from mine. His breath reeked of alcohol and perhaps some dope, but I couldn't be sure. I shouldn't say he was a boy. Nathan Martindale was pushing mid-twenties.

The older man sauntered back into the house.

The sludge of a man must have been his dad, for Nathan

looked exactly like a younger, slimmer version. Cleaner too. Nathan wore black slacks and a sweater that had to cost more than the house was worth.

"Leave me alone. I got nuthin to say."

"Do you want to help Amanda?" I said, keeping my voice low, but firm.

His eyes rolled upward as if asking the heavens for help. "I can't help her. She's dead. Don't you read the news files? That ship, fine little ship it was, has set out down the Mississippi."

"Someone killed her," I said icily.

Wimpy boyfriends didn't impress me much. Besides, Amanda was a very good girlfriend to him if the silver watch and nice clothes were any indication. Not to mention the aerocycle he rode. It was a newer, more expensive model than Jane's and Jane spared no expense when it came to her aerocycle.

He plopped down on the porch steps, the crunch of fallen leaves protesting the placement of his rear-end. "What do you want?"

"Tell me about Amanda. I've been hired to find out who killed her, and I need to know her. Hobbies, favorite hang-outs, you know, stuff only her boyfriend would know."

With a strangled sigh he closed his eyes. His face crumbled and without speaking a word more, fat tears spilled out and slipped down his face.

"Ain't your friend found out enough? Lookit!" he held up his arm as exhibit A. "I outta file violation charges."

"I'm asking for a little more. She's dead, Nathan. You can help with this."

I waited while he cried in quiet sips.

Without asking, I sat down next to him on the porch. Across the street were historic houses and numerous Victorian-style structures. The trailer parks resided on the eastern side of the street, while the historic homes lined the west. Most of the Victorian houses were in need of repair, but still retaining their grand shapes and extended porches. Some seemed to be lived in, while others definitely were abandoned.

"I dunno what you want from me," he said, his voice leaden. "I already told your partner, the one who broke my arm. She didn't believe me, and twisted it until it fractured."

"I'm sorry about that. She can be a little impatient, and she's very upset about Amanda's death. Just like you."

He nodded. "Gettin' this off tomorrow. Advanced healing through injections of calcium and other crap the doctors come up with. All healed up."

"Can you tell me where you met her?" I asked, trying to prompt some answers. The day drifted on towards night.

He sighed, but a dreamy expression spread across his face. "I met her at this club called the Joker's Pun. I know the name's stupid, but Amanda liked to dance there."

I nodded with a smile. "Seen it myself the other night. Why did Amanda go there? Was she stripping?"

"Nah," Nathan said, his head shaking. "She wasn't in it for that. She liked slumming it. Getting away from it all, you know? Being anonymous, like not the mayor's daughter, but who she wanted to be. You know?"

It was my turn to nod in agreement. I had the same thought myself.

"She-she wasn't alone, but with this older man. He was way older than you," Nathan continued. "I asked her why she was hanging out in with her dad, and she said he wasn't her dad."

An older man? Where had I heard that before?

Note to self, check on the older man in Amanda's life.

"She gave me telemonitor i.p. address and I called," he said. "I didn't know the mayor was her mother."

Nathan wasn't Amanda's age, but older. I guessed he was about twenty-three.

"So, you were initially attracted to her even though she was with another man?" I smiled at him, working him to put him at ease. He seemed tense, shifting, and while sitting still appeared to be moving. I'd guess he was some sort of addict, because he had to work at sitting still.

He smiled back and I saw, perhaps the handsome, well, wholesomeness that drew Amanda to him. The slightly slip of devilish too.

"I dunno, I- I had to have her, you know?" he said with an immense sadness. "Now she's gone."

His sadness and loss seemed to cover me like a wet blanket.

"What are you gonna do?" he asked. "Whatever you do, don't ask her mother about me. That woman hates me."

He laughed, but it wasn't one filled with mirth.

It was hollow and empty.

"I'm going to try to find out who killed her," I said as I stood up. It grew darker and I wanted to get back to Henry's. "Tell me, was Amanda a Zenith user?"

He scratched his head and laughed that dead, empty laugh again. His face closed and I saw a small glimpse of Nathan when angry. The super cool boyish act he'd given me since I met him was an act. He was behaving the way he thought I expected him to act. That didn't mean though that the information he'd given me on Amanda wasn't true.

"No. Who told you that? People who didn't like us being together used to say that, you know? That she was only with me 'cause I got her Zenith."

"Did you peddle Zenith?" I asked him, knowing he did whether he admitted or not.

He stood up too and his eyes held mine. "Yeah, before I got with her. But once we got together, I gave it up. Sex with her was better than Zenith ever was."

With that said, he stalked up the stairs and entered his house.

I guess I got all I came here for.

But should I believe him?

CHAPTER 23

"That's total shit!" Jane bellowed from her position by the window. Smoking like a chimney, the smoke floated out the open windows into the night slower than she was contributing to its haziness.

I wouldn't put up with her smoking in the rental room or in my wauto, so she was smoking at this restaurant that came complete with filters imbedded in the sections around smoking tables, were her only refuge. Lung cancer not being an illness I wanted to openly court, I told her cut back on the amount she smoked or do it some place else.

O'Shea's Bar rested on a deserted, lonely strip of road that ran parallel to Beale Street and only a few blocks over from Regulator Headquarters. After the incident at Henry's Restaurant, we decided we'd try something a little seedier, since the upscale place had robotic waiters and lousy food.

Seated on the patio designated for smoking, Jane consumed bottle after bottle of Peck, while I drank a cup of strong coffee. Our waitress, Katherine, an older woman in her forties, with good legs and heavy mascara, seemed hungry for a smile and a bath. But she kept my coffee filled and Jane watered up.

Heaven knows we could use the break.

When we first arrived, the place hardly contained any people, except for the bartender, a third-generation O'Shea and a few regular customers from the look of it. Right around ten minutes after nine, the old crowd shuffled in and started singing Old Irish songs and drinking heavily. Fifteen guys, hanging and slobbering all over each other kept to the bar.

With tomorrow being Saint Patrick's Day, they must have been practicing for the big Irish celebration. Indeed the decorated bar had blinking green lights as if sectioning off a spot for an alien concourse and landing. Plastic four-leaf shamrocks dangled from the ceilings as if an indoor shower of clovers. An electronic sigh flashed "green beer for Irish cheer, ten silver pieces." The tables had been covered with green and white patch tablecloths, plastic too like the shamrocks.

"Shhh! The window's open," I hissed at her. "That's what I heard from a reliable source."

"No, no," she said firmly, her head shaking. "Mandy didn't do drugs."

"How well did you know her?" I asked, thinking of how addicts kept their addiction a secret until the addiction took over. Then it wasn't a secret for anyone.

She looked up at me really fast and sighed. "I saw her about four times a year. But we wrote a lot to each other. Daily emails, you know, telemonitor calls, instant messages, you name it we used it to keep in touch."

It was nearly ten o'clock at night. I had shared the autopsy report with Jane because she demanded to see it. The one condition was that she try to act more like a private inspector and less like a female reincarnation of Batman.

She agreed.

We'd been at O'Shea's since 8:45 or so. I had the soup du jour while Jane had a hamburger, a rare treat since beef was ludicrously priced. Finding unmutated cows and threading out the mutations was a costly business and not one many farmers could afford to do.

"It's possible," I said careful and soft, which I found to be a pain. I wanted my old Jane back. The one who knew me and one I didn't have to handle with kid gloves, "she might have hidden her drug use from family."

Jane closed her eyes and opened them again. "Yeah. It's possible. I know it is."

"Tomorrow, follow the boyfriend. I want to know his friends, his habits, everything. Let's start with him since we got nothing else. Besides, what's the saying? Once a Zenith dealer, always a Zenith dealer?" I said. "I'm going to talk to your aunt about her daughter."

With a deep drag of her cigarette, she nodded. "I'll head out tonight."

"Don't get caught. He knows you, remember," I said with a wag of my finger. "Stealth."

She laughed, which was good to hear.

"Don't harm him, Jane."

She shrugged with one shoulder.

"How many have you had?" I asked, counting two bottles on the table.

"Four," she said with a grin. "I can handle it, you know. I'm an ex-Marine." She took out two capsules called E417, which was supposed to sober you up after taking them. With a quick toss, she had downed both pills with the remainder of her beer.

I smiled. Tough and stubborn was my Jane.

"I'm going now," she said, her speech slightly slurred. "I want to find him before he disappears into the nightlife."

After grabbing her bomber and slapping down a few coins, she left through the patio door.

I signaled for Katherine who wore green ribbons in her hair, and a shirt that read, "Kiss me, I'm Irish." She filled my empty cup. Seated and relaxed, my own thoughts turned to the mayor. It was high time she told the truth about her girl. How could I get the media ready mayor to release the not-so-good things about her daughter to me? I needed a plan of attack.

With Jane back on board and recovering from her spell of revenge, I felt good about finding Amanda's killer(s).

I was on my third cup of java when the door to O'Shea's opened and in walked Captain Hanson. Seated back on the patio, I could make out his turquoise sweater as he took up residence at the bar and greeted O'Shea. The others at the bar waved and nodded to him. He must be a regular as several of the "boys" referred to him by name.

Katherine strutted over to my table. "Need anythang else?"

"Can you tell me who the handsome man is that just came in?" I asked politely.

She grinned, showing her crooked teeth. "Oh, yeah, that's Tom Hanson."

"He's really well dressed. Is he married?" I asked innocently, as I glanced up to the bar.

Katherine chuckled. "I don't think so, miss, but I think he got somebody. I tried all ready…Handsome though, ain't he?"

I nodded, acting disappointed. No wife, but he must have someone like a girlfriend.

"You know," Katherine said, her tray resting on her hip, speaking low as if we were suddenly best friends. "He usedta come in here with a grin, you know, happy. But lately, he been drinkin' more an' stuff. Sometimes, cries a little to O'Shea…"

"Maybe the girlfriend broke up with him," I said, sipping my coffee. Again faking innocence while snooping on the captain. Sometimes I was just damn nosy.

She shook her head. "I asked him, thinkin' the same, but he said she died."

Died.

"Recently?" I asked, a little enthusiastically.

Katherine nodded. "I think last week."

I paid her with a big tip and got up from the table. She smiled again, forcing me to shudder. When she didn't smile, her face was pleasant to look at. The teeth, crowded on top of each other and decaying right before my eyes, disturbed the symmetry of her face.

"Hey, maybe we can go out together sometime," she said. "I work most week days, you know, but I'm free on Saturdays."

I said, "Sure." Thinking to myself, never, never, never.

Katherine sauntered off toward the bar's direction. I exited through the side patio door, not wanting Captain Hanson to see me. No doubt, he'd figure it out once Katherine described me to him, but I needed time to find out the identity of his light 'o love.

I climbed into my wauto and cranked the heat up to seven. Chilly, the night's air, calm and crisp, dropped steadily toward freezing temperatures. Without a coat, I hunched over and forced myself to think about some tropical island with nice, hot weather, and studly men.

Drowning his sorrows in a mug of beer wasn't exactly how I thought Captain Hanson spent his nights. Sipping wine and eating extremely rare steaks at the Chop House came to mind, but instead he's at a dumpy little bar. Strange.

Yeah, I know I ate there too. But a man of Hanson's caliber shouldn't be seen in dives like O'Sheas. There's more to the good captain than meets the eye. My curiosity was peaked and that meant I'd dig around in Hanson's life until I found out what he was hiding. Might not pertain to Amanda's murder, but then it might. I wouldn't know until all the bees had flown out of the hive.

Placing the wauto on autopilot, I pulled out my handheld and scribbled furiously the stuff I heard from Katherine. It would all have to be checked out, because Katherine might have overheard Captain Hanson's drunken ramblings. Hearsay and nothing more, the prosecutor would argue and win. All the dots needed to be lined up correctly, for it one thing was off or tarnished, the entire picture could crumble.

With a sigh of relief, I zipped into the air. I had somewhere to start with Hanson.

We were back in business.

CHAPTER 24

In less than twenty minutes from the time I left O'Shea's, I reached Henry's doors.

The flight back wasn't pleasant; it was glorious! Clear, nearly empty lanes stretched out in front of me as I cruised. The traffic signals changed to green as I approached. Normally, I caught all the red ones.

The Fates were with me.

By the time I had parked, climbed the steps to the second floor and entered the rental room, it was after ten-thirty. The room shroud in shadows came to life with the flick of the lights. I didn't expect to see Jane, because she was out hunting Nathan, but the lights revealed...

"Good evening, Mr. Schmuckler," I said, dropping my satchel on the floor next to my travel bag. The good mood I was in slipped away. He was seated crossed leg on my bed.

Fickle Fates.

"Good evening to you, Miss Lewis," he said, as he stood up, seemingly undeterred that his presence in my room didn't surprise me—at least on the surface. Tonight he wore a pinstriped suit of burgundy and gray, his hat a matching accessory. There's something obscene about a man who's color-coordinated, probably right down to his boxers. He removed a mauve handkerchief and wiped his forehead. "Quite humid in here, don't you think?"

"What do you want?"

Asking him how he had got in or how he had found me would have been completely pointless. The man I saw stalking me must have been a T.A. agent, keeping tabs for Schmuckler, if not Schmuckler himself. My temper flared at the obscene, heavy handed gall of the Territory Alliance, but I didn't let any of that come out of my mouth.

"I am requesting you to tell me the location of Trey Ohornon," he said plainly. He opened his jacket casually to reveal a midnight black gun. "I am asking politely."

Tsk, tsk, you know how I hate intimidation tactics…

"I don't know," I said icily, brandishing my own weapon. =From here, he couldn't see if I had bent down to tie my shoes or grab my piece. He knew now.

"I know you and the pug are acquainted already," I said with a shrug. "You want to make it personal, and become more intimate with it?"

He glared at me, the cheery demeanor melted off like snow on a wauto engine.

"Trey and I are no longer a couple and haven't been for some time. I told you back in D.C. Should've saved yourself the trip."

"Perhaps if I tell you why his whereabouts are important, you will tell me," he said, his voice polite and soft as if he hadn't heard me. His eyes continued to stare at me, rarely blinking.

"I don't care why you're looking for him," I said, holding my gun along my side, ready to draw. "I don't know where he is. English isn't your first language is it?"

"He killed two T.A. agents while undercover. He's gone rogue," Schmuckler plowed on, continuing to ignore my cracks. He smiled, but it was a twisted, a wry smile. "The Raymen Cartel has a price on his head as well for other murders he committed while undercover. You're a woman of good moral upbringing…"

Trey. Kill two people for no reason. Nah, it didn't wash. As for the good moral upbringing, he didn't really know me, did he?

"One more time, genius secret agent. Find...him...your ...self!"

No way was he going to shoot me in this rental room. Mayor Christensen and all of the Memphis regulators knew I was here, knew why I was here, and hated the Territories Alliance for no other reason, than the T.A. was always stepping on their toes and interfering in their cases.

Schmuckler stood up and said, "Well, Miss Lewis, I'm afraid my superiors don't believe you..."

"I don't give a shit who believes me!" My voice escalated like my temper. It sounded high and terrified. I hated that. "So, you can go back to them and tell them to kiss my ass. Find him yourself and leave me alone."

He tipped his hat to me and placed it back on his head. Then he removed his gun from its holster and lifted the safety off. "That's too bad, Miss Lewis..."

As Mr. Manners slowly raised his gun, I dipped to the floor, rolled toward my travel bag and pointed my own gun at him. "Don't do this, Schmuckler. You can't win this!"

He pointed his gun at me. I could see it in his eyes; he knew I was faster.

Before he could tug on the trigger, I shot him in the shoulder, the pug's blast forcing him to his knees. His gun flew across to Jane's bed as if ripped from his hand by an invisible giant. It slapped into the wall and fell with a *thud* to the carpeted floor.

"Oh!" Schmuckler groaned and fell face forward to the carpet, writhed around in anguish a bit, muttering to himself before promptly passing out.

I raced over to him, and using my foot, kicked him to see if he was faking it. Satisfied that he wasn't, I got down on my knees, and rolled him onto his back. His face was pale and the burnt hole in his jacket ruined a perfectly good suit, though the color sucked. The wall behind him contained blood sprayed like water from a sprinkler. The hole was through and through. I could see the carpet through it, if I stared hard enough past the cartelized wound.

The bastard was going to kill me.

He really was...

Shaking my head to dislodge the cobwebs, I went over to the telemonitor and contacted the regulators.

Less than ten minutes later, the rental room quickly filled with people. Mr. Schmuckler, strapped to a metal stretcher and devoid of his hat, jacket and shirt, hovered as the floating alloy platform floated out of the room. I could see his flabby, white chest. Beside him the paramedics were busily taking notes and readings as it glided a few in feet ahead of them on out into the hallway.

Captain Hanson, smelling strongly of cigarettes and beer, leaned against the bathroom door, his eyes unfocused and his face red, his own suit, rumpled and smelly. The violation scene team, three guys in turquoise coats and large metallic boxes, went around gathering evidence to support my claim of self-defense. They did locate and bag Schmuckler' s gun and some other stuff, so I wasn't too worried about it. I'd been in this situation before, but not with the Memphis Regulators, the D.C. ones.

"So, he's a T.A. agent," Captain Hanson called over to me. It was a statement, not a question.

The interrogation had begun.

I sat on the floor, across from the bathroom, beneath the telemonitor. It was wall- mounted so there was space beneath it for me to sit. Despite this short distance, Captain Hanson's voice sounded far away as if he was down the hall. Over the roaring sound of my blood, pumping fast and hot through my veins, his voice came across as being very small, timid against the tide of adrenaline.

"That's what he said," I mumbled, my ears ringing and my body extremely tired.

"Why would a T.A. agent try to kill you?" he asked, certain

that I was hiding something. If he didn't believe me, I couldn't tell. I couldn't tell if he did believe me either.

"I don't know. He was here when I came in. Ambushed me. Took out his weapon and told me he was going to kill me."

Lying was a natural habit for me, but it wasn't the lying that made my throat feel like it had been scraped with a blunt knife. It was the fact that the entire T.A. would come at me with all their ammo. They could forbid me from being a private inspector; they could audit my office files, and much, much more. They didn't have to kill me to make my life a living hell.

Was Trey worth it?

"...Cybil...you all right?" Captain Hanson was saying. He'd come to stand in front of me and was now waving his hands in front of my face. "Hey! You all right?"

I blinked rapidly. "Yeah, yeah...How much longer are your guys going to be?"

Captain Hanson glanced around and said, "Another hour at least...Plus, we're going to have to seal it until your story can be collaborated. Did you know he was staying in a room down the hallway from you?"

"No." It was already going on eleven. "If I knew, why would I continue to stay here?"

He shrugged. "I have to ask."

"I'll going down to get another room."

He nodded. "Just let me know which one it is."

Before I got my satchel hoisted over my shoulder, Jane appeared in the doorway.

"Cybil?" she called, her eyes roaming over the scene until they landed one me.

"Here," I called standing up, trying not to look at the blood splatter still on the walls.

She glanced at Captain Hanson as she walked by him and further into the room. With quick eyes she took in the blood and the scientists swarming our shared space. Already one of the guys came over to her and tried to get her to go into the hallway before she contaminated the scene.

"What happened?"

"Tell you on the way down to the front desk. We're going to need another room," I said, taking her arm and pulling her out with me. Captain Hanson raised his eyebrows, but did not ask who she was. He may have already known her from the funeral.

Once we reached the front desk and out of Hanson's earshot, I whispered, "Schmuckler tried to kill me tonight. He wouldn't take that I didn't know where Trey was..."

"You killed a T.A. agent?" she balked, her eyes filled with fear. Jane wasn't easy to scare. But the T.A. was no laughing matter. Pulling a gun on them was one thing, actually firing it was another.

"I didn't kill him. I shot him in the shoulder," I muttered. "Self defense."

"But still, the T.A. won't be happy about it," Jane said, her voice a little shaky. Her eyes flickered as she took in the lobby as if waiting for T.A. agents to leap out from behind the furniture and kidnap us. Or worse, kill us.

"I know, so can you knock it off? Why can't they take no for an answer?" I grumbled as I stepped up to the desk.

Jane shook her head. " I dunno, but I've got something you should hear."

We quit talking when the robotic front desk clerk, which looked strangely like the waiter at Henry's restaurant, glided from the back and asked what we needed. He gave us room one-thirteen and we headed back up the stairs to reclaim our belongings—the ones we were allowed to take anyway.

When we reached our new room, Captain Hanson had left and two of the three lab guys were still working the room. Jane and I gathered our travel bags and clothes. Before we could we go, I had to change out of my clothes, give them to the techs. Dressed entirely in sweats and a hoodie, I glared at the techs, who were lowering my silk thong into a plastic bag with raised eyebrows. I told the senior man, Eric, where they could find us and we headed back down the stairs.

Our new room was on the first floor had more space. Wider and larger, the two beds were full sized, but the outer room held a sofa and a table with two chairs. It looked more like an apartment and less like someplace to lay my head.

Though I didn't want to start thinking of Memphis as home.

Jane took the bed closest to the window, like before, and I took the one beside the bathroom. She didn't bother unpacking. She tossed her travel bag in the closet and her armful of dirty clothes on to her bed.

"What the hell has Trey done that's got T.A. agents looking for him? Ain't he one of them?" she asked as she removed her boots. "And worth killing you for?"

I recounted the story about the Raymen Cartel and Trey's firing without telling her he'd been in my apartment. I also left out the stuff Schmuckler said about us being lovers. She didn't seem to be listening because she stared out of the window, where nothing stirred and when I finished she didn't say anything for a few minutes.

Then she said, "He knows more than he told you. Something about the T.A. probably, which is why they want him dead."

I believed that also, and nodded as I sunk onto the sofa in the outer room. It wouldn't be the first time a governmental agency put out a hit on one of their agents for knowing more than what was good for them. I guess that would count as a job hazard. Wondered if he got paid extra for that?

My head throbbed from too much coffee and the surge and fall of adrenaline. "Tell me what you found out about Nathan." Anything to take my mind off of Trey.

Jane came into the outer room and sat down in one of dining chairs. She took out her cigarette pack and soon was smoking. The fogbog struggled to gulp down the toxic billowing from the end of her stick.

"Well, I found out something," she began, than stopped.

Her tone more than anything made me lift up my head and focus. "How bad is it?"

My stomach twisted into a tight, lumpy knot.

"I followed Nathan tonight, like you said. Totally worried about the nightlife thing, but I find out he works nights. Guess where he works?"

A sickened look on her face didn't do anything for inspiring hope in me that this was a good thing. Something stirred in the dusty corners of my mind, but I couldn't drag it out into the light. Too much coffee, the gun battle with Schmuckler and Trey's troubles clouded up my vision.

"Okay, I give up. Where?"

"He works at Regulator Headquarters," she said and took a deep drag on her cigarette. "He's a reg, Cybil. A goddamn regulator."

"What?" I asked as if I hadn't heard. My body tingled as I sat up fully. “Impossible! He's a Zenith dealer.”

"Yeah. He's in the drug enforcement section," she grinned. It was cold and bitter. "I talked to one of his fellow regs, a guy named Johnson. Said that Nathan used to be a snitch for them, but about six months ago, he joined the team," she said, her lighter falling to the floor.

"Academy?" I asked, following a hunch and knowing full well what Jane was going to tell me.

She snorted and shook her head no. Her smile thawed from her own excitement, she said, "Checked. No one fits his description or name in the last six months. One of the guys at Regulator Headquarters is searching further back. I told them I was with the T.A. as a consultant, researching their files and looking for new recruits."

"Pull his bank account," I said. "I want to know how and why he's working for Captain Hanson, as you might recall said he didn't know him. He hired everyone who worked for the Memphis reqs."

"Liar, liar, pants on fire," Jane sang with a cough.

I leaned back against the sofa. The outline of the puzzle came sharper into focus. This was huge, a super big clue. "Your aunt hook Nathan up with Hanson?"

Jane stubbed out her cigarette in a ceramic cup that was normally used for coffee and said, "I don't think so. Aunt Belle despised Nathan. Said he was beneath Mandy's standards."

She bent down to pick up her lighter. "Johnson also said, he swore it was rumor, Nathan used to be a small time Zenith dealer here in the quad. Nathan keeps denying it. He didn't know if Nathan actually used, but he said Nathan knew a lot about the trade. That's why he was such an important snitch."

I lay down on the sofa and stared up at the beige ceiling, which became a canvas for my mental puzzle.

"What's he doing in the drugs division?"

Jane shrugged. "I think undercover."

I laughed out loud, spooking Jane.

"Have you lost it over there?" she asked as she lit up another cigarette.

"No. Think of it, Jane. Nathan has the perfect cover."

"What?"

I sat up again and looked at her. "It's the perfect cover. Nathan told me that he *used* to be a Zenith user. He probably still is, but if his drug tests come back positive, he can always say he *had* to take Zenith because he's undercover. Had to fit in…be believable…"

Jane laughed, the light bulb finally going off in her mind. "Yeah, yeah. Nice cover though for both."

"Listen, tomorrow, find Nathan and stick to him like a bad email virus," I said, after stifling a yawn. It was nearly midnight. "I'm going to talk to Captain Hanson in the morning about his latest rookie."

I told her about Katherine's comments about Hanson after she had left O'Shea's.

"Freaky," she said and she stretched, uninterested in Hanson.

We changed into our pjs. Jane changed in the room; I changed in the bathroom. When I emerged, Jane's eyes once again gave my camisole and short shorts the once over. I crawled into bed. Across from me, Jane fell immediately to sleep and I lay awake only a few minutes longer.

As I drifted to sleep, I had an aggravating itch that I was failing to recognize something. The zzzs came and it was lost in the clouds of slumber.

CHAPTER 25

Tuesday came too swiftly and when I finally rolled over, Jane's empty bed lay deserted in rumpled sheets and scattered covers. I groaned and stretched. My body was achy from too much sleep. A new bed usually didn't allow me a descent night's rest, but I was too exhausted last night to notice. A bit disoriented, I rubbed my eyes and suddenly last night's tango with Schmuckler came back to me. Images of a wounded Schmuckler swooped down on me as I thought back to the minor gun battle.

Is it really a gun battle if only I fired? It was more like a draw.

Something nagged at me, something I had lost during the hours of dreamless slumber, but I couldn't capture it. I turned a sleepy eye to the clock that rested on the table between Jane's bed and mine and I sprung out of the bed.

One o'clock!

Captain Hanson might be engaged in meetings at this hour. Why didn't Jane wake me when she left at the crack of dawn? I could have ambushed the Captain before his day was underway. Before he devised a sober explanation for Katherine's comments about a girlfriend.

Swearing loudly, I dressed quickly and hurried from the rental room.

My wauto lifted up to join the partially filled lanes. The lunch hour crowd from the courthouse building inched their way back to work, the hour drawing to a close. I entered the coordinates for Regulator Headquarters and raised my fist bitterly at an invisible Jane.

With any luck, I'd still be able to see him and to question

him about the girlfriend he said he'd lost and why a known Zenith dealer, and possible addict, was on his staff.

Perhaps after I talked to him I'd drop by Mayor Christensen's office and talk to her about Captain Hanson. I'm sure her comments about him would be nothing but coos of good things. The outer shape of the puzzle came together quite beautifully. Two lovers plotting together.

Once the lunch traffic exited at the downtown lane, I coursed through the sky and zipped over to Regulator Headquarters. Again, I left my weapons in the vehicle. This was a friendly chat between two people who wanted justice for Amanda Christensen.

Riiight.

I winked at the two regulators guarding the entrance and exit to headquarters. One shot me a confused look while the other one grinned at me before catching himself. Once again Herman sat high up in the elevated seat watching all who came and went through the three hallways. No prostitutes today, but a gang of young boys, all wearing the color red. Tough chins jutted out and arrogant smirks littered their faces as they stood against the wall, to the left of Herman's desk.

"You again?" Herman asked gruffly as I approached. He still wore the same tired, bored expression and watchful eyes.

At least he remembered me.

And people thought I was forgettable. Yeah, right.

"I need to see Captain Hanson," I said, calmly, trying again to catch his attention. Hoping I wouldn't have to sink to threats. The man's eyes never rested. Like a swivel, they moved constantly.

He didn't argue, for which I was grateful, and twirled around to contact Hanson. I waited, feeling the warmth of the heated air blow gently against my face. The din of the people making their way through the conjunction of the corridors reduced Herman's voice to a low mumble.

"Hey, baby," called one of the thugs posted up against the

wall across from Herman, grabbing his crotch and gesturing in my direction. As if he'd ever get within five feet of me without getting a face full of pug.

"Nice package you got, suga. Come on over and let me handle it!" called another, blowing me kisses and rotating his hips in a lovemaking gesture.

I ignored them and turned back to Herman, who rotated around to me.

"Captain ain't in," Herman said, his eyes not resting on me, but scanning the pack of people. "You punks, shut your traps!" and then to me. "You missed him."

I stared at him intently, trying to decide whether or not he was telling the truth. Herman must have thought that too because he said, "He went home for the day. Sick."

With a shrug, I left headquarters, secretly cursing Jane for not waking me up earlier.

I stood beside my wauto, allowing the sun's rays to wash over me though they did little to warm me up. Icy patches littered the sidewalks and streets as last night's temperature plummeted to seventeen degrees and was struggling to break through the freeze.

Captain Hanson, sick? He didn't seem so ill last night when he came to the rental room. What was he doing there anyway? Regulator Captains did not come to violation scenes; they pushed electronic files and budgeted currency. No way did they voluntarily get their hands dirty with real work.

I climbed in and started the vehicle, my mind racing. What if he was only playing hooky? What if he was getting nooky from the mayor?

While hovering over my parking space, I punched up the Memphis Quadrant directory, and scanned through the names for Hanson, Tom. I wanted to get his address. With a little bit of luck, I might catch the two of them together.

The telemonitor screen whirled and returned a message of "no address found."

I pressed clear and than typed in the number for Mayor Christensen. Within moments, I was connected to her administrative assistant, a handsome, Hispanic lad with nearly clear blue eyes and caramel toned skin. Hatchling maybe? The result was striking and I could use one of him to be my administrative assistant.

"I'm sorry Miss Lewis. Mayor Christensen is out of the office," he said after I had introduced myself and quit slobbering.

Fighting back the desire to invite him over for dinner and desert, I said, "That's okay. Maybe you could help. I need the address for Captain Hanson's home."

Looking a bit uncomfortable, but still gorgeous, he said, "I-I am not allowed to give that information out. Even to those on the mayor's payroll."

"I'm not a stranger! I'm trying to solve her daughter's case. If you must know, Captain Hanson wanted me to stop by his house to discuss the case, but failed to give me the coordinates."

With me the lying never seems to stop…

He sighed and glanced around. "Since you are working for her, I'll tell you. He's at 3024 West Nightingale Drive."

"Thank you," I said and flashed my it's-your- lucky-day smile. "You're a life savior."

"Just catch the guy who killed Mandy," he said with a sniff and disconnected the feed.

A little put out that he hadn't asked me to dinner, especially after the smile I gave him, I typed in the address, and the coordinates filled themselves in. With a smile firmly planted on my face, I headed toward Captain Hanson's home to ambush him and his mistress.

Both of them out of the office, they probably didn't think I'd put it together so damn quickly. I recalled how offended Mayor Christensen looked when I told her I wanted to meet with Captain Hanson. Not to mention, that when I *did* meet with him, he lied about not knowing I would arrive so soon. He knew. The entire thing was too put together for my arrival to be solely a shock for him.

Tsk, tsk, lovers, you're about to be caught.

Saying his girlfriend died was a cover. Hanson really was trying to hide his relationship with Mayor Christensen because her daughter was dead. The press was all over this, and with the upcoming governor's race, an affair would ruin Christensen's chances in office. Despite how technologically we've come as a human race, some deep seeded issues of morality and family could not be unearthed, especially in the Southeast Territories.

I hummed happily as I made my way out to Nightingale Drive. It rested outside Memphis primary section one, and into section six Germantown. The sky continued to be clouded with thick, graying clouds, but held off with releasing any precipitation. No amount of snow, sleet or rain was going to douse my good mood. I was really close to solving this case and that meant I could go home soon.

The lanes leading to the luxury of Germantown remained clear and free of suffocating traffic. About one-thirty, I wondered how Jane was doing with Nathan. Who would hire an addict, ex or otherwise, to be a regulator? It seemed dumb to have him around so much Zenith and Ackback. It would be like asking an alcoholic to tend bar. Temptation would drive the person nuts.

And what about Nathan? Why would he sign up for such torture?

I didn't know, but I hoped Jane could find out. Again, a smile tugged at my lips as I thought about Jane's turn around. It could be that she truly wanted Amanda's killer brought to justice and for that she worked hard. Or it could be that she realized that biting my head off at every remark or staying holed up in the rental room crying, wasn't going to help capture the dunce who did this to Amanda.

Either way, I was glad to have her back in the game.

As it were, the afternoon remained dreary as I sped onward. As I dipped downward closer to the old pavement, I slowed down as I passed by magnificent homes, hidden mostly by shrubbery and tall trees. Every other home or so, I could make out the beginnings of a pathway that led back, far back, into a shadowy piece of land and a house.

I found Captain Hanson's street. His lodging was the only one, and made a left. As I flew under overhanging trees that arched over Nightingale Drive like acrobats at a circus, I again thought back to money and prestige. Two things I never had, and had long since stopped wishing for. Along the edge of the paved road, I could make out the brownish grass that in spring would be a bright green, or maybe pink. How could a regulator captain be able to afford a home like this?

Maybe Mayor Christensen wasn't just a momma to Amanda; maybe she was a sugar momma to Hanson.

At the end of the long driveway, I found myself draped in partial sunlight as I flew around the cul-de-sac that had a small fountain of Venus rising up from her shell, clad in only soft clouds with water spraying around her. It looked a lot like my sister's driveway up to her house (minus the fountain). I guess the rich liked to be private and secluded.

The three-level brick house rose majestically over the paved cul-de-sac and its porch. The porch, stone gray and flat didn't extend outward past its overhang. It wasn't the kind of porch reserved for outside sittings and barbequing. It was the kind of porch that served as a place for people to wait to be let in. Vines crept up the left side of the wall as if desperately working their way toward sunlight.

Impressive.

To the right of the porch was a three-wauto hanger, brick red, like the house, but newer. The bricks were still somewhat red and shiny, not weathered like those of the house.

Could the mayor's vehicle be hidden in there?

I pressed the doorbell and waited. The maid might not let me in without a good reason. Racking my brain, I developed a good lie to infiltrate the Hanson residence.

To my surprise, Captain Hanson opened the door himself, dressed in a satin, navy robe, striped flannel pajama bottoms and navy slippers. He wore reading glasses and they rested precariously close to the edge of his nose.

"Can I help you Miss Lewis?" he asked, his voice tight and unsure. He removed his glasses, folded them and placed them in the pocket of his robe. And people thought women were vain. "Just doing some light reading."

Only a little after two in the afternoon and he looked ready for bed. I wondered who he was sharing his bed with. I tried to peer over his shoulder, but could not see anyone.

"I wanted to talk to you about something that's come up in the investigation," I said, putting it out there. The lie wouldn't have worked on him anyway. I did want to talk to him about Nathan working for the Memphis Regulators.

Was it me or did he pale a little? His eyebrows rose and he smiled weakly. "Come in."

In the foyer, canvases around me bustled with traders handling slaves, and showboats lit up with lights and decorated for entertainment. These detailed portraits conveyed the South and the Mississippi that separated it from the west in historical art and reflective colors. To the right of the front door was a staircase that arced upward to the second floor. The carpet, a warm beige, didn't subtract or add from the room. Two large square mirrors set in ancient, hoary frames above two end tables faced each other. One contained an elegant white and beige vase filled with wiry twigs and the other nothing but a cream colored dish, where silver coins had been deposited.

"Welcome to my home, Miss Lewis," he said as I followed him through the foyer and back, through elegantly designed rooms filled with antiques and expensive furniture, on out to a stone-slab patio. A canopy covered the patio from the afternoon sun. The back of the house also contained a fifty-foot covered swimming pool.

"It's warm enough today to sit outside," he said, as he remained standing until I took the seat across from him. Always the gentleman, he sat down in one of the three caramel-tone wicker chairs facing the pool. A matching table with a glass top was between him and me. Overhead three gigantic heaters warmed the deck. He picked up a mug full of something steamy as he gazed outward, over his property. "Nice day, isn't it?"

Past the pool and its tiny supply house was an extensive amount of acreage. Currently a dull brown, it would be a magnificent green in the spring and summer. Unspoiled land as far as my eyes could see was silent except for few intermittent animal calls and cries.

"Would you like some cocoa?" he asked, his eyes turning back to me. He rose out of his seat.

"No, thank you," I said, my voice hoarse.

Nature, undisturbed and clean, often choked me up. I loved beauty in any form and nature presented some of the best acts of beauty I have ever seen. I pondered how Hanson had managed to keep all of the land free of development. Often developers gobbled such pieces of land up into high rises, condos, or apartments.

"Beautiful home."

"Yes, well, it belonged to my great-great-great grandfather," he said with a proud smile that fleshed out both his dimples. An inviting bon vivant, Captain Hanson, sipped more from his mug. He sat down and gracefully crossed his legs. On the table, a handheld computer, much like mine, rested in sleep mode. "Much of the furniture belonged to my great great-grandfather, a voracious antique dealer. This used to be a plantation home, but my grandfather had it dismantled and rebuilt this estate instead. Pieces of the original home are imbedded into the structure and the third floor. He said he didn't want to be associated with slavery, but he gladly kept the inheritance."

He chuckled. "I am the last Hanson. I will leave it to the historical society to turn it into a museum for the large amounts of antiques here. Others should be able to enjoy their beauty as well. Besides, this place isn't for children."

"Wonderful idea," I said, meaning every word. "You know, I think I will have some cocoa."

He smiled and got up. After he disappeared into the house, I nudged his handheld to see what he'd been reading. It was Amanda's autopsy report.

Light reading indeed!

I clicked the sleep mode button and hurriedly sat back down.

Captain Hanson returned, a steaming pink mug in his hand. He placed it gently on a coaster beside me and returned to his seat.

"I stopped by headquarters, but they said you were here, sick."

He nodded gravely, the proud smile gone along with his dimples. "I-I needed some time to rest, to be alone. The job isn't so wonderful and exhausting."

"There's no one here with you in this humongous home? Staff? Girlfriend?" I asked, moving back to the task at hand. I hadn't seen any wauto parked outside the house, nor had I seen or heard any other voice in the house. It didn't appear that there was another way out, other than the way I had flown in on.

"A gentleman never kisses and tells, Miss Lewis…" he said, his voice rough. He sipped from his mug, cleared his throat and asked, "Why do you ask? Are you interested?"

I grinned. Direct wasn't he? "Well, uh-, no, but there must be *someone*."

"No, no one. Not now," he said with a heavy sigh, his eyes

turning to me and giving me his full attention. "Miss Lewis, what is this about? It is uncommon for people to come by my home—even for work related topics I am a private man, as I'm sure you've gathered."

"Call me Cybil," I said, feeling suddenly small and a little guilty. The sadness that seeped into his eyes bore into my heart. It was an emotion I was all too familiar with. Loss.

"Cybil," he said with a sigh. "I want to know why you've come here. You said you had developments..."

"Uh, no. I said I had questions. There's been some questionable things surface in my investigation," I said. "Tell me why a known Zenith user is employed as a regulator at headquarters?"

As the question left my mouth, I could see tiny lines appear on his forehead.

He turned back to the view of the pool and sighed once more. He closed his eyes.

A minute passed and he opened them, sipped his cocoa and stared back out into the yard, holding the mug as if for warmth or maybe strength. Far in the distance rabbits could be seen chasing each other. Even still I could tell that one of them had an extra leg.

"When we first spoke, you said you didn't know him. But surely you must because he works on your staff," I said, pressing him to give some sort of comment or explanation. "I mean, you hire everyone at headquarters, do you not?"

"Yes, yes," Captain Hanson said testily, slamming his mug onto the glass tabletop. "I knew you'd find out about him. I told...never mind. Yes, he's on my staff."

I waited. He didn't tell me why Nathan was on his staff, but I let him talk.

Finally he began to speak, his voice grew louder as he spoke. "Nathan is an undercover regulator. He's caught numerous dealers and pushers, all of which are serving time up in the quadrant's Montgomery Cradle. Each sleeping away about fifteen years and in some cases life," he said, his voice stiff with an undercurrent of annoyance. "So, that's your answer. What else did you want?"

"I found it interesting, a possible clue as to why Amanda may have been killed," I said, twisting the lie as I stood up. "You know, if she found out about Nathan working as a regulator, he could have killed her to keep her from telling her mom. How would you explain that to Mayor Christensen?"

Captain Hanson's eyes burned with restrained fury. He stood up so fast; he knocked his wicker chair to the patio floor. He glared at me as if the idea was ridiculous.

"How- how dare you…a footless accusation! Get out! Out!"

"If you're hiding something, captain, I will find out," I said smoothly. "Tell me now and save me the trouble."

"Out!" he bellowed, the vein on the side of his head throbbing in rage. "You have no idea!"

"Good afternoon," I said with a nod and left, feeling the 350 under my coat.

As I crossed the threshold into the still brightly-lit outdoors, I glanced back to the front door. Captain Hanson did not follow me out or even check to see that I had left. In the far distance, I could hear something smash, possibly one of the mugs.

I thought I had him. He almost told me something back there before he caught himself. I still didn't know for sure who his girlfriend was, but I had to find out.

Why was he reviewing Amanda's autopsy report?

There could be a simple explanation for it. Her death must be the largest case of his career. Hanson may want to make sure that it was carried out to the letter, that no stone was left unturned, and that every item was duly noted.

Still, I couldn't shake the feeling that he was hiding something. Tonight, I would fly back to his house and follow him. Maybe he and the mayor met after dark, under the cloak of night if you will, to meet.

Clandestine rendezvous.

Oui?

CHAPTER 26

A few hours later, night and day struggled for control of the sky. I sat outside Captain Hanson's long, solitary driveway. He had not left and my butt was getting numb from sitting too long. I couldn't get out of the wauto and walk around because someone might see me. That's all I needed was the regulators to come to investigate a reported suspicious character by a nosey neighbor. Convinced he and Mayor Christensen was an item, I sat stubbornly, waiting.

The grounds were wet, soaked from layers of melted ice and snow. Patches of the frozen snowy heaps lay strewn across the grounds and the treetops. With the heat on three, I had removed my coat and my 350. I wasn't going to shoot him once emerged, only follow his wauto.

The yellow rays of sunlight faded as puffs of nearly black clouds shoved their way over the Memphis sky. In moments, snow showers fluttered down from the ominous sky as if the heavens suddenly had a bad case of dandruff.

With a heavy sigh, I realized that Hanson wasn't going to leave in this mess. I clicked on the headlights, when suddenly, Captain Hanson's sleek, black-four door vehicle slipped past me and onto the illuminated lane.

"Yes!" I said and went to follow him. "Lead on!"

A surge in excitement zipped through me. The downpour of white flakes created a curtain of snow, I could barely make out his rear taillights. Confident he was going to lead me right to the mayor, I tailed. I'll be able to dismantle their scheme, which may or may not have lead to Amanda's death, but it might be information enough to get them to tell me what they do know.

Captain Hanson glided through the lanes, winding around curves and eventually downward toward the city's limits. This didn't look good, as the mayor's home lay in Germantown, probably not too far from Hanson's own house. The flight over from his house to hers shouldn't have taken him downtown.

After nearly thirty minutes of following him, he finally landed at the O'Shea's bar. I didn't stop, but sped on by as if I had business elsewhere.

For the life of me, I couldn't believe Mayor Christensen would be caught dead in such a dive. Perhaps tonight was one of the nights they didn't see each other.

Wautos, a few banged up aerocycles, and a cargo craft cluttered O'Shea's normally vacant lot. I circled around mid-air and parked down on the pavement across from the bar where someone had recently vacated. I could see inside O'Shea's through spots where the windows weren't foggy. I lowered my wauto's window a little to allow in the cooler air and waited.

The music boomed and from here I could see people dancing, laughing and tossing back a few bright green beers. Katherine and a couple of other waiters I'd never seen before navigated through the throng of people, spilling beer, and shouting to the bartender.

They partied, oblivious to the dangers of life that, for now, where suspended. I wondered how Hanson did his job well when he drank like this every night. A couple of patrons stumbled out, laughing into the cold air. They held onto each other, leaning like that tower that used to be in Pisa. I could hear their conversation, even from my distance across and down the pavement. Drunks had no idea how loud they were…

"...Mike, stop it! Stop! I'm gonna tell your wife…(Laughing)"

"All right, Lily… tryin' to have fun…"

"Da both of ya knock it off… 'fore I bust ya traps…"

Ah, so much love in the air tonight…I watched them until they disappeared into the dark shadows at the corner.

I sat for another hour watching people come and go from O'Shea's. The snow stopped, but left an icy, slick ground covered by a thin layer of snow. None of the people leaving or arrived were the mayor. If Hanson and the mayor's affair were a secret why would they meet at such a public place?

I pushed on toward the rental room, my hopes dashed.

Tired and a little befuddled, I entered the rental room and found Jane seated on the sofa, her feet up and over the edge of the right armrest, facing the door. A beer cradled in her arm, she looked totally satisfied with herself.

"About time."

I laughed and collapsed into one of the two chairs. Jane wore her cat-that-ate-the-cream smile, which meant she found out something worth telling me. But of course, I had to ask her.

"You look awfully pleased."

She nodded and sat up. Without looking at me she took the package of cigarettes from the table and lit up.

"Okay, I'm asking," I said wearily. "What did you find out?"

"Guess who Nathan's partner is?" she asked, her eyes twinkling with her newfound information, her voice full of amusement.

I shrugged, my brain dead in the water, my stomach growling. I flicked on the room's filter, and it began to suck Jane's cigarette smoke up and out of the small space.

"Some guy named Jameson," she said with a ring of smoke escaping from her mouth. "Followed them to the less than stellar parts of the quadrant in their unmarked wauto. They rousted a few corner dealers, but nothing else worth reporting."

Jameson and Nathan as partners. Jameson was a creepy kind of guy. Partnered with Nathan, there must be hundreds of regulations they've broken.

How did Amanda fit into this puzzle of drugs, regulators, and politics?

"So, now what?" Jane asked. "Hungry?"

I hadn't eaten all day and smiled. "Famished."

"Well, Aunt Belle invited us over for dinner at her home, tonight. I told her I'd call her either way by six," Jane said hesitantly and stubbed out her cigarette, half smoked.

"Fine."

This would be a good time to meet Mr. Christensen and to observe their relationship. After years of following and photographing wayward husbands, wives, girlfriends, and boyfriends, I could usually tell when things were amiss in a marriage or relationship.

Except my own.

P.I. heal thyself.

"She's got this really good cook, Cajun," Jane was saying as she headed for the bathroom to wash her hands. "I promise it will go well."

Yeah, right.

ꙮ

The drive out to the mayor's mansion passed swiftly and before I had summoned the patience and honey needed to endure the night we were there. Around the west and east sides of the house, bushes rose from frozen earth. Their naked branches weighed down low with chunky ice. The paved cul-de-sac lay covered in fluffy snow.

Her house was about fifteen minutes from Hanson's estate home. They were practically neighbors.

I climbed out of the wauto, but Jane had already beaten me to the double, metallic doors. I reached the edge of the porch when Mayor Christensen answered them.

"Janey, so good to see you," she said as if she hadn't seen Jane in a year. "You made it."

With a brief hug, Jane moved forward inside. Mayor Christensen turned her hazel eyes to me and said, "Cybil."

Definitely not feeling wanted, but not really caring, I followed her through the foyer, this one decorated in soft desert rose and mauve carpeting, to the sitting room.

The sitting room contained a couple of two-person sofas with matching floral prints of pastel pink and white. They faced each other while two stiff-looking armchairs covered by some white gauzy fabric completed the rear of the U arrangement. The chairs faced a fireplace that burned on gas, not wood. In the center, between the sofas and chairs, an oval oak coffee table was placed on top of a striped mauve throw rug. Unlike the foyer, the floor here had been buffed and polished so the hardwood floors could be seen and admired.

Already seated on one of the sofas, Jane met my eyes and gave me a half-shrug. "Aunt Belle, about the case..."

Mayor Christensen clucked her tongue. "No business talk tonight. I invited you so that we could relax with a good solid meal. Not even a synthetic slice of bland."

I fought to keep the frown from my face. I didn't think a daughter's murder was *business* nor did I think Mayor Christensen truly wanted to relax. She wore a Christmas red pantsuit with sparkling gold high-heeled shoes. Her Afro bore two gold encrusted barrettes. Two long golden chains complete with golden charms hung from her neck. She looked ready for a party, not dinner at home with her niece and a p.i.

When I relax, it's in my pjs, maybe my favorite pair of sweats, but not a holiday formal outfit.

The fireplace warmed the room, and I turned my gaze from it to look around at the walls. No pictures of family, oversized oil paintings of various landscapes and a few modern art pieces.

"Dinner will be ready soon," Mayor Christensen said as she took up the seat next to Jane on the opposite sofa. "Tell me, Janey, what do you plan to do once you get back to D.C.?"

I snorted and Mayor Christensen ignored me. Jane's going to do what she always did, work cases with me and try to solve crimes. But I kept my mouth closed, trying my best to be good.

"Well, I might take some time off," Jane said, slowly, her voice low.

"What?" I balked. Jane taking a vacation? It was news to me…

Jane hesitated, and kept her eyes on Mayor Christensen's face. Seated across from her, on the opposite sofa, I watched the conversation unfold without further commentary from yours truly.

The two were pretending that I wasn't there anyway. They talked about family, etc., nothing that I could add to the conversation. That was fine with me. I liked people watching anyway.

After about ten minutes, a slender, dark-skinned girl with silky, waist-length hair, came into the sitting room. "Madam, dinner is served."

Mayor Christensen gracefully got to her feet, her posture perfect. "Thank you, Maria, dear."

The dining room draped in feathery yellow and dark woods had already been set for a party of three. The cloth napkins, a mixed pattern of yellow and creams, were large enough to cover my entire head. The fine china and heavy silverware only reinforced the ideal that Amanda had a very good, if not wealthy, life. Why would she run away from it?

I waited until the "family" had sat before taking my place beside Jane. The place setting for Mr. Christensen was missing. Damn, and I wanted to get a look at the guy, get to meet him, and try to read him. He was missing again.

The first dish was soup du jour, a more seasoned blend than the one I had at O'Shea's. This one came full of chopped celery, carrots and peppers. I sipped gingerly as Jane and Mayor Christensen resumed their conversation.

"I wanted to ask you, Janey, if you would like to work for me," Mayor Christensen said, and this time she looked at me. If she wanted to catch my reaction, she must have been disappointed because I didn't give her any.

I kept eating my soup, my face blank and empty.

Jane's reaction, on the other hand, startled her. "What!"

Mayor Christensen dabbed at her mouth gracefully and repeated her invitation. “Less risk, more pay.”

"But, you have to go through all kinds of exams to work for the mayor's office," Jane said, her neglected soup growing colder by the minute. "I-I’m not all that good with regulations."

Spoken like a true inspector-in-training. I beamed with pride.

"I wasn't thinking about the mayor's office. I was thinking I could appoint you over, say regulators for the Southeast Territories, as governor, I could do that," Mayor Christensen said smoothly, a hint of glee in her voice as if she'd already won the election.

Jane's eye grew wide with excitement. "You'd put in me as attorney general? Wow! Aunt Belle, I-I..." She faulted and stared at her aunt, misty-eyed.

"The election isn't won yet," I said, breaking into the happy scenario.

Jane was my assistant, and not that I couldn't get another one, I could. I didn't like seeing Mayor Christensen revving up Jane's motor when the election was still some eight months away.

Mayor Christensen laughed shrilly and said, "I know, I know, thrusters before the wauto and all that." She rolled her eyes away from me and said to Jane. "I want to know if you're on board for it, *when* it happens."

Jane readily accepted and Maria came into to take away the soup bowls. Empty, my bowl took the most usage, for Jane's and Mayor Christensen's bowls were still three-quarters full. I thought of all the homeless people who'd love a small sip of that soup. The wealthy never ceased to amaze me.

"So, will Mr. Christensen be joining us for dinner?" I asked, breaking the temporary silence and thus shattering their cheery mood.

I didn't do it on purpose.

I couldn't help it. I had to know. The suspense of his whereabouts was killing me.

Behind Mayor Christensen, I watched Maria hesitate, her shoulders rising in a defensive move, before she disappeared back into the kitchen.

Mayor Christensen's mouth drew into a thin, aggravated line. She opened her mouth and quickly closed it as Maria bustled in with the salads. Mayor Christensen sat one hand under the table, probably in her lap, and the other hand lay on the table in a tightly coiled fist.

When Maria left the room, Mayor Christensen said, "Mr. Christensen is unavailable to dine with us tonight." She said it as if she'd said it a hundred times before.

Jane glanced at me. A questionable look briefly appeared on her face before turning back to her salad. She shoved in a forkful of lettuce, and chewed, though her eyes were on me.

"Why don't you tell the truth? There isn't a Mr. Christensen?" I asked, nearly playfully. "You had Amanda out of wedlock, didn't you?"

A curveball, and it socked Mayor Christensen right in the stomach. She dropped her fork into her salad plate with a clang.

"This is *my* house, Miss Lewis," drawing out the "s" as if my name was a dirty word. "And when I say there'll be no such talk of business, I mean it!"

I'm like a vampire, once you invite me in, you'll never get me out without giving a little blood…

Jane's eyes widened and she forcible swallowed her mouthful of salad. Then she said, "Aunt Belle, what's the big deal? Just tell Uncle Richard to come down and that'll shut Cybil's mouth. She's like a cat. Solving her curiosity will probably get her killed one day, but…"

"She can't call him down, because he doesn't exist," I said

calmly between bits of salad. "She's been playing, us, Jane. She's secretly sleeping with Captain Hanson."

Mayor Christensen's media smile was gone and in its place a sneer so animalistic, she resembled an enraged wolf. "What did you say?"

Jane too twisted in her seat to face me. "Cybil, that's down right stupid ass…"

"She knows it's true," I said, my salad plate partially clean and awaiting Maria to cart it off. "Tell me it isn't."

Mayor Christensen said heatedly, "It's not true! I would never, never sleep with a man who-who…"

"Who did what?" Jane asked, her eyes bouncing like a tennis match between her Aunt Belle and me.

Here it is again. For the second time today, I have shoved people so far that they were close to confessing something, telling me something I'm not supposed to know. Sometimes I could press so hard, people shattered into a million pieces and nothing could be savaged. Sometimes they'd let loose something they wanted to hold close. I'd have to risk it. Not wanting to loose the moment, I pushed harder.

"Who works for her!" I shouted, slamming my own hand on the table making Jane jump.

"Who slept with Amanda!" Mayor Christensen cried and as quickly clapped her hands over her mouth.

Jane gasped. "W-what?"

Mayor Christensen rolled her eyes in disgust. Beneath her make-up she had gone a greenish color. Her hands still covered her mouth, the bright ruby red nails dug into her cheeks.

"Mayor…"

She sighed and pushed back her chair, sickened, and said, "Follow me."

Numb, for I hadn't expected that answer, I slowly scooted back from the table and rose. Jane fell in line behind me. Neither of us spoke.

We took the stairs up to the second floor, down a short

hallway into the only door on the right. Inside the bedroom was painted a girlish pink with white lace, like Amanda's casket, throughout. An ivory, four-poster bed, complete with lacy canopy, occupied most of the space.

Mayor Christensen stood in the doorway, unable to enter. Jane walked in and looked around. Nothing had been disturbed or packed away. Nothing. “Mandy’s room…”

"I found her journal one night when Maria was off and I was looking for one of my sweaters," Mayor Christensen said, her voice far away, her eyes staring off into the distance. "She-she used to always borrow my clothes, you know? She'd grown up and could do that now…In a little less than a year, she’d be going off to college."

Jane whirled around to me, her face haggard and her eyes narrowed to slits. Yeah, she was angry with me for pressing the mayor, but now we had information we didn’t before. She’d have to get over it.

"…I read about two or three files. Most of it teenage girl stuff, when a note fell out of the back. It was his handwriting, to her, as if I hadn't seen it a zillion times—his handwriting was drafted into a common font for memos and reports…" Mayor Christensen said, softly. “Who uses paper in this day? Who could afford it?”

Jane brushed past the mayor and out in to the hallway, her face diverted from me. I alone remained standing in the room, looking for clues. Anything Amanda might have left to give me a clue as to who killed her.

"He talked about how he loved her. How he wanted to marry her once she came of age…the usual horseshit…"

I looked back to Mayor Christensen. It was the first time I'd heard her curse or use any language that wasn't appropriate or ready to print.

"Did you confront Captain Hanson about the affair?" I asked, interrupting her beginning rant and snapping Mayor Christensen from her reminiscent spell.

"Oh, ah, no, no I did not," she said, her eyes focusing and locking with mine. "And I forbid you to discuss this matter with him. I don't see how this can help your case to find Mandy's murderer anyway. That's what I'm paying you for."

Jane must've snapped out of her foggy emotional dip too, because she said to Mayor Christensen, "Aunt Belle, we need to know everything. If you're holding back, it ain't going to help us find out who killed Mandy. We need to talk to everyone who could've harmed her."

The words, although logical, were spoken with a harshness, that even I flinched.

Mayor Christensen leaned back against the hallway wall, but Jane wasn't finished. She rounded on the mayor with avid anger. "You knew about her and Hanson and yet, you kept it from us. Why? Because she dated an older man? We needed to know this yesterday! We've been focusing all of our energy on Nathan when it could damn well be the regulator captain who murdered her. Damn, Cybil warned me and I was too, too caught up in your horseshit to see different. Arrgh! Don't you see?"

Mayor Christensen's eyes were wide with disbelief. "I-I never thought that Tom would do something like-"

"It's obvious you haven't been thinking about anything, except yourself!" Jane barked, her hands in fists, her eyes narrowed to burning slits of rage. "What? You afraid the press would get a hold of it and line the story up next to the article about spotting Elvis in Anchorage?"

I had all these thoughts too, but hearing them come from Jane shot them into perspective both for me and for the mayor, I would guess. Jane and I have been chasing our tails because we didn't have all the information from our client. It wasn't the first time this had happened with a client, but remember what I said about personal cases? Secrets get lost, hushed up and piled into a closet until someone yanks them out into the open.

Jane would not allow her aunt to pass to go down the stairs

to the first landing. The mayor had to hear Jane's grief, frustration and pain all wrapped up and stabbed into her psyche.

"...and where is Uncle Richard? Huh? Speak! You've been silent long enough!" Jane spat and spun around back toward the opposite wall. Fuming, she opened her pack of cigarettes and without asking, lit it up.

The mayor's famous media smile and southern grace dissolved as she slid to the floor, her eyes brimming with tears. They spilled and splashed down the front of her suit. "Janey, I-I, oh God..."

She wept, sitting there on the floor outside Amanda's room.

This time the tears were real.

CHAPTER 27

"Pink shells or purple butterflies?" I asked Jane over the top of my handheld. "She's seven this year."

"Butterflies," Jane replied disinterestedly, her eyes glued to the telemonitor. A short, bushy man dressed in a leather brown coat and jeans reported on the story of the 2149 model aerocycles was on. "New color coordinated duel blasters…"

Wednesday afternoon stretched out lazily. On the table lay half eaten sandwiches of peanut butter and jalapeno jelly, cups of cold coffee and Jane's cigarette butts piled into a Styrofoam cup-turned-ashtray. Jane relaxed, sprawled across the sofa, transfixed by the pictures of shiny slick aerocycles zipping through crystal blue skies.

"Hmmmm… I'll get a child's size pajama shirt and a young girl's pajama bottom in purple. I think she's still small in the chest area, but her legs are growing like vines," I muttered to myself, clicking on the items to add to my shopping cart. I added gift-wrapping (purple balloons) and a note from me (Love, Aunt Cyb) and paid. I prayed Nina would get it by Saturday, her birthday. Laughing, I imagined the look on Tisha's face when she saw my gift arrive and Nina discard all the high, overpriced stuff from Marcus and her, in favor of my present.

Last night, Mayor Christensen took two sleeping injections and bid us goodnight. Jane tried to get her to tell us more about Amanda and Hanson, but Mayor Christensen refused, her media smile slapped back onto her face. Jane didn't speak on the way back to the rental room, her anger spent.

My investigation stymied and emotionally drained; I decided to take a day off to relax. Nothing like a nap and lounging to recharge the batteries. Jane agreed and we had deliberately omitted talking about the case at all. We were stuck and we both knew it.

It all comes back to objectivity. As I said earlier, it's a p.i. essential. Ours were gone. Personal cases always found a way of dismantling it.

I knew it and now, so did Jane. She had so wanted me to be wrong about her aunt, to be wrong about Amanda, and to her horror, I wasn't. I, on the other hand, had wanted to be so right about the mayor that I too had made a mistake in accusing Christensen and Hanson.

"Go grab us some beer," Jane said lazily. "It's after four."

Feeling like a wife instead of a partner, I said tartly, "Get it yourself."

With a deep, exaggerated sigh, she clicked off the program and stood up. Without a word, she put her naked feet into her boots, laced them up and left the room.

Gross. No socks!

Shuddering, I turned back to my handheld, and pulled up the case notes. We weren't supposed to be talking about it, but that didn't mean I couldn't read up on it. I knew Jane wasn't mad, but more irritated. I clicked on the last entry date when three *dings* spooked me from my thoughts.

Jane's back quick. Probably forgot her money, leaving so hastily.

"Hold your wauto," I said and opened the door to…

"Hello, Cinnamon. 'Member me?" Jarold Montano said, his hot breath brushing my face, forcing me to want to gag.

I slammed my fist into the close button and he fired at me. The doors clipped off the beam. He forced his foot into the space at the last moment, making the doors retracted. He stalked into the room, his face perverted into a mash of glee and fury.

I wanted to spit into his smooth face. But then I'd be too close when he fired.

I raced in to the bedroom, and picked up my 350 from the nightstand as Jarold fired repeatedly. One shot nicked my calf, forcing me to collapse down between Jane's bed and the wall containing the room's sole window.

Fear settled into a cold, hard lump in the pit of my stomach. I tried to settle down, but my breathing came in fast, rough gulps. How the hell did he find out where I was?

"Just tell me where he is!" roared Jarold. "Tell me now, Cinnamon!"

His voice drew nearer, and I readied myself to try to stand and fire. Blood seeped into the carpet from my leg and the pain made my eyes watered. *Bastard!*

"Come out, Cinnamon, come out sweet little thing," Jarold sang hysterically, raising goosebumps across my arms. The sing-songy voice was disappearing like melting snow. "Now!"

He stepped closer to my direction, judging by his voice. The two-room rental place didn't leave me many places to hide or get cover. Fish in a barrel.

Exposed, I knew that I was an easy mark.

But then, so was he.

I wore only my black camisole and shorts. I felt naked. I pressed my hand hard against the laser wound, but blood squirted up between my knuckles and fingers. It ran into the carpet, making it squishy. I felt a little dizzy, but I shook my head to rid myself of the cobwebs.

A laserbeam shot burst through the bed's overhanging covers and right above my head. A mere one-inch lower and he would have shot me in the head.

The bastard was shooting under the bed.

And he'd nearly scalped me.

Quickly, I flipped up the cover...

"I see you," he said and laughed with malicious cackling from the opposite side of the bed, where he had lifted up the bed's overhanging covers. His black eyes shined. He fired again and I felt the hot burn of the laser burrow into my arm and out. I dropped the 350 and gritted my teeth to the agony.

No, no, h-he wasn't going to kill me this time…

"Bye, Cinnamon," he said with an icy smile as he let go of the hangings and stepped around to the side of the bed, where I lay on the floor, bleeding and in major pain. "Those breasts look so yummy all pushed up and exposed."

He pointed his gun at me, his eyes glazed over and dewy. "I will enjoy nibbling on them when you're sipping your last breaths."

I had a good life. Well, at least it was adventurous.

I closed my eyes to the coming blast.

It never came.

I heard something hit the window, grunt, and then to my relief I heard…

"Freakin' fucker! Take that!" Jane growled.

I opened my eyes to see a dead Jarold Montano slump to the floor beside me, the lasergun hole dead center in the middle of his forehead. The shininess poured out of his eyes, which stared at some far off place without seeing. He flopped down beside me, underneath the window.

Another gaping hole in his stomach allowed me to see the blood smeared wall behind him. What a mess. Hanson wasn't going to like this at all.

"Jane," I said, my throat felt dry, my strength ebbing out onto the carpet in a dark red stream. My voice only came as a croaked whisper. Strangled and sore, I couldn't get enough air to speak.

"Don't talk. There's blood everywhere," Jane said as if she hadn't killed someone. She moved out of sight and I heard the telemonitor click on. There were voices, but they were muffled…

….and then the blackness

…swallowed me.

ꟈ

"Cybil," called a man's voice, gently with a soft hint of southern twang. Soothing like a sunny patch of light, the voice called again, "Cybil."

I gradually opened my eyes to find my body strapped to a stretcher hovering above Jane's bed. The overhead lights seared into my head. I closed my eyes against the brightness. I thought back to Mr. Schmuckler, but wished that vision away. Stubbornly, the pictures plowed through the mental roadblocks until I conjured up memories of Trey, which exorcized him.

Trying once more, I slowly opened my eyes. I raised my hands to shield my eyes from the horrid, glaring fluroscent lights, and groaned. The room was filled with turquoise clad people who puttered around with scanners, kits and digital cameras. A strange sense of déjà vu swept over me.

Captain Hanson loomed beside me, his manicured hands holding one of mine. "Cybil, are you all right?" His eyes skimmed over my partially clad body, taking in my exposed legs and my tight, short top. Perhaps he enjoyed the blood splatter across my breasts. He hastily moved his eyes back up to my face.

I licked my dry lips and with a mouth full of spit that felt like paste, I said, "Sure, for someone whose been shot twice."

"Can't be hurt too badly if she's cracking jokes," said one of the paramedics.

I wasn't too sure about that hurt too badly part. The room seemed to spin around, slowly, as I was on a carousel…up and down, around and around. My stomach didn't like it very much. I could feel it churning.

Hanson blushed and said, "Sorry. Listen, I am sorry about the other day. I-I have a lot of things to talk to you about. Get better first, and then we'll talk."

Jane finished her statement to the regulator and came over

to the stretcher. The paramedics, one slender young man with dreadlocks scowled at her, but she growled at him and he stepped back, allowing her room up to the stretcher.

"They're taking you to the hospital. With luck, you'll get a room with Schmuckler," she said, with a grin.

CHAPTER 28

That first night passed in a blur of nurses, bland, tasteless food and visitors. I awoke on Saturday afternoon. To Jane's disappointment, I did not end up sharing a room with Schmuckler. I was given my own room where two armed regulators were positioned outside—a gift from Hanson. They only allowed in Jane, Captain Hanson, and Mayor Christensen.

During a lull in the activity, I punched up the number for Tisha with my left hand. My right arm from the wrist down to the elbow was bandaged rigidly. Itching like wildfire beneath the tight gauze, I rubbed the thing, but couldn't get any relief.

Tisha's face filled my hospital room's monitor within moments, her braids slick and curled in ringlets. "Hello. Oh, it's you."

"Just calling to talk to Nina," I said, biting back my name-calling urge.

"One minute," Tisha said, her eyes searching my hospital gown and bandages. "Are you hurt again?"

I nodded, feeling her icy disapproval wash over me. "Two laser shots, one of which could've been fatal. Fates were lookin' out."

Her eyes grew wide, her nostrils flared. "Cybil." She sounded like mom.

The laughter of kids and music crept from the background as 'Tisha traveled to the ongoing birthday party.

"How's the party?"

"Fine," Tisha said, her eyebrows knit together. "About

your chosen profession, it is entirely unladylike…no wonder you haven't had a real husband or boyfriend…"

The telemonitor shifted sharply and Nina's face came into focus. "Aunt Cyb!" she squealed happily.

A smile so big it covered the distance, from ear to ear, appeared on my face. "Happy birthday!"

"I love my butterfly pjs. Purple is my favorite color," she gushed, her eyes bright and her voice filled with joy. Indeed, for she wore a purple long-sleeved shirt. Her quick eyes took in my gown and the joy ebbed out of her face. "Are you-uh-okay?"

"Yeah, it's nothing," I said waving her off, trying to bring back the smile and her joy.

She frowned disbelievingly. *Damn. She looks just like Tisha when she makes that face.*

"Listen, blow out your candles and make a big wish," I said around the lump in my throat. "Make it good so that you'll enjoy it all year long."

"Okay," she said, her smile gone, perhaps for the rest of our time on the telemonitor. Darn.

"Hey Squirt, do me a huge favor. Don't spit all over the cake," I said playfully although my insides were twisting in knots at the horror this would bring to my little niece.

She laughed and said goodbye, the edges of a faint smile on her face.

Tisha's scowl replaced Nina's giggles.

"One day we'll talk about your other job options," Tisha muttered. "She cares about you and here you are taking chances with your life. DO you know what it would do to her if you were killed?"

And what that would do to you, Tisha?

"I like my job," I said, not wanting to think about the effect my death would have on Nina. My death would put me in a sour mood too. "Until you get a job of your own, Tisha, don't try to tell me about mine. I love that little girl with my heart and soul, so don't think I take my ass getting shot off lightly!"

Tisha gasped and replied tartly, "I am a mother. Something to which you will never experience…"

"Sure," I said, suddenly exhausted and slightly winded. "Later."

I clicked off the telemonitor with Tisha's mouth wide open to speak. I couldn't deal with that right now. Fatigued streaked along the inside of my body like thread through pipe. Achy and still sore where the laser shots burrowed through muscle and flesh, I lay back against the pillows, my brow sweaty and my hand, the good one, shaky.

The doors slid open and in walked a nurse. She was young, about twenty-ish and carried a big vase crammed with artificial flowers—real ones being extremely difficult to find and expensive to boot. With a rattled sigh, she placed the vase on the stand beside my bed. There wasn't a card or note. No electronic pinnings or animated card.

"Someone sure likes you," she said as she briskly checked my vitals and left.

ℰ℘

When I woke up again, shadows stretched out across the wall and cast the room into dusk. Across from my bed, beneath the room's sole window sat Jane, avidly watching the news on the telemonitor with the sound turned down low. Flashes of the program spilled over her and she didn't seem to know I had awakened.

"Anything nasty going on?" I asked quietly, for my throat still felt like rubber. I didn't think I could stomach any food without it being rejected and sent back up the opposite way.

"Oh, the sleepy has arisen," she said, turning in her seat to face me. "How you feel?"

"Like I've been ran over by a cargo craft," I said scooting up to a sitting position. During my nap my bandages had been changed; but already pink, watery fluid bled through the white wrappings on my arm. I knew that scar tissue, lump and thick, would decorate this arm.

"This should make you feel better," Jane said as she got up from her chair and clicked off the telemonitor.

She came over to my bed. Dressed in a black, long-sleeved tee-shirt and black jeans, she looked lethal and dangerous. Her dreadlocks were tied high at the top of her head in a ponytail. They swept over her shoulder, brushing her neck and middle back. She didn't wear a jacket, but I could see the outline of her knife holder she kept on the right side of her waist, beneath her shirt—only because I knew where to look.

"I spoke to Captain Hanson a few hours ago and he's unearthed some stuff you should hear," she said, a smirk on her face. "Hold on to your night gown. Jarold Montano is sleeping away at Frazier's Cradle Corporation for theft and your attempted murder. He hasn't been awake or out of the cradle since the day they loaded him in and injected him."

"Then-" I sputtered.

Jane held up her hand. "Left me finish."

I closed my mouth, albeit grudgingly. Someone was trying to make a fool out of me and I didn't like it. Jane had shot someone in our rental room. He looked exactly like Jarold Montano.

"The body in our rental room was a hatchling clone," Jane said, her voice even and firm. "Jarold was a hatchling. So, they kept his mix on file. Someone duplicated it, grew it and pushed it out into the streets with one purpose-kill you."

"What?" I gasped, leaning forward. "He wasn't anywhere near perfect. I never even saw the tattoo!"

"Apparently, Montano wasn't a legal hatchling authorized by our trans-territory legal genetic system, but by some rogue, independent geneticist. This genius created a second Montano at the original's request. Probably from Mexico..."

"But, he had crooked teeth, a twisted sense of humor..."

Jane nodded. "Well, before Montano went to the cradle, he

had some guy produce a clone. The specific details are fuzzy. The original idea may have been for it to take his revenge out on you."

"But..."

"Something happened to derail that pleasant plan," Jane said with a grin. "This second Montano started using Zenith and other stuff that makes a brain go wacky. Remember, independent geneticist don't have to follow the territory's guidelines for creating a hatchling...we're talking black market work. Under belly basics, based on currency—nothing more or even close to being regulated."

"Someone hired and redirected him to come after me," I said, my heart hammering inside my chest. The idea that someone created another Montano increased my blood pressure...And if they created another one, there could be more.

Jane sat down on the edge of my bed. "But, of course, no one wants you dead." She snorted in laughter, her eyes sparkling. "Yeah, it could've been anyone."

"Funny, oh, funny," I said as I tried to ingest the news. I had a laundry list of enemies. Still, Montano only cared about carving out information concerning Trey. Otherwise he would have killed me outright that night outside Padre's. The other night, though, his orders had changed. He asked about Trey between firings. He came straight away to kill me. Like Schmuckler. They were both going to kill me, even if I did have Trey's information and gave it to them. This could only mean that Trey had been found by whoever was looking for him and I, a loose end, had to be eliminated.

"Smells like the Raymen Cartel."

"Probably," Jane said, with an air of boredom, her eyes drifting back to the telemonitor as she turned to face the blank screen. "Though I don't know why you put yourself out there for a hatchling. Christ, I'd give Trey up. Anyway, I told Hanson."

"What did you tell Hanson?" More sharp than I had intended, I erased the frown on my face.

"That we've had past dealings with the Cartel," she said, her face pointed away from me. "Keep your gown on, I know the rules. I gave him enough to make him feel like he knows what's going on. He suspected something, and I gave him something to back off us."

"I know, I know," I said, my throat starting to sear in pain.

"Oh, I had to move us to a different rental property. We got kicked out of Henry's," Jane said, a big grin on her face. "They said we were bad for business. Two rooms, three days, and the regs constant attention. Nope, the owner sent us packing.s"

I laughed. My eyes felt heavy, as if weighed down with bricks. Must be the medication repairing the muscles. It took a lot of out you and I felt sleepy just thinking about it.

Relaxing, I lay down and was soon asleep.

CHAPTER

29

I woke to a world of damp gloom. Jane lay asleep only a few feet away, awkwardly positioned in a chair, chin tucked into her bosom, her legs sprawled outward in front of her. The telemonitor, blank and dim, in the wee hours of the day, was finally silent.

As if sensing I was awake, a nurse, a man named Tim, came bustling into the room. His chubby, ruddy cheeks pushed out as he smiled. Tim had the shrunken look of a person who lost a lot of weight in a short time. Except in his face, he kept the jolly, fatness in his face.

He whispered, "You're awake. Good. Good."

I nodded, yawned and sat up for his usual pricks, pokes, and prods. He'd been my early morning nurse for the last two days.

"Thought you were off on Sundays," I said, lifting my arm for the blood pressure test.

"I am, but they were giving out overtime. Can't pass that up," Tim said, his eyes glued to the monitor behind me. He slipped the pad around my arm, secured it and went back to watching the monitor. "Your blood pressure looks good, although I don't see how with your profession."

He removed the I.V. and placed a bandage over the spot where a tiny bubble of blood had appeared. Next, he took the blood pressure pad off of my arm and scribbled onto his tiny handheld. He kept his eyes between the monitors and the handheld, writing notes and readings.

"You're all better. No more leakage from your wounds.

Healed and sealed, as we say. Promise me you won't get into any more gun battles."

"I can't promise you that."

"Well, the medicine also cleared up those nasty scabs and cuts on your face," Tim added distastefully. "You are much too pretty to be getting into so much trouble." He wagged his finger at me. "The scars on your body read like a road map of violence."

"You're right about that one, partner," said a smooth, southern voice from the doorway.

I shifted to see around Tim, and there stood Captain Hanson. His dimpled smile beamed across the room like a beacon slicing through fog.

Tim turned his handheld around to me and said, "Thumbprint, please, for checkout. We'll bill you, later."

I placed my thumb in the area and groaned. Stiff and sore, I crawled out of bed. Tim left with a quick glance back to Hanson and then me. As soon as the doors shut, Hanson came over to the bed. He leaned over the bed's railing and nodded in my direction.

"I heard you'd be getting out today," he said, in the muted light of the room his bright blue eyes seeming to loom like headlights in the rain. "I thought you'd like a ride home, with me."

How would he know when I didn't even know until Tim told me I was being released? Hanson must have been talking to the nursing staff, and as a regulator captain, why wouldn't they tell him?

Jane stirred awake and said with a throaty voice, "You goin somewhere?"

She rubbed her neck and stood. With a short nod toward Hanson, she came over to the bed and bent down to touch her toes, stretching and twisting her back to dislodge the kinks.

When done, she stood up again and said, "They trust you to leave?"

Hanson laughed and said, "She's safe enough, I guess. You're the one who shot and killed someone. She only wounded one." He turned to me, "Speaking of Schmuckler, he's out all recuperated and such. Sent a couple of regulators to pick him up for attempted murder, but he's gone. In the wind, as they say."

Jane's eyes narrowed, but she didn't say anything else.

"Let's get out of here," I said, breaking the silence as I glanced at Hanson. "Give me about five minutes to get out of these hospital greens."

"Sure." He disappeared through the doors.

"You goin with him?" Jane asked, her voice suddenly hollow as soon as the doors hushed closed behind Hanson.

I knew what she was thinking. Jane's been with me long enough to know when I'm attracted to someone. She wasn't stupid. And it bothered her because of Hanson's relationship with Amanda. Besides, getting involved with someone in a case, is a big no-no. Of course, Hanson was attractive and very, very naughty, which was apart of the allure. I wasn't going to jeopardize the case for him. He could be a killer after all.

I pulled a murky gray sweatshirt over my head. Jane must've brought them to the hospital, because I didn't own a gray sweatshirt.

"Whose is this?" realizing that it wasn't mine because the arms were too long and the width too wide.

"Mine," Jane said, a fresh unlit cigarette dangling from her lips. "Didn't think you'd want to wear your sleeping bikini out of here." She snorted and said, "You didn't answer my question."

Nodding, I slipped on my jeans, dotted with dried brownish blood spots, probably from blood splatter. I ran my fingers through my braids, strangely aware that I was stalling Jane. My naked feet and disheveled hair were excuses not to answer her right away.

"Yeah," I said hoarsely. "I'm going to ride with him. See if I can't get something out of him. I know your aunt told us not to, but, you know."

"Yeah," Jane grunted. "Make sure you get something out of him. Don't let him get something into you. We're at Roger's Rental Rooms over on Bale and Lincoln."

With nothing else, she stalked out of the hospital room.

Jane is always blunt, but to the point. Oh, yea of little faith. No way would I engage in the horizontal hello with a suspected killer. Jane had to know me better than that...right?

I've never endangered a case; well, not counting that case involving a lovely stripper named Jose several years back. I've learned my lesson since then.

Hanson walked in. "Jane probably filled you in on Montano," he said, shoving his hands into his tight jeans pocket. The hunter green sweater gave his skin an air of warmth. Raindrops glistened like jewels in his hair. "I went out to Frazier's yesterday, myself, and saw him. Montano is in the cradle, sleeping away."

He drove all the way out to Frazier's to check on Montano? For me? He could have sent any first year regulator to do it. Why?

"Thanks," I mumbled. "Am I cleared on Schmuckler?" I wanted to move the conversation somewhere else. Away from me, back to the case. Schmuckler was middle ground, part personal and part business.

"Yes," Hanson answered, his gaze burning into my skin. "We have a great deal to talk about, Cybil."

"Like Amanda Christensen?" I asked, bringing my eyes to connect with his.

He quickly retreated his gaze, and downward to the floor. "Y-Yes, I guess that's one thing."

The doors opened unexpectedly, spooking Hanson. Jane came back in and went over to the chair, grabbed her backpack and stalked out without another word to me. Before the doors closed, she shot me a two-finger code that meant she would follow Hanson and me.

"I'm ready when you are, lady," Hanson said, his voice sweeter than sweet potato pie. Sweat droplets dotted his forehead, making him skin look moist. Nervous? About what?

I quickly put on my socks and boots. Heavy silence pressed down on my shoulders as I bent to tie my laces. Was I walking into a trap with a killer? Did he mean to shot me the moment I sat down in his leather-seated wauto? Weaponless and partially defenseless, Jane wouldn't be able to get to me in time.

With a fast twist, I knotted my hair into a ponytail.

"Ready," I said breathlessly. Minus the suit Hanson still looked wonderful. Within the close confines of the room, I was more than aware of his scent, rustic and powerful.

He nodded and he waited until I had passed him and followed me out. We walked down to his parked, sleek wauto in the hospital parking lot in silence. The hallways were empty as if the rain had somehow stopped accidents, shootings, killings and beatings from happening. No one wanted to get wet.

"Nice," I said, destroying the rain bubbles that stood erect on his wauto's polished finish with my fingers. Brand new, it still had that new wauto look and smell to it.

"You've seen it before," Hanson said cheerlessly and he slipped into the driver's seat.

In minutes we were off and headed toward the downtown area. The bleak day traveled on, oblivious to the tension unfolding inside the vehicle. I fiddled with the console, remarking how much his LCD screen and touch music panel acted in concert with the balancing of his HD system.

"You made me," I said, my pride bruised and smarting. "No one's caught me before."

"First time for everything," he said, this time with a smile, fleshing out his dimples. "Don't be mad. I let you follow anyway."

"Why?" I asked.

He shrugged. "Got nothing to hide from you, Cybil. By the way, where are you staying at now?"

"Rogers."

"Nicer place than Henry's," he said, his eyes darting between the lane and me. "Annabelle footing the bill?"

"Sure," I said. "Captain, why didn't you tell me about Amanda?"

He sighed, his smile gone. Water splashed down on us. The sky leaked freely without pause. "Please call me Tom. I-I, well, how could I tell you? How could I tell anyone? She was a minor. And I would have been accused of her murder. I-I needed to be free so that I could find the murderer, not tied up with trying to build a defense."

"If you're innocent, you shouldn't need to worry about building a defense."

"You know as well as I do how crooked and unbalanced our justice scales are…His eyes flashed into a feisty fury. "You know I'm right. Besides, Annabelle forbad me to tell you. Especially with the election in November coming up…a scandal could've tipped the scale against her. That's all she's angling for right now—being governor of the entire Southeast Territories"

I knew that much. But I let him talk. He needed to talk. A few short days ago, he was ready to tell me what he was going to tell me now…

"…for that woman," Hanson was saying and he shivered, "if the fur isn't flying, you're not doing anything. Except now she's worried about the governor's race."

The splatter of raindrops drummed on the roof. The lanes, empty and deserted, allowed Hanson to sneak looks at me without totally taking his eyes off the lanes.

His grin vanished in the shadows of his face. "You might not believe me, but I did love Mandy. My whole world was wrapped into her little finger."

The urge to hold him was overwhelming, the immense sadness was similar to the feeling I got from Nathan. Is it possible they both loved her? Truly? Instead I folded my hands in my lap.

Ha! True love is a farce.

Cynical? Who me? All the time. Love caused so much damage, how could it ever be true?

"You would have loved her too," he continued, his voice saturated with pain and sorrow. "Beautiful, funny, and smart. Very much like you."

Yikes! I blushed.

"Tell me why Nathan's working for you? Where does he fit in? He's on record for being Amanda's boyfriend," I said, swallowing hard. I cleared my throat and waited.

Hanson hesitated and then gravely said, "He was her boy friend. They'd been pals for a while, but no sparks. I think, well, I'm quite sure that Nathan was in love with her. Of course, Amanda was with me, so she spread the rumor that he was her boyfriend, romantically, to keep people from suspecting us. Sadly, this was where things got sticky."

"How sticky?" I prodded, trying to keep my voice from growing louder. I wanted Hanson to reveal the missing pieces to my puzzle and hopefully help me solve this case.

Hanson sighed. "Nathan started blackmailing me.

"Blackmail?" My brain sagged under the new load of information. Even still I stood ready for more. "You're a regulator captain! You could've had him arrested."

"Yes, I could…if I wanted a scandal and a one way flight out to Montgomery's," Hanson said, his eyes now firmly planted on the clear lanes in front of him. His knuckles turned white where he gripped the steering wheel. "He had pictures of us together. Threatened to send them to every online tabloid and community sites across the quadrant. God only knows how he got those. Sent me a few to prove he had them. He was bleeding me dry...every month…"

Sweating profusely now, Hanson's lips pressed together into a tense, thin line. The wauto dropped downward as we approached Roger's.

"So, I wanted him to stop," Hanson continued. "He agreed, in exchange for a job, a regulator job. I don't know why, but if he would stop, leave us alone, I thought," he said, his voice growing quieter. "It was stupid to hire him, but I-I couldn't lose Mandy."

I shrugged. "You lost her anyway. Don't beat yourself up though. People do all kinds of things for love."

"Sounds like you know a lot about that," he said with a sly glance in my direction. "Well, to end this tale, I hired him. Amazingly, he kept his word and left me and Mandy alone."

"He hasn't asked for anything since becoming a reg?"

"No. He does a good job," Hanson said, his voice high and shaky. "I-I can't fire him."

"Can't or won't?"

Hanson briskly wiped his face with his right hand. "Both. I guess. I've gotten reports from others about Nathan and Derrick supposedly stealing from the evidence warehouse, but when I make an inquiry into it, it nets a big fat goose egg. They've got help from others, but I can't catch any of them."

"Are they wiping it out of the computers somehow?"

Hanson shrugged. "I don't know. Maybe, but our computers personnel can't find the trail if there was one to find in the first place."

We rode in silence for another ten minutes when Roger's appeared on the horizon. Hanson sat down the wauto directly in front of the lobby doors. He turned to me, his face glazed with tears.

"She was so lovely. And I miss her terribly. But I did not kill her, Cybil."

"Who did?" I asked, feeling a sore knot in my back burn. Why was Hanson still trying to defend himself? "She was only a teenager. No enemies."

He shook his head, his hair flawlessly staying put. "I've been asking that same question since the day I got the call she'd been found."

CHAPTER 30

Roger's Rental Rooms took up nearly all of a city block. The massive brick building resembled a converted school and several of the windows were still glass with cranks. Captain Hanson turned off his wauto and rotated in his seat so that he could look directly at me. For a few moments, he simply stared. My eyes and his connected and finally he blinked first.

"Cybil, I-I'm sorry I shouted at you the other day," he said, his southern twang emerging in his speech, somehow making his apology seem more heartfelt, sincere. "I was so offended by the fact that you thought I was capable of killing Mandy and sleeping with her mother that I …lost it."

"Tom, you did carry on a relationship with a minor," I said gently. "I mean, that's serious enough. You were hiding something. I was wrong about what you were hiding."

He nodded. "I didn't want you to believe that I was capable of murder. I didn't want you to think less of me. I-I…wanted you to like me."

"Why do you care what I think?" I said, my stomach tingling as if a bucket of ice had been shoved into it.

"I want you to like me, because I like you. It matters to me what you think," he said. Then he cleared his throat as if nervous. He wiped his hands on his pants. "You're so beautiful and feisty…Being near you, makes me sweat. Hot."

"Tom," I hesitated and then stopped. Hot?

"I know you're trying to find out who killed Mandy," he said, his hand reaching out and caressing mine. "We can talk about this later. When the air is clear and when I'm surer of this. I mean-if you want."

I shrugged and gave him a "we'll see."

With my heart pounding in my ears, I fled into Roger's lobby. To my surprise, no robots awaited at the front desk. Two uniformed women, one named Deborah, the other Melissa, smiled pleasantly as I approached the desk. I didn't know what names Jane had reserved the rooms under, but I was saved from embarrassment when Jane walked into the lobby and came up to me.

"We're in room one-ten," she said, slipping me my own room keycard. "What did he say?"

"He admitted to having a relationship with her," I said. "Claims to have loved her. I asked him about Nathan. Said Nathan was blackmailing him and eventually the final payoff was the regulator job."

We reached the room and Jane entered her keycard. The doors opened up to a wide room with a kitchenette, a tiny table with two bar stools and a second room with two double beds. The bathroom was directly across from the kitchenette. It smelled clean and that's truly all I cared about at the moment.

Piled high on the table in front of the bar stools were CDs.

"What's that?" I asked as I pointed at the CDs. I opened the miniature refrigerator and smiled. Jane had included the necessities. Peck beer, jalapeno jelly and coffee. I snagged a beer.

"Nathan's bank statements for the last four years," she said as she grabbed my beer out my hand. "I should've gotten them earlier, but my contact in D.C. was on vacation. And then I was going to go through them today, but the nurses told me you were being released today, so I went back to the hospital."

"Hanson said that Nathan was bleeding him dry before he hired him on to be a regulator," I said as I climbed awkwardly up on a stool; my right arm was stiff and tight. "If he was, then there should be proof of that in these."

Jane took the second stool. She removed her laptop, waited for it to boot up and inserted a CD. "This one is from January of last year."

"Start there. He's only been a regulator for a little over six months."

The doorbell blared and I jumped, feeling my muscles tense. My gun hand was rigid and that wasn't good. I couldn't even curl my hand, only wiggle my fingers. Yeah, this I wasn't good at all.

"You expecting someone?" I asked, as I got up from the stool. "Where are my guns?"

"Pug's in the top drawer in the nightstand," Jane said, removing her knife from its holder, underneath her shirt. "The 350 is with the Memphis Regs."

"Shit."

I took out the pug into my left hand as the doorbell blared once more. I nodded to Jane and she pressed the release.

The doors slid back to reveal…

Mayor Christensen.

"Aunt Belle," Jane said stonily. "What are you doing here?"

She lowered her knife and stuck it back into its holder. I lowered my gun and sighed.

"I came to see about Cybil," she said sweetly. She wore a navy suit with a skirt that stopped above her knees with matching pumps.

"Did hell freeze over?" I mumbled as I went back to the stool, slapped the gun onto the counter. I drank a big gulp of beer from Jane's open bottle, trying not to spill any of it. Drinking with my left hand wasn't nearly as smooth as using my right.

Mayor Christensen pretended not to hear me and answered Jane instead. "I heard Captain Hanson drove her home. Surely you did not disobey my orders and discuss- -uh, well, you know."

"Yeah," I said. "I'm investigating a death of your daughter. Remember."

Mayor Christensen pressed her lips firmly together. "Well, I thought you should know that I am hosting a charity benefit tomorrow night, here in the ballroom to raise money for recovering Zenith addicts. Here are your invitations."

She tossed two electronic badges that read "Mandy's Memorial Fund.

"Here is a guest list. I thought you would want to review it. Everyone will be there," Mayor Christensen said. "I trust the conversation you and I had would remain a private matter."

Jane grunted in disgust. Without looking back she disappeared into the bedroom and almost immediately the noise of the telemonitor could be heard. The 24 hour new broadcast's jingle flowed into the outer room.

"For now," I said, my eyes level with the mayor.

"Well," she said, her voice slightly quivering. "I-I will see you there."

Jane came back into the kitchenette area once she heard the doors click closed. She sat back down at the table, picked up her laptop and opened the file. Her back to me, she drank beer and scanned the files without comment. The telemonitor's volume pumped news stories into the kitchenette area.

"You want to talk about it?" I asked, getting her another beer from the mini fridge.

"No," Jane said, her voice low with an undercurrent of hurt.

Leaving Jane to it, I went into the bedroom and lay down. I stared up at the ceiling trying to picture why Mayor Christensen was having a benefit for her dead daughter. She said it was to raise money for recovering Zenith addicts, but the good mayor had said that Amanda didn't engage in drugs. Coincidence that the charity cause was Zenith users? Why not alcohol or some incurable disease?

I scanned the list of guests.

The fundraiser list held all of Memphis's upper echelon citizens and several regulators including Nathan and Derrick.

Funny, Mayor Christensen said she hated Nathan, so why allow him into a private party? The mayor may be holding back more important information. I didn't want to think she'd be stupid enough to anger Jane and jeopardize the case to find Amanda's murderer, but then…

I yawned, still feeling the after effects of the drugs to repair my muscles. My eyes closed and I slept until I heard…

"Gotcha!" Jane shouted from the kitchen.

I hurried into the kitchenette and found Jane hunched over her laptop, an ashtray stuffed with cigarette butts at her elbow. She mumbled to herself as she scanned the file's entries.

"What?" I asked, my eyes roaming over the figures and entries on the laptop screen.

Jane smirked. "He has been getting a regular deposit of ten thousand SE currancy, starting in January a year and a half ago." She pointed to a highlighted entry. "See this is the same account number that the funds comes from. It's identical to the other deposits after January's. Unless he has other accounts under different names, this is his only income."

I could see that Nathan was very frugal. He hardly removed any of the hush money, a few fifty extractions here and there, but nothing excessive to arouse the suspicions of the quadrant revenue division.

"Here," Jane said as she clicked another button, "is a month after he gets the regulator job in October."

"No entries of ten thousand dollar deposits."

Jane shook her head no. "That's because he started getting a salary." She scrolled downward and highlighted a deposit. The first in a few weeks according to his account.

"A much larger one."

There, highlighted by Jane, were deposits by the Memphis Quadrant Treasury from October to March. If multiplied by twelve months, Nathan was being paid a sum of fifty-two thousand dollars.

Jane whistled.

"More than I make," she said with a quick glance at me. "No wonder he left Hanson alone. This was easily five times more than his previous take."

"Yeah," I said breathlessly. "So it would seem that Hanson was telling us the truth."

Jane nodded. "Don't mean he still isn't a slimy creep."

"About the fundraiser tomorrow night, Nathan and Derrick are on your aunt's list," I said, swiftly changing the subject away from Hanson.

"Nathan?" Jane frowned. "Aunt Belle hates him."

"Seems that Mr. Martindale may have found himself a new blackmail victim," I said as I climbed onto the stool beside Jane. "She may be keeping it from us."

Jane's eyes narrowed to slits as she dug into her pocket for a cigarette. "Figures."

"But most importantly," I said with a grin. "What are we going to wear?"

CHAPTER 31

"Are we ready to go?" I asked from the kitchenette. Monday's afternoon had been filled with reviewing of notes, scanning through Nathan's bank statements and paying bills for my apartment, office and other utilities in D.C. This only made me homesick and renewed my desire to finish and solve this case.

The clock read seven p.m. and the charity fundraiser was slated to begin any minute. Already the parking lot outside Roger's was filling with expensive cargo crafts, wautos and even a few aerocycles. The night's sky seemed to be dressed for the fundraiser because even it was absent of clouds and a few brightly twinkling stars could be seen, like diamonds tossed in its hair.

Jane walked out from the bedroom, sporting her jeans and long-sleeved tee-shirt.

"What's this we stuff?" she scoffed. "I'm not going."

"You leaving me to go at it solo?"

She nodded. "I've got a date tonight."

"A date? Jane, we're working a case here!" I said, my hands on my hips.

"You're always saying that I don't have a personal life. Now that I've got one, you're yelling at me. It'll be a bore and I'm sure it ain't nuthin you haven't done before."

"Who could you possibly know here?" I asked, exasperated. "We're in Memphis."

"Her name is Susan and we're going to go dancing and later to dinner at someplace on the west side. This isn't my first time to Memphis, Cybil, my aunt lives here," Jane said breezily.

I've known for some time that Jane's sexual preferences wavered between the sexes, landing on the one she favored that particular night. Most often it was women. She has kept her private life private and she didn't share much of it.

"All right," I said defeated again by her verbal argument. "I'll see you later."

I watched her leave and headed out myself. The hallway that led to Roger's Meeting rooms and the ballroom had been sprayed with scented air fresheners, something floral and gagging. Once I got inside the ballroom, I noted that the ballroom's air contained some misty, scented perfume and it made my nose itch. All around Memphis's wealthiest and most powerful people mingled, drank slivers of champagne from flutes and opened their wallets. Several beefy security guards and chunky robot guards prowled the area, looking for anyone suspicious.

They kept their eyes on me.

I wore my newly purchased black dress pants and a silk red blouse. My braids had been pulled up into a ponytail and wrapped around in a bun. Jane placed sparkly barrettes in it to make me look more glamorous. I wore a black suit jacket. Even though it added to the over all polish of my outfit, I only wore it so that no one would see my gun.

My feet ached. New shoes, courtesy of Nero's, pinched, but still I circled around the crowd, mingling, smiling although not many knew who I was. The lure of the free buffet pulled me toward it and I had reached down to take a carrot stick when I heard someone laugh.

I looked down the buffet to see Mayor Christensen laughing with a very nice looking man and woman. The couple wore a lot of diamonds. The lights glistened against the rocks that littered around the woman's neck. She seemed to smile, but it never really seemed real to me. Fake, maybe like those diamonds.

"Mr. and Mrs. Harvey," said Captain Hanson as he picked

up several carrots sticks. "They own several stores, including Nero's and Marco's clothing stores. Big contributors to her campaign. Mr. Harvey," Hanson pointed with his pinky finger, "wants to be appointed as the ambassador to the northeast quadrant when Annabelle wins the governor's election."

"Really?" I said and bit into my stick. I crunched and watched the mayor move away from the Harveys and work the crowd. "She's damn good."

Hanson nodded, his lips curved into a smirk grin. "Only on the surface, sweetheart. Only on the surface."

I moved away from Hanson to do some working of my own. The robot guards drifted along behind me, as if I couldn't see them tailing me. I had already shown my pass once, and yet they continued to follow.

The section by the stage seemed empty and I walked closer to the audio speakers. Music, supplied by a robotic deejay swirled from four boxy speakers that were taller than it. I leaned back against the stage, watched and listened. I noticed that Hanson and Christensen made sure not to bump into each other or circulate in the same groups.

A temporary lapse in the music revealed the loud guffaws and murmurings of conversations. I thought back to my situation with Trey. How many of these events did he attend as an undercover working with the Raymen Cartel? It was rumored that the cartel had their tentacles into everything from politics to prostitution. I looked around, trying to guess which person worked for the Cartel.

"You still hangin' 'round this fuckin' city?" asked a raspy voice.

I looked to my right and caught sight of Nathan Martindale strolling toward me. Dressed in a charcoal gray suit and black shirt, he seemed in good spirits. Minus the cast, his right arm held a slender glass of champagne. He leaned beside me. He smiled, sparkling, white teeth and a pound of charm.

My right hand shot a spasm but I still couldn't close it fully. The muscles pulled tight when I tried, but locked out full mobility. Damn.

"Yes," I shouted over the beginnings chords of a waltz. "Surprised to see you here."

Seems Nathan had dipped into his hush money because his black leather loafers alone cost more than my retainer. Either that or my suspicion that he was blackmailing Christensen was dead on.

He smiled. "Funny thing…"

The rest of his conversation was drowned in a bath of trumpets so I never got what was funny.

Tired of shouting, I strolled away from the stage and he followed. The ballroom's side entrance lay in partial shadows. A few feet away, several solo people held up the wall.

"Tell me. How does one go from being a petty Zenith dealer to an undercover reg?" I asked smoothly. "Without going to the academy?"

He lowered his head, his mop of curls cascading forward. With a laugh, he said, "Nuthin' a secret in this town. Who you been talkin' to babe?"

My eyes briefly connected to his as he tossed his back his head, still laughing.

I didn't see what was so funny and I had a sneaky feeling he was high.

"No. In fact, I know Amanda wasn't your girlfriend and I also know your dirty black secret for soliciting funds from fellow guests." I gestured around with my hand to the crowd at the buffet table, which included Hanson.

He stopped laughing and his voice became pitiless. "So what? He's a freakin' child molester. Pervet. Freak."

I shrugged, thinking so are you.

"…he's what? Twice Mandy's age?" Nathan was saying. "Guy's a fuckin' sham. All good and regulation bound, but can't follow the shit himself. Fuckin' hypocrite."

"The real molester is the guy who raped and killed her," I said.

Nathan's rant wavered and he paled. "S-she was r-raped?"

"Brutally," I said, watching him closely for he seemed genuinely surprised at that tidbit, but surely he'd looked into Amanda's autopsy report.

"You said sex with her was better than Zenith. Was that because you liked it rough? Play acting a little rape scene with her that got out of control? Or maybe you didn't have sex with her at all and her constant flirting became too much for you? You lost it and killed her."

His mouth moved but no sound came out. With a rough cough to clear his throat, he said hoarsely, "Mandy loved me."

"Yeah, you say that now. And how convenient she's not here to dispute it," I said back, my voice low and bitter.

"That old idiot was her money bag!" Nathan shouted, his jaw rigid with anger. He drew several quick looks from a couple of aging wallflowers. His eyes held unshed tears.

He took in a deep sip of air and ran his fingers through his hair, snaring some of them on his tangles. He let out his breath, slow and deliberate. Lowering his voice he said, "I was her true love. We did have sex and I didn't kill or rape her. I-I loved her."

His face was damp from sweat and he rubbed it vigorously.

Nerves?

"You know, Nat old boy, that doesn't add up. Amanda came from money. Why would she need his money?" Amanda didn't strike me as greedy, but…

I was painfully aware that both of us were avoiding saying Hanson's name.

Nathan leaned in to me. He smelled of honeysuckles and mint. "See, I got news for you, inspector, her mother cut her off."

"Why?"

Despite this surreal conversation, I felt somewhat sorry for him.

"Becuz. Mandy was still on it," he snapped.

"Zenith."

"You got it," he said with a terrible twisting grin on his face. "For real? She was raped? You ain't makin' it up or nuthin?"

"You're a big time regulator now. Check her autopsy report," I said as I walked away.

Across the room, I saw Mayor Christensen's eyes peer in my direction, despite her flashy smile. When she saw me walk away from Nathan, she excused herself from a trio of gawky women with bluish-tinted hair and jeweled glasses.

We met at the buffet, which had cleared out and was temporarily deserted. Most of the food looked like dyed paste, but my tiny plate filled up quickly. Hunger is the best spice and I was starving.

"You are associating with scum," Mayor Christensen hissed through her plastered on smile. She gracefully sipped from her glass and glanced around, nodding at guests…smiling.

"You invited him," I said carefully while staring away from her. "That's not all you've been doing with –uh- what did you call him? Scum?"

She stiffened as she looked around widely. "I have no idea of what you're talking about."

"Sure?" I said, studying her reaction. "I mean, Jane could come and ask you about your relationship with scumboy over there. I don't think she'll be very nice about it, though. Considering how you've kept important info from us before."

I looked directly at her. Her Afro, fluffy and glittery, sparkled under the track lights. She placed her drink on the table; nodded in my general direction and drifted off to some other cluster of elite guests.

Did I hit a nerve?

That's two for two tonight.

I took my miniature platter a few feet from the buffet when my eyes landed on Derrick. He sat moodily across the room in a section of small tables set up for those who didn't like to eat while standing. A cigarette rested in an ashtray, its smoke spiraling toward the ceiling. Both of his boots rested on the table's clean surface. He drew several frowns from other guests passing by, and I noticed he sneered at Hanson when he strolled by with three other people.

Hanson didn't seem to notice.

Suddenly, Nathan plopped down into the seat beside him, his face contorted in fury. Nathan clapped Derrick on the shoulder so hard, Derrick nearly toppled over. He removed his feet, rotated his chair to face Nathan's and leaned into to listen. Whatever they discussed, Nathan wasn't happy about it. And soon, neither was Derrick. His scowl distorted his face and he pounded his knee as he spoke.

After a few minutes, Nathan caught me looking and the two got up from the tables. I watched them stalk out of the party.

The next few hours dwindled down to dust and guests began filing out in drunken clusters of people.

As people left, Jane came in, her eyes bright. "So? Learn anything new?"

"Tell you later," I said, my feet screaming to be released from my shoes. "How was your date?"

"Tell you later," she said with a small grin.

Hanson nodded in our direction before exiting through the front doors.

Alone.

CHAPTER

32

The blare of the telemonitor woke me with a start. Groggy from too much champagne, I fumbled to a sitting position and yawned. Tuesday's morning was underway. I awaited my eyes to adjust to the screen's glare and then I caught the time at the bottom of the monitor.

Seven thirty.

"Jane, do you have any idea-"

"Shush!"

Already awake and fully dressed in noir jeans and another tee shirt, Jane sat Indian style on her bed. Her eyes reflected the telemonitor's images. "I want to hear the news."

I hated sharing a room with her, for this very reason alone.

"This is Roberta Rodriguez with your early morning news," said the beautiful news anchor. Her curly locks spiraled down her back and some was artfully tossed over her shoulder. She wore a navy suit with pinstripes, her lips a glossy burgundy.

"The news?" I asked with a groan. I collapsed back down to the bed, covered my head with a pillow and tried to get back to my dream of vacationing in the Bahamas with Mayor Christensen's administrative assistant.

"Mayor Christensen's fundraiser for local area recovering Zenith addicts was a huge success, earning some two million dollars in donations..." Roberta continued in her crisp professional voice.

"That should make her look good," Jane mumbled. "Even though it doesn't bring Mandy back."

"...The fundraiser was in part a memorial to Mayor Christensen's slain daughter, Amanda Christensen, who had volunteered at the Zion Zenith clinic and was found dead earlier this month..."

The telemonitor clicked off and the room dipped into darkness. I heard Jane get up from her bed and in a few moments, the doors open and close.

Jane was on the prowl. Heaven knows what she'd find when she was restless like this.

I dozed for a while and woke a few hours later. I made two jalapeno jelly sandwiches and drank two cups of coffee. Jane returned while I was on my second cup. She strolled back in and sat on the stool next to mine.

"Cybil, do you think we should pack it in and go back to D.C.?" she asked quietly.

"I thought we were here to find Amanda and who killed her," I said, my plate empty as my mug growing more so with each passing second. I love coffee.

"I dunno. I mean, I like Hanson for the crime, but it seems like he's told us the truth so far. And," she said with a sigh, "Aunt Belle doesn't really want us here. She still isn't telling us everything we need to know. I mean, how badly does she want the murdering rapist caught?"

"She's paying our rental room fees, plus my usual retainer," I said. "She's not doing that for nothing. Nevermind her, we're interested in finding the killer. Right?"

Jane tossed her dreadlocks over her shoulder. "Yeah. I mean she's doing it so that it looks like she cares, but she doesn't. Like that fundraiser last night. That was only to try to boost her ratings with the public. Susan said last night that Aunt Belle is favored 82% above the next competitor for the Governor's seat."

"So what?, Don't you want to put the bastard who killed Amanda in the cradle?" I asked, trying to lift her spirits. "Justice, you know, for your favorite cousin."

Without speaking, she put her hand in her back pocket, and took out a tiny, metallic CD. She slapped it down on the counter. "Here."

"What's this?" I asked as I picked up the CD. Designed for handhelds, the CD fit snuggly into my palm. I waited while it booted it up.

"It is Amanda's birth information," Jane said, the undercurrent of hurt rising to the top.

I didn't have to ask if Jane had already seen it, because she had, judging by her actions. Jane wore it on her sleeves. If she felt it, you could see it. She was as transparent as a piece of glass.

Once the file booted up, I clicked on Amanda's name and read the mother's name and the father's name listed on the certificate. "Jesus Amador Raymen?"

Jane nodded with a sickened look on her face. "The son of Jose Raymen, head of the Raymen Cartel. The same cartel that's chasing down Trey and trying to kill you."

"Amanda's father is that Raymen?" I couldn't believe it. I felt like I'd had the air sucked out of my lungs by a vacuum cleaner.

"I met him, once," Jane said. "Once, at a family reunion, he came when Amanda was like four. Ever since that time when we ask about him, Aunt Belle always says he's away on business. Traveling, making dollars, and such. He might've been at the mayor parties when she won the mayoral seat about a decade ago."

"He missed Amanda's funeral," I said, staring back at the file. "I bet he's doing a lot of business between Mexico and the Southwest Territory. Who has access to this?"

"Memphis regs, upper government, the people at the clerk's office," Jane said, her voice heavy and tired. "How'd you think I got it? Birth records aren't public any more."

"Where did you get it?" I asked, my eyes moving over to her.

"Susan."

"Ah," I said. Susan worked at the quadrant's clerk office.

"Do you think he would have had Amanda killed?"

Jane shrugged. "From what Amanda used to say about him, she knew even less about him then we do. He would write to her, give her money, clothes, you know the whole dotting father act, but always from afar. Of course, she knew him as Richard Christensen, not as a Zenith drug dealer, Jesus Raymen."

Amanda, the daughter of a Zenith dealer was a Zenith addict herself. Now, I was beginning to see the picture. Trey while working undercover for the Territory Alliance, arrested Amanda for being a Zenith addict. Her mother, a popular mayor and maybe a shoe in for governor, couldn't let her daughter's arrest come to light. If it did, it might also come to the public's attention as to whom Amanda's father was... So, Mayor Christensen had Trey fired, thinking it would all hush up and go away. The Raymen Cartel wouldn't let it go at that. They wanted him dead.

But how does any of it tie in to who killed Amanda?

I debated as to whether I should share Jane's discovery with Hanson or not. For now, I kept it to myself. The day's events were slow and I lay on my bed, reviewing my notes and thinking, which took a great deal of energy. So does napping. Jane had left again, restless as she often was when a case was stalled.

Sluggish, I got up to get myself a fresh cup of coffee. My batteries needed to be juiced. I had reached the mini-fridge, when the doorbell rang, and expecting Jane, I ignored the opened doors and bent down to get my sugar from the mini-fridge.

As I stood up with the sugar in my hand, I heard a voice that was too deep to be a female but it was faintly familiar.

"Do not turn around. Leave Memphis now! This is your only warning, Ms. Lewis!"

Why? Why did people feel like they could threaten me off of a case?

I allowed my shoulders to slack and with a sudden spin, spun around and whacked the threatening menace on the wrist with such force a bone cracked. The gun clanked to the ground. I shoved my hand under his chin and plowed him back against the wall using my forearm. I pressed the sugar against his larynx, which brought me up on my tiptoes. He was tall.

"Trey?" I whispered as I yanked the mask from his face. "What the hell are you doing here?"

He smiled, but it was nervous. "Uh, let me explain…"

Angered I shoved my hand higher, lifting his chin to an angle that had to be uncomfortable. "Do it."

"I-I, I didn't go underground," he muttered, calmly without even breathing hard. "I can't breathe."

"No? Really?" I released his chin and leaned back against the min-fridge. "Why the hell have you been following me?"

He shook his head and rubbed his chin. "I haven't! Listen to me. It isn't safe for you to be here. I should've told you, but I, I…listen to me…"

Here I was worrying about him being dead in his attempt to go underground and he was in Memphis. Furious, I could only glare at him.

He sighed and glanced past me toward the bedroom. "Amanda Christensen…"

"Yeah?" I barked. Was he going to tell all of it now? He'd been keeping something from me. The look on his face betrayed that much. Nothing he could say was going to sway my fury at being lied to.

He fell silent, but his eyes grew larger. Something I couldn't define shined out from them.

"I heard you were nearly killed," he said with a painful grin. "I came here at once."

I knew he wanted to protect me, to keep me safe, but I'm stubborn. "Get to the point."

Trey swore softly and then plowed on. "You always know how to treat a man."

"Will you stop sneaking up on me?" I snapped and sat down on the stool across from him. "I could've shot you. Never mind, tell me what the hell you're doing here?"

Thinner than when I last saw him, he seemed happier despite the fresh crop of wrinkles around his mouth and across his forehead. His clothes bore button size rips and tears. Broad greasy streaks marked his sweater as if he'd been crawling through the sewer.

"I've come to see if you're still breathing," he said as he crossed the room and sat on the stool next to me. "I told you. Your listening skills are slipping, baby."

I flexed my muscles, feeling my right arm muscle pull tight and stiff, but good enough to use. "Good as new. If you're not going to tell me what's going on, then leave, now! Get out!"

Instead of leaving, he said, "I told you about that Christensen woman. Just pack it in and go home."

"Come off it, Trey," I said, tired and irritable. "Tell me what's going on. Quit stalling."

He said, "I haven't told you everything because you didn't need to know everything."

"I have shot a T.A. agent and was nearly killed for you! You've got about two seconds to clue me in. Or you pack it in and hit the fucking road."

He bit his lip. "Schmuckler and Montano aren't T.A. agents. They're the cartel's hit men. Schumuckler is actually one of the lower level newbies. I heard Jane nailed the clone really good. Thank goodness she was here..."

"Hit men?" I asked, ignoring his comments about Montano. If Schmuckler wasn't a T.A. agent than who was following Jane and me? Whose fingerprints are on the cigarette butt that was left at the scene?

"Don't look at me that way," Trey said. "As an agent I can't tell you everything. You know that. Sometimes, well, you know confidentiality and all that. Come on Cybil, I had to keep you safe. Smile for me, baby. Let me hold you."

"So the stuff back at my place was all horseshit?" I snapped. "To keep me safe?"

"Not all of it," he said softly, his eyes staring off into some spot on the wall. "I'm still an agent, but my cover was blown by someone in the Memphis government. I wasn't fired, but to appease the complainer, we faked my termination. My boss thinks the snitch is also the one allowing drugs to come into this quadrant. There are so many ties and connections, it's a tangled web."

I snorted in disbelief. Why? There was nothing to be gained from faking Trey's termination. But why lie to me?

I had been a pawn. Bait for whoever was in the government that had connections to the Raymen Cartel. If I could unearth that, then Trey and the T.A. could get information to arrest that person. "Do you know who killed Amanda Christensen?"

He closed his eyes and swore. "No. I'm not in Memphis investigating Amanda's death. And neither should you. It's a Memphis regulator problem."

"Don't tell me what I should be doing," I snapped. "I can't believe anything you tell me anymore."

"You don't believe me? Despite everything we've been through?" he asked, turning his gray eyes to me. "Don't you see, I couldn't tell you? And I still can't tell you all of it."

"I don't know what to believe," I said, my voice escalating on believe, my heart doing somersaults in my chest. We had been through a lot together, but these last antics of trying to keep me safe was his way of trying to make me into the good little girlfriend who made cookies and wore skirts. "I don't even know you. It was best we ended our relationship. You're a liar and a deceiver."

He hopped off the stool, his hands balled into fists. "You mean that?"

I didn't answer.

I didn't have to.

He left a few minutes later.

I hadn't wanted to fight with him, but lying to me had been too much. My right arm tinged. Laser shots, being followed, all for him and he can't even trust me enough to tell the damn truth.

The telemonitor buzzed again and I hurried into the bedroom to answer it. I clicked it on.

Captain Hanson appeared. "Cybil, I-I was wondering if you'd like to come by the house later, say seven tonight? I really need to speak with you."

It was already after five o'clock and I wondered why he wanted me over at his place. Because he told the truth about Nathan's blackmailing, didn't mean he wasn't a killer.

"Sorry, I've got other plans, Tom," I said.

He smiled, but it seemed tired as if weighed down by grief. "Later than, about eight? I-I really need to talk to you. "

"Why not now? What's going on?" I asked. From the background, it looked as if Hanson was at his home. The swimming pool's cover could be seen behind him. Hanson was on the patio no doubt.

"I-I can't talk about it over the monitor, Cybil. Please…" he pleaded.

"Fine, I'll be right there. Let me-uh- reschedule some appointments," I said, still unsure of what I was walking into.

He clicked off still muttering to himself. Something was up and I needed to find out what. Sitting here in this rental room moaning over Trey's ethics wasn't getting me closer to finding out who killed Amanda.

I grabbed my satchel, holstered my pug, and left.

CHAPTER 33

Half an hour later, I sat down my wauto once again in front of Hanson's home. The doorway opened out into the tidy cul-de-sac. He leaned casually against the door, dressed in his satin robe and matching slippers. Lights from the house flowed out and onto the steps and the statue of Venus. The goddess of love, illuminated in yellow light, as if coming to life this very night, stared across to Hanson. The night's sky held bits of clouds, some obscuring the full moon's illumination. The crickets' songs raised up against the cool air as if the beginnings of a crescendo.

"I'm so glad you've come," Hanson said as I crossed the path up to the door. He reeked of alcohol and sweat. His breath held the scent of sour beer.

"You called and I'm answering," I said, my stomach fluttering.

Was he going to try to slay me after or before the entrée? Ever since that first meeting with him in his office, I've felt that Hanson wasn't telling me everything. Whatever it was could mean the difference between him being a killer and him being an innocent man. The speech he'd given me, in the wauto, about loving Amanda the other day wasn't a total package of lies. It was like my first conversation with him. There was just enough truth in what he said for me to trust him, nothing more.

He led the way back through his house to the living room. The oval room held a fireplace and skylights that revealed the partially clouded sky. The fire burned lazily. A sofa and antique, leather recliner were the room's only furniture, except for a bar that took up most of the east wall. Hanson strode across to his fire, his back to me.

I scanned the cream-colored walls. Three nearly door-sized paintings consumed most of the wall space. I wondered: Had Amanda sat in this very same spot on the sofa?

Hanson remained standing by the fire, his shadow falling across the floor. "I have a confession to make. About Mandy, I wasn't completely forthcoming…She, oh hell..."

He wiped his face and went over to the bar. It was a stocked filled cabinet and a littered with crystal glasses of all shapes, sizes and uses for alcohol. I still drank beer out of the bottle so those various sizes meant nothing to me. Perhaps the more civilized people used them correctly.

I remained silent and watched Hanson fix himself a drink. Never thought of him as a boozer, but the people at O'Shea's did know him by name.

He poured amber liquid into a short, stocky glass. After his first grimacing swallow, he said, "I killed her."

My stomach fell. "What?"

Another shot of courage and he continued, "N-no, I as good as killed her." He sighed. "Annabelle came to see me down at headquarters. Her hair was on fire, she was so furious. Threatened to sue me, have me fired and on top of all that file charges against me if I didn't stop seeing her daughter immediately. So, I-I ended my relationship with Mandy like her mother requested."

"Let me get this straight. You paid money to Nathan to keep your relationship a secret, but her mom threatens lawsuit and you buckle?"

He shook his head. "I paid the money to stay out of Montgomery's. I'm a captain now, but I used to be a regulator investigator. Imagine how many of those guys in the cradle I put there. Not all are sleeping. Some get active detail. I'd be dead in a few hours," Hanson said, his eyes swimming in their sockets. He drained the remainder of his glass. "So you see, Annabelle wasn't going to be paid off. Not like Nathan. She wanted a pound of flesh for her daughter's supposed virginity."

"Mayor Christensen told me she hadn't spoken to you about the relationship," I said.

"She's lying," Hanson said as he got up and returned to the bar. "She came right over."

"What day did you end it with Amanda?" I asked.

Mayor Christensen was hell bent on being governor. She'd do anything to keep her image clean and family oriented. With the decay of society since the fall of the United States, the focus on family units has been huge. The governor of the Midwest Territories won solely on his platform for marriage tax breaks.

"The day she disappeared," he said as he sat back down in the recliner. He lifted the glass to his mouth and took another gulp. He looked old and tired.

"So initially the regs didn't follow up on her kidnapping because you thought Amanda was being angry, not because she'd run away before," I said, thinking back to Hanson's first conversation.

"Yes," Hanson said, his mouth down turned in a frown. "I should've searched for her right away, but I thought-I-I was protecting myself. If any of the regs found her while she was still infuriated with me, she might have said anything, hell, everything to them. Then I'd be under investigation…"

I had been wrong about Nathan being the wimpy boyfriend.

Captain Hanson was loosing his allure in my eyes. Pale, wrinkly and sloshed, Hanson lifted his drink, realized it was empty again and got up to refill it.

"If only I had been firm to Annabelle…" he moaned, slurring Mayor Christensen's name.

If only…yeah, well, hindsight is a perfect twenty-twenty. I would've dumped Amanda too. No one wants to spend thirty years in the cradle and Hanson's point about regs going to the cradle had merit too. But if he and Amanda had kept it secret for months, why not tell Annabelle that he'd do it and then continue to see the daughter anyway? Maybe Hanson had tired of the teenager and used the mother's demands to piggyback his own exit from the relationship.

A loud sob caught my attention and I looked away from the fire to Hanson. He was crying and babbling about love and loss. I guess I wasn't going to get any more answers from him.

I let myself out as Hanson returned from the bar, this time with the bottle, not the glass in his hand.

As I lifted off, I thought about where Amanda went after Hanson's rejection. If I could find that place, I'd find the crime scene and the person who killed her.

CHAPTER 34

This case was like looking under a rock and seeing all the ugly stuff underneath. Wednesday was waking up and I felt like a fish out of water. I waited outside Mayor Christensen's house, armed to the teeth with both guns and my sharp tongue. All the major players seemed to act as if an individual life, Amanda's, didn't really mean piss. Hanson was only concerned about his job and staying out of the cradle. Amanda's own mother used her to further her political goals, and her boy friend, Nathan, used her as a stepping stone to cut himself a slice of the Raymen's Zenith trade.

A stream of golden sunlight was falling across the porch, bathing it in warmth. For perhaps the fourth day in a row, I was up before my usual time of noon. In fact, it was nine o'clock on the nose and I knew that Mayor Christensen was seated in a board meeting right this moment.

I wasn't here to talk to Mayor Christensen.

The doors slid open and Maria's face appeared in the open space.

"Hello?" she asked, her eyes darting across to the areas behind me.

"I came alone, Maria," I said. "I need to speak with you."

Maria's eyes widened and she shook her head. "The missus is not here…"

"I know that," I said, stepping up closer to the open doors. "May I come in?"

"I-I do not think that is a good idea," she said, drifting

back into the house. The doors begin to close. "Come back when the missus is here."

I shoved my foot between the doors and they opened back up automatically. "I'm here about Amanda, Maria. She's dead, and I think you can help me."

She sighed and allowed me to enter the house. Carefully, she locked the doors after one final glance outside the house to make sure Mayor Christensen wasn't with me.

"You are alone?" she asked as she led the way back to the sitting room.

"Yes," I said as I sat down on the same sofa as a few days before. "I made sure to check. Mayor Christensen is in a board meeting."

This seemed to relax her and she took a seat opposite me. Her shiny black hair had been tied back today and she wore an apron over a red dress. In the pockets, dusters and a few well worked toothbrushes could be seen. She didn't wear any jewelry and I didn't know if she was married or not.

"What do you want, Miss Lewis?" she asked, her voice soft and somewhat hesitant.

"I want to know about Amanda's life here at home," I said, taking out my handheld from my satchel. "I am trying to put together who killed her, but I need to know how she was here."

Maria shrugged, her face a mixture of confusion and…fear. "I do not know…"

"Please," I said, putting away the handheld and leaning forward, my elbows resting on my knees. Often in wealthy families, the hired help is viewed as part of the furnishings. Maria probably witnessed many things in this house, but Mayor Christensen didn't even know Maria knew. If Maria were to write a tell-all book about the mayor, Ms. Christensen would be shocked at the details. "This is strictly between you and me. I won't tell the regulators, Mayor Christensen or anyone. But I must know…"

Maria sighed.

"Miss Christensen, she no like it here," Maria began, wringing her hands while they lay close to her lap. "She hate it. Always crying in her room. Fight all the time with…with, the older missus Christensen all the time. Missus Christensen yelled at Mandy for smoking and for her drug use. Nothing Mandy ever did was good enough for her momma. Never perfect enough. The great mayor had to keep a…a wholesome image. The governor's seat and all," Maria shook her head, her eyes brimming with tears. "But...but Mandy get a boyfriend. An older man, she tell me, Oh, Maria, he is so awesome and cool. He let me drink wine. We make love on the patio outside with nature all around…"

I smiled for I knew mothers like Mayor Christensen. Their children, especially their daughters, were thought of as extensions of themselves, something to be controlled. When the children reject their ideals, the mothers apply more pressure and dominance. Those types of cases were always messy

Maria's face took on a dreamy expression as if she too was experiencing Amanda's joy at having a secret relationship with Hanson. "I tell her to be careful…older man not always good for girl her age. She laugh at me. Says I'm an old maid. She was a good kid."

Maria's face became cloudy and dark like an approaching storm blocks out the sun.

"Tell me about the day she went missing," I said, keeping my voice calm and even. I didn't want to demand anything from Maria, or rush her. She might leave something important out if I did.

Maria became rigid. Her eyes were miserable and tears gathered at the corners.

"Awful day that day was. Mandy come home, her face streaked with tears and her heart broken. Oh, how she screams at the older missus. She say that her mother don't love her or want happiness for her. She say that the older missus only care about her career not about her. Oh, the screaming and then and then the missus slaps Mandy hard across her beautiful face…"

Maria broke down into sobs. Her face buried in her hands, I waited. The mayor would be in the meeting for several hours. The board wanted to build a new courthouse and the mayor, trying to curb government spending to look good for the governor's race was against it.

After a few minutes, Maria collected herself and went on, her eyes staring off into the fire. "Mandy, such a good girl, had so many problems. Father always working. The missus said that she would whip her from here to spring if she breathed a word of her relationship to anyone. Said that it was for Mandy's own good, and that as her mother she had to step in. Called Mandy a tramp, a whore..."

"Did Amanda flee to her bedroom after the fight with her mother?" I asked, my stomach clinching into a harshly coiled knot.

Maria wiped her eyes and looked at me. "Uh, no. Mandy said she couldn't stand another day in this house. Called it a hell and a prison. Packed a bunch of her things and left. I think her ride was waiting outside for her because she couldn't fly. She wasn't old enough yet."

"This friend wasn't the older boyfriend?" I asked, the knot churning around and around in my stomach. This was a big clue and perhaps the final nail in the coffin of this case.

"I don't think so," Maria said, but then shrugged. "I do not know. I did not see her leave the house. Only the missus chased her to the doors. I-I was in the service bathroom crying for Mandy. Poor, poor girl…"

"Thank you, Maria. You have been a bigger help than you know," I said as I stood up to leave, trying to leave the excitement out of my voice. "One more thing. Have you ever met Amanda's father?"

Maria's eyes stared at the floor. "I have only heard of him, but I have never seen him. Richard Christensen—he's always working."

"He doesn't live here with the mayor and her daughter?"

"I do not know who comes at the end of the week," Maria said, her voice low and strained. "Sometimes Missus Christensen has a guest over. A man, I think, but have never seen him. Only uh-leftovers in her bedroom that she had not been alone. Could be Mr. Christensen. Could not be."

She shrugged.

"How long have you worked for them?" I asked, my eyes carefully watching her, because I had the feeling that Maria was smarter than her broken English conveyed.

"That is two questions over your limit, Miss Lewis," she said her eyes attaching themselves to me.

So I was right. Her English was perfect, as I guessed. "Right you are. Tell me who you really are, and I'm gone."

Maria smiled, but it didn't seem to be the warm inviting grin of a domestic servant. It was cool and calculated. "You don't miss much do you?"

"No, not really. I am a private inspector, you know," I said, my hand on my gun. Not that I thought I would need it, but one could never be too careful.

She noticed my piece and said, "There's no need for violence. But please, indulge your, uh, theory."

"You're a T.A. agent, posing as an undercover maid," I said. "You're investigating Mayor Christensen's link to the Raymen Cartel."

"Damn, you are good," Maria said casually, leaning back against the sofa, her posture straighter, her poor-servant act was gone like the embers in a fire. "Trey said you were better than average. Couldn't ever possess him to go out with me. Now, of course, I see why."

"Thanks," I said, sitting back down across from Maria. "So, who are you?"

A genuine smile spread across Maria's face. "I am Maria Sanchez. I'm here trying to fit the pieces together on how deep the Raymen Cartel's dirty money goes, while Trey is out hunting down the other loose ends. He and I are partners. That's all I can tell you, of course. So I can't tell you about Mandy's father because I didn't know him, nor have I ever seen him. In fact, the mayor has nothing in this place that even has his name on it. She never speaks of him, not even when I'm around and I'm beginning to wonder if the man exists at all."

"Immaculate conception?" I asked with a grin.

Maria snorted. "Hardly. That child was good, like I said. But her mother's demands would drive anyone to smoke and do zenith."

"So you have no idea who Richard Christensen is?" I asked. Ha! I knew something the T.A. didn't know. Score one for Cybil and Jane. The Territory Alliance, zero.

"No," Maria said and I could tell she was telling me the truth. "I also don't know who killed the girl. I liked her. I've been here for about a year, and Mandy was a good kid. A Zenith addict. Once she started dating this older guy, she'd kept herself clean. For him. Said she loved him and all that. Maybe she did. But the night he dumped her because of her mother's interference really shattered her."

"Any idea who the boyfriend was?" I asked, just for giggles.

"None," Maria said. "But I'm not here to investigate the daughter's death. Just the Raymen Cartel connection, a bigger fish."

Wow! Cybil and Jane two. The T.A. Zero.

I reached across the coffee table and shook Maria's hand. "Thank you."

"No problem. I liked the kid. Hope you find out who killed her," Maria said and removed a duster from her apron's pocket. "Oh, wait a minute."

She hurried out of the room and through the dining room. Within a few minutes she returned, a little out of breath, her face red. "Here, I found this while cleaning Mandy's room. I haven't looked at it but it might help you out."

I took the cd from her hand and said, "Thanks again, Maria."

"No problem," she said. "Just get this bastard. Listen, I gotta get back to work."

I left the mayor's mansion with more than a bee in my bonnet. I knew that Maria probably witnessed the night Amanda disappeared, but I had no idea she was an undercover agent until I started listening to her speak. She had her cover down to a science though, and I doubted Mayor Christensen could see past her own nose to the spy in her midst.

I laughed as I climbed into my wauto.

I wasn't going to tell the mayor about her spy, but I wondered where Amanda went after she left the mansion?

Not wasting any time, I pulled out my handheld, booted it up and loaded the cd. It was indeed Amanda's diary and the password was easy enough to break. It was Hanson's name, a secret that only she and Nathan shared.

I skipped ahead and read her entry dated the day she disappeared:

> Today the burden of being the only child of the mayor has grown to be too much. Mother only cares for her stupid career. She busted up the good thing Tom and I had. Sticking her nose where it doesn't supposed to be…again. This is not something new to me, but I still feel the stinging of the slap from her hand. I have dealt with it for too long. She gonna pay for this! I love Tom and she ain't going to stop

me from being with him. What am I trash to her? Something to be thrown out? I hate her! Bitch! I'm nothing to her. Nothing.

I pulled back from the paragraph, my heart aching for Amanda. Where would she go? All of her contacts had deserted her. Hanson broke up with her because he no longer wanted to deal with the secrecy and the payouts. Her mother had selected her campaign over her daughter's happiness and had belittled her to the point of tears. She didn't know her father, from what Jane said, the family hadn't seen Amanda's father, Richard, aka Jesus, since Amanda was four. Who would she run to when her world was crashing down? Where would she go?

To her best cousin in the whole world, who was more like a sister to her.

That's who.

CHAPTER 35

Twenty minutes later I entered an opened O'Shea's bar. It was a little before eleven o'clock in the morning. I met Jane at a table back on the patio. She'd been up when I left to go visit Maria and we agreed to meet at O'Shea's for breakfast to talk about the case. Katherine was nowhere to be seen, and O'Shea himself waited on us. I ordered a coffee and toast. Jane ordered the same, but with sugar in her coffee. It was a late meeting for her, still very early for me.

"Sugar? This early in the day?" I asked with a small smile on my face.

She nodded, her dreadlocks loose and her face grim. "I finished going through Nathan's bank reports up until last month. He hasn't received any additional money from Hanson, only his regulator paychecks. I did, however, move off the bank statement to his credit report and recent purchases. Did you know that computers can check everything you've ever purchased?"

I shook my head. I didn't want to think about it as I remembered my purchase for a red lace teddy which cost too much to be a liner in the bottom of my panty drawer.

"Anyway, he purchased a 2149 EX model aerocycle last month. All paid in full. He has also been buying a lot of expensive clothes; all paid for in SE currency and his shoe buys alone would pay my rent for a year."

"Where's he getting that kind of dollars? Dipping into his hush money?" I asked, my stomach growling. O'Shea caught my attention and pointed to the coffee maker brewing fresh java.

"No, I went back over the bank reports. Nothing. He doesn't withdraw any money," Jane said. "So I thought maybe he was taking it out before he deposited his check. Nothing doing. His paychecks are all wire-transferred in. So, it's not like he's keeping out three hundred dollars and depositing the rest..."

"Then it could only be one of two things," I said, falling silent as O'Shea brought in our coffee.

"Toast be out in a minute," he said gruffly and stomped back up to the bar.

I got the feeling he didn't like being a waiter.

"Either he's dealing Zenith again, or he's found a new blackmail victim," I finished. "We're going to have to ask your aunt about her relationship with Nathan. But I prefer to catch them together first."

"What makes you think they're an item?" Jane asked with a scowl. "You thought she was also with Hanson."

Okay, true I'd been wrong before, and I'm sure it won't be the first time. Still, I let the comment pass. Jane caught my look and quickly added, "Not that it wasn't a good hunch..."

"If you want me to lay it out fine," I said, placing my right hand out for her to see all five of my fingers. The clump of twisted scarred flesh lopped into the middle of my forearm caught my attention, but I pushed by it. "One," I held up my index finger. "Nathan ended up on her guest list. Two, he smelled of honeysuckles and mint, your aunt's favorite perfume, and three, when I asked her about him, she nearly passed out. And four, the Raymen Cartel connection. All I need is five and it counts as a conspiracy."

Jane nodded, a smile on her face. "Sure, you got a good argument, but will it cut the mustard? Now, what did you find out with Maria?"

I filled her in on the conversation with Maria, keeping Maria's role as an undercover agent out for now. Jane didn't really need to know that, and it added little to our case. The

Raymen Cartel was Trey's and the T.A.'s problem, not mine. Not Jane's. Unless they killed Amanda, which I doubt they had done. Family is family. Most of cartels didn't mess with family, unless family messed with them—which it hadn't in this case.

"...so once Amanda had exhausted all of her family members in Memphis, I wondered who would she turn to next? Not to those who had already betrayed or used her up. Who, Jane would she go to for help?"

I finished the tale and looked at Jane.

Jane's eyes stared at something behind me. I waited.

O'Shea dropped off a small plate filled with toast. I took out my jar of jalapeño jelly out of my satchel (what did I say about being prepared?) and spread some across a piece of lightly browned toast. I bit into it, tasting its fiery sweetness. Jane sipped her coffee.

After a few minutes, she said, "You're right, even though you didn't come right out and say it. Yeah, Mandy called me the night she went missing."

Of course she did. She'd turned to everyone one else in her family.

"I knew you'd find out," she sighed, rolling her eyes. "I wanted to tell you, but there never seemed to be the right time. Really, Cyb, I did."

I understood that. I really did, but I felt incensed anyway. That night at my apartment instead of slamming Jane with my irritation, I let her deal with it. Guilt would chew away at her, if for some reason her failure to disclose her cousin's call would make it impossible for us to find her murderer.

"I know you're disappointed in me," she said, her eyes moving to my face and searching it. "I never meant to let you down, girl, I was just so, so hammered by the fact she was gone. I got lost, you know, in her disappearance and then her death..."

"Personal cases," I said. I drank some of my coffee and took another bite of my toast. "Eat, Jane. It happens to everyone."

She nodded numbly and took a piece of toast from the plate. With swift swipes of the knife she'd jellied her toast. She took a big bite, getting jelly in the corners of her mouth.

Patience was my goal today and I waited for Jane to finish eating. I had another piece of toast, and Jane had two more in that same time frame. Our plate finally littered with crumbs and rogue spots of jelly, Jane sighed once more as if to talk was an exhausting task.

She said, "She called all upset and crying."

I nodded, nursing my coffee.

"I couldn't understand her at first. Once I got her calmed down, she said her boyfriend had broken up with her because of her mother. Well, I knew Aunt Belle hated Nathan. Who else could it have been? Mandy had insisted and talked Nathan up as the boyfriend for so long, how was I to know it was Hanson? I didn't even question it."

I shrugged. I didn't expect her to know it was Hanson or to think it was anyone else but Nathan. But Jane's questions were rhetorical, not intended for me. So, I sipped more of my coffee and listened.

"…And I asked her if Aunt Belle threw her out or if she left on her own. She said that Aunt Belle called her a whore and she couldn't take it any more. Could she come and stay with me?"

Jane's voice took on that far away sadness that comes from thinking back over your actions and regretting them. Hanson had the same tone in his voice when he spoke about his breakup with Amanda. Now that the girl was dead, everyone wanted to do something different about their actions.

But life doesn't have a restart button.

"I couldn't let her stay with me. I kept thinking about how that case with the Change nearly got your sister and your niece killed. I didn't want that for Mandy. What if we got a hot case and they blew up my apartment or shot out my windows and killed her? So, I told her she needed to go home and to work things out with her mother. Can you believe that? I totally sounded like an adult, not like her friend or even her family. I could've taken her for a few weeks, you know, until Aunt Belle simmered down. If only I'd done that, she would have been somewhat safe, alive…"

"Jane, you did what you thought was right at the time," I said. "How could you, heck, how could anyone have known that Amanda would be killed? If you had some mystic vision, you would have done something different to save her. But we don't have that kind of power."

She nodded, but her eyes held a glassy look. She signaled to O'Shea for another round of coffee and he came, removed our plate and vanished back behind the bar. "I was supposed to be there for her, and I wasn't. She kept saying that night that her Zenith vision showed water, cold icy water…"

"So, you knew she was using Zenith?"

Jane's head snapped up as her eyes eagerly sought mine. "No, but, but I suspected it. She called it a waking vision and deep down, you know inside, I knew it was Zenith."

"And you didn't ask?" I asked, my voice soft, non-judgmental.

Jane croaked out a "no. I—I didn't want to know. You understand? I didn't…"

"Regardless, you were there for her. You answered her call, gave her advice and listened to her. This wasn't your fault. Her own mother didn't listen the way you did, Jane," I said, trying to put Jane back in the game. The situation with Amanda was much too complex for one person to shoulder the blame for chasing her out of the house and into the waiting arms of death. In fact, the only person to blame was the person who shot, raped, and killed her.

Jane gave me a smile, and said, "Yeah, well, little girls aren't supposed to die that way, Cyb. Anyway, there you have it. That's her telemonitor call in a nutshell. A couple days later, I got another telemonitor call from Aunt Belle telling me that Amanda was missing."

"And the rest we know is history in the making," I said with a final draining gulp from my cup.

O'Shea arrived and filled up our empty mugs. He grunted and sauntered off.

"She didn't come to D.C., then where did she go after she called you?" I asked.

Jane shrugged with a sigh. "I dunno."

We sat that way, thinking about the many facets of this case and where Amanda would go when she had no one else. Who was her best friend?

"Nathan," I said.

Jane looked up, puzzled. "Yeah, I'll follow him tonight to see if he and Aunt Belle are together."

"No, not that. Who else would Amanda go to? She'd go to him. Tom said that they'd been friends forever. When she needed a cover to hide her relationship with Tom, she used Nathan. When she needed a Zenith fix, she went to Nathan..."

"And when she needed someplace to hide, she went to Nathan," Jane said. "Christ, Cybil, he told me that she left his house to go to the embankment where we found her body!" I smacked my forehead in disbelief. I've known about it this whole time, but have left that tiny piece of information in my handheld buried under other notes.

"Nathan must've killed her," Jane whispered.

"He was definitely infuriated at the charity ball when I mentioned that she wasn't really his girlfriend and how he might have been jealous of Hanson or tired of waiting for her to pick him, so he killed her."

Jane stood up and tossed a currency carddown on the table for breakfast. It landed with a smack. "Let's go find him and ask."

I took another sip from my cup of steaming coffee and said, "What else we going to do today?"

CHAPTER 36

We stopped by the rental room in order to drop off Jane's aerocycle so that I could drive the wauto. Feeling a little lightly prepared, I went into the room to pick up my laser gun 350. Hanson had returned it. Jane clicked on the telemonitor, and the mid-morning edition was on. Roberta Rodriguez still worked the counter as news anchor, her slick, black hair tied up in a bun with a few strands spilling down her to her shoulders.

"In other news, the Memphis Regulators are seeking any information that will lead to the whereabouts of Regulator Derrick Jameson. Jameson, a relatively new member of the force, has been missing since Monday night. He was last seen at the benefit for Mayor Christensen's daughter, Amanda."

"What?" I asked, as I looked away from the bedside stand to the telemonitor, my gun in my hand. With a quick shove, I placed it in my shoulder holster and glanced at Jane who was as transfixed by the news as I.

"...If you have any information regarding the disappearance of Regulator Derrick Jameson, call the MR hotline at 555-555-6891..." Roberta said briskly before moving on to other news. "In other news, the society for the better treatment of robots has petitioned the local quadrant government..."

"Derrick Jameson is missing," I said, thinking back to the last time I saw Derrick.

"What's it to us?" Jane said casually. "Let's go find his partner."

The buzzing of the telemonitor interrupted us. I clicked it on and Captain Hanson's haggard face appeared.

He seemed worst for wear, his face a sick reddish color. Deep creases etched themselves across his forehead. He was definitely looking his age today.

"Cybil, have you been in contact with Derrick Jameson?" he asked, his voice strong, but quivering slightly.

"Not since the fundraiser the other night," I said, sitting down on the bed. "I heard the news. He's missing…"

Captain Hanson cleared his throat and said, "Well, uh, that seems to be the case. We can't find him."

"What does that mean?" I stood close to the telemonitor. "What do you mean we?"

"He's missing, well, officially missing. It's been forty-eight hours and he didn't report in for nightshift. We've been by his home and no one's there. I've contacted his relatives and they have not seen him either."

"Could be that he's late," I said, knowing in my gut that this felt wrong. Derrick wasn't late for work. "Maybe skipped town?"

"Yes, well, that might be, but he's never been late before," Captain Hanson said, his face reddening. "Been two days. Of course there is a first time for everything."

Hanson clicked off.

We headed out. Although it was my wauto, Jane drove us downtown to Nathan Martindale's house. We reached the decrepit neighborhood within half an hour, but my thoughts were still back in our rental room.

Where was Derrick Jameson?

Derrick was a bit of a jerk, but he was a hard, rigid man for regulations and rules, even if those rules came from a wicked book. I wondered if his dealings with Nathan had somehow gotten him killed or buried under someone's new house.

Jane sat us down in the cluttered yard and in the broken paved driveway. She was out of the vehicle before I could even ask her how we were going to approach Nathan. I followed her out of the vehicle and stood at the steps.

She rang the bell, her boots tapping impatiently on the porch.

No answer.

Nathan's aerocycle wasn't parked anywhere near the house. I scanned the deserted lane and didn't see any aerocycles at all.

"He's not here, Jane," I said, but she didn't seem to hear me.

She rang the bell again, but no one answered.

After several more attempts, Jane finally sighed and gave a sort of strangled growl of frustration. "Where is he?"

"It's the day shift, perhaps he's working overtime," I said, glancing down at my watch. It was fifteen till noon. "Or he could be out searching for his long lost partner."

Jane smirked. "Yeah. Sure he is..."

"Let's go check out his job," Jane said, her hands clutched into tense fists.

"Sure," I said as I climbed back into the passenger seat. As Jane sat down, I entered the address coordinates for regulator headquarters. I could see the numbers in my head; I'd been there twice already. It seemed I could recall the details of headquarters better than I could the items in my apartment at the moment.

The murky Memphis sky painted the landscape in bluish shadows and bleak buildings. Below us, the sidewalks lay undisturbed and the only movement came from the wind as it whipped through alleys and wrought iron fences. Who knew it rained so much in the city of blues?

"He'll probably be out looking for Derrick. Or with any luck, we'll catch him before he leaves."

Jane shrugged. "I know his usual router. We'll find him."

Fury slithered under her words and tone. Nathan had a lot of explaining to do. The odds leaned toward him as Amanda's killer, but I couldn't shake the amount of pity I felt for him.

That pity came from my gut. Hunches and impressions that burst from there usually were dead-on accurate, with or without evidence. I thought back to the first time I met him, sitting down on that ripped and scarred piece of porch. He spoke of Amanda with love and a deep loss that seemed to slice right into the center of his heart.

I believe then that he loved her unconditionally and without judgment. Something Amanda rarely received at home or from her lover, Hanson.

So why kill her?

Why would he kill the sole person who believed in him? Was the cut into the Raymen Cartel's Zenith business worth enough to exchange for Amanda's life?

My gut was rumbling a solid no.

Jane flew over to headquarters in minutes. She stepped out into the cool, garbage-scented air and said, "Creepy."

Indeed headquarters resembled a creepy, something-out-of-Frankenstein- building that thanks to its few lights only added to its eeriness. Only a few illuminated ancient windows spilled arcs of watery circles onto the sidewalk.

"Let's do it," I said, walking past her and up the steps.

She followed, her hand on her knife. I didn't have time to tell her to leave it.

The security regs confiscated Jane's knife and I moved up to the information desk that Herman manned during the daylight business hours.

At this time of the day, Herman went to lunch and a robust blonde, named Sherry began to watch over the foyer for that hour.

"Wha' can I do for ya, hon?" she asked, her puffy eyes drifted over the desk's edge and down to me. She leaned on the desk, her arms squished beneath her overflowing bosom.

"I'm here to see Nathan Martindale," I said with a smile. Honey, honey opens more doors than vinegar, my grandmother used to say.

"You press?" she asked, her blue eyes searching over my outfit, looking for cameras, recorders or other devices that security may have missed.

"No," Jane said, her voice hard like flint. "Martindale. Where is he?"

Sherry reared back as if slapped and pointed with a somewhat shaky finger to her right, our left. "Follow da signs to da narcotics unit. His desk is marked."

Jane didn't smile as she led the way back to the narcotics unit. She felt for her knife, remembered that it lay in a pile at the checked in articles cage at the front of the building.

At the end of a rather short corridor lay a room that contained roughly twenty-two desks, each with a telemonitor linked to a laptop computer. Some were decorated with rotating pictures, coffee mugs and electronic calendars, while others lay decorated only with cds and disks.

As soon as we entered, we found three narcotics regs huddled in a small group towards the rectangular whiteboards at the front of the room. All over the walls were maps, diagrams and flowcharts of the Memphis Quadrant. On the right hand wall, before the whiteboards, were mounted jpgs files of violators that rotated every minute in a slideshow of wanted rogues.

"Hey Jane!" shouted a thick-necked hunk of a man from the trio at the front of the room. He wore a fitted azure shirt and his badge swung from his neck on a black rope.

Jane stopped scanning the desks' nameplates and glanced up. "Johnson!"

She met him halfway between the whiteboard and the rear. They shook hands briefly. She turned back to me and said, "Cybil, this is Regulator Johnson. Avid aerocycle fan and a very good regulator. Knows everything and anything about Zenith and Ackback."

I shook his enormous, meaty hand. He had to be at least six feet nine or so. His turquoise shirt hugged his chest and his hardened muscles. He flashed me a rather bright smile before saying to Jane, "Listen, Jane, if you're here to talk to Martindale..."

He moved further away from the front, taking Jane by the shoulder and lowering his voice. They bent their heads together.

I gravitated with them.

The doors to narc unit slid open as Captain Hanson strolled in, dressed in a gray suit that accentuated his hair. He wore a grim expression. He saw me immediately and slowed until he reached me.

"What are you doing here?" he asked, his eyes bloodshot. "How did you know he was working a double shift?"

"Looking for Martindale," I said, a little miffed at his tone. "I didn't know he was working a double."

"Captain!" one of the regs called a short man with a round afro.

"One second," Hanson hissed. His voice stiff, but still authoritative. He turned back to me. "Nathan is on suspension, starting today."

"Why?" I asked, tension quickly flooding the air. The two regulators hovered, their arms crossed over their chests, above the two guns that each had slung over his hips. One cleared his throat loudly.

Hanson glimpsed Johnson whispering to Jane and said, "Johnson."

Startled, Johnson stopped whispering, saw Hanson, and left to rejoin the group. Hanson stalked off from me and joined the men. His voice rose above the silence and I caught about every third word or so.

"Day shift already heard...." said one of the regulators.

"...Martindale...for...from the ....locker," Hanson said. He tossed me a quick look before continuing, trying to lower his voice even more. "...Derrick...may..."

"Well now," Jane whispered from behind me, spooking me.

"Pow wows are fun. Come on, I've got someone we should see."

I turned around and followed her out of the room. Questions buzzed about in my mind, but I kept them to myself for now. Who did Jane want to see? Did Johnson tip her off with more information?

Jane wore her I-know-something-you-don't-know smile as she opened the doors labeled locker room.

She skipped over the fourth set of metal lockers and seated in his black regulator pants and a dingy, once-white tee-shirt was Nathan Martindale. Locker number five-sixteen was opened and a hand-size rectangular mirror reflected the overhead lights.

"What do you want now?" Nathan asked as he pulled back his curly hair into a snug ponytail. "I've gotta report in five minutes. I'm late as is. Working a double."

Jane snarled, her anger once again up front and center. "We won't keep you."

"Nathan, I have a couple of questions," I said, taking a seat beside him on the bench.

"Ask, but I've gotta go," he said with a sigh as he pulled on his long-sleeved turquoise shirt, the Memphis Quadrant crest on the shoulder.

"Did you pick up Amanda from her mother's mansion the last night she was seen?"

He buttoned his shirt without answering.

Jane paced behind him, cracking her knuckles. "You deaf?"

Finally after the last button had been done, he said, "Okay. Yeah, I picked her up. Mandy was cryin'. Her and that bitch of a momma got into it." He shrugged. "Her momma had busted up Mandy's relationship with, well, you know."

He fastened the buttons on the cuffs and said, "That it?"

Jane punched a locker behind him. Nathan jumped and scooted away from her. He quickly glanced down at his arm.

"No, that ain't it by half," she barked.

Nathan peered at her before saying to me, "The rest you know. I took her to the bank, her favorite spot. Then I left her there. She-she said she'd get a ride back home after she cooled off."

"Where did you go after you left her?" I asked quietly, playing the good p.i.

Nathan's face seemed to close. He stood up and stepped into his boot. "I had some private business to take care of."

Jane stepped over the bench, her hand reaching out toward his throat. He swatted it aside, and Jane swung. Nathan dipped and punched. She blocked it.

"Martindale!" Hanson shouted as he jogged up to the fifth set of lockers.

The locker room was filled with the three narc regulators and Hanson.

"Martindale, until the Quadrant's Internal Interrogation team complete their investigation and has cleared the charges of theft and trafficking," Hanson's clear his throat, "you are suspended with pay."

Nathan's face burned a bright red. "What?"

"It starts today," Hanson said icily, a small smile tugging at his lips. "Now."

"Who?" Nathan growled and then stopped. His eyes scanned the three narc regulators who stood behind Hanson with naked disgust. "You!"

Hanson swelled up to his full height. His blue eyes flashed as he spoke. "You know I cannot tell you more. The QIs will be contacting you during the course of their investigation." His voice echoed and bounced around the locker room as if the heavens had opened and the gods had spoken this to Nathan.

Smiling broadly now, Hanson said, "Good day."

He and the other narc regulators left, two with short glances back at Nathan. Those eyes held glee and in one, relief.

Nathan ripped off his shirt spilling buttons across all directions. He glanced over at us. "Satisfied?"

Jane said, "No."

"Good," he snapped as he slammed his locker door closed, threw his ripped shirt into the trashcan and left.

"Let's follow him," Jane said, her eyes still pinned to the spot where Nathan has been sitting.

"You go," I said. "I need to talk to Hanson. He'll drop me off at Roger's."

She nodded and we parted ways at the information desk. Jane reclaimed her knife. One of the security regs said, "Nice piece," before giving it back to her.

I hurried up to Hanson's office. Sherry seemed asleep. Her double chins flattened against her chest as she dozed. The quiet of the corridors swelled out into the day.

Hanson's doors had opened as I reached his nameplate on the outside wall.

"Ah, Cybil," he said, a broad smile on his face. "Forgive the cold shoulder earlier. Work, you know."

He beamed. Getting rid of Nathan had definitely been a huge rock lifted from his shoulders.

"Tom, can you tell me about what he did to get suspended?"

Hanson said in a hushed tone, "He stole Zenith from the evidence locker."

Temptation had led to action.

Seeing the look on my face, Hanson added. "He's done it before, but we couldn't catch him. I suspect that Derrick used to do it, hell, he was smarter, but with him gone, Nathan had to do it. He got caught." Hanson shrugged.

"How?"

"After that talk you and I had that day from the hospital, I asked the QIs about a hidden camera. They said okay. So I set it up. Sure, I could've done it before, but I was, was afraid for my career. I owe to Mandy to be more of a man."

"Good for you, but that won't stand up in court."

Nathan could argue he was set up, but of course, the QIs

would have thought of that already before agreeing to Hanson's request.

Hanson shook his head, his hair flawless. "Doesn't have to. One witness and Nathan's hair with DNA left at the scene of the missing Zenith. He's toast."

Nathan had this habit of trying to run his fingers through his tangled, curly hair. He'd snatch his fingers through it and rip a few strands right out from the roots, leaving DNA attached.

"Any news on Derrick?" I asked as we started down the corridor to the staircase.

"No," Hanson said, a little less thrilled. "Two of my best regs are working on it. Nothing. Could've left the quadrant, leaving Nathan to take the fall for theft. I wanted it taken care of before it hit the newsfiles…"

But leaving didn't seem like Derrick's style. He liked being a reg and he liked issuing orders.

Hanson said, "I owe you an apology for the other night. I-I shouldn't have, well, you know. Anyway, I'm back on the wagon. Going to my first AA meeting tomorrow."

"Good for you," I said. I didn't know what exactly I was looking for here, but something had to point to Amanda's killer. If Nathan had left Amanda on the bank, who came along later and killed her?

We reached the bottom of the stairs when I saw Jane storm in. She stalked up to me and said, "We gotta go!"

She yanked me forward by the arm and I pulled it from her grasp before she dragged me out like a sack of potatoes. I followed her out of headquarters and into the wauto. She was practically running.

"I thought you were following…" I said between breaths.

"Maria called. Nathan is on his way to the mansion!" Jane spat, already starting the flight sequence. "We've got to get there before he harms Aunt Belle!"

I hurried around to the passenger seat. Before I could close the door, Jane lifted off.

"Slow down!" I shouted, while feeling around under the seat for my gun.

"I can't," she said, her voice shaky. "He's going to kill Aunt Belle!"

CHAPTER
37

"We don't know what he's going to do," I said, my voice louder than I wanted.

Jane's eyes stayed focused on the lanes. She must've been a racecar driver in another life. We went from downtown by regulator headquarters to the mayor's mansion in half the time it's supposed to take. She set down the vehicle and hurried to the mansion's doors, where Maria opened them so fast I suspected she was standing by them, waiting for us to arrive.

With wide eyes, Maria shushed us and pointed to the staircase that snaked behind the foyer's wall and up to the second floor. It wasn't the same staircase that led to Amanda's room towards the rear of the house. This upper floor section overlooked the cul-de-sac and our parked wauto.

"They're in her bedroom," she whispered, pointing to the staircase. With bright eyes, Maria wiped her hands on her apron. "He got here about ten, fifteen minutes ago. Boy was he in a terror. Yelling, cursing…" Maria shook her head. "I nearly went for my gun."

Jane led as we took the stairs up to the second tier and down the hallway towards the western end of the house. Along the cream-colored walls were awards the mayor had won or been awarded due to citizenship, contributions, and community service. Too bad she didn't give her daughter all that time.

As we reached the top of the stairs, the giggles and moans greeted us with intensity and heat. Like dripping water, they fell into the hallway, naked and unrestrained.

Jane tossed me a look of shock and her face mashed into disgust.

I knew what Mayor Christensen and Nathan were doing and I've had the sneaking suspicion all along. But Jane was taken totally by surprise when we reached the doors, opened them to the lewd scene. Nathan's naked body, amazingly hairless, was pale beneath the room's lights. I prefer the dark or candlelight, but others needed to see everything.

Tangled in a mass of sweaty desire, Nathan and the mayor continued with their romps of joy until Jane cleared her throat. Nathan's head snapped up, a look of astonishment on his face. His spill of curls in his eyes turned him into slightly sexy. The mayor's eyes were tightly shut, her teeth firmly holding on to her bottom lip and her forehead damp with perspiration, continued to engage him with upward thrusts.

He froze, his eyes skipping over to me and then to Jane.

Mayor Christensen struggled to sit up, her eyes searching Nathan's face and then following his gaze to the doorway to us.

Outraged filled her face, turning it into a mask of fury where seconds before it had been relaxed in pleasure. "What the hell are you two doing here?"

Nathan rolled back on his heels away from her and toward the window. I saw his exposed buttocks before he pulled on his pants from their spot on the bed's edge. His back bore circular bluish-black bruises. His neck burned a bright red.

"That's what I want to know about him," Jane said. She gestured with her head in Nathan's direction, her voice amazingly calm despite the situation. "I thought he was trying to kill you."

Firm and slightly athletic, Mayor Christensen boldly walked across the room to her vanity table and collected her robe. Her body wasn't bad, despite her age.

"What goes on in my bedroom, Janey, has nothing to do with either of you, so get out!" Mayor Christensen crossed her arms over her now covered bosom and glared at us. "You aren't in charge here," she continued, her eyes whipping over to me. "You're fired! Get out!"

Behind her Nathan smirked across the room at me. His tousled hair scattered and skewed made him look wild. He folded his arms across his bare chest as if to say there.

"You'll fire us to protect him?" Jane balked. She stepped closer to Mayor Christensen, her fist raised. "He cares nothing for you. What about Mandy? What about her killer?"

The mayor laughed, but it was without heart. "Please, this has nothing to do with him or Mandy. I'm weary of you. Always barging in, popping up and questioning people. I'm trying to win an election."

"You can fire me, but I'm still going to investigate Amanda's death," I said, crossing my own arms, feeling the 350 move beneath my jacket. "Though I don't know why you're so eager to protect him. He called you a bitch only a few minutes ago, back at headquarters. Didn't you Nat?"

The mayor pretended she didn't hear me, although the corners of her mouth turned downward in a slight frown. Jane's eyes bore a hole in Mayor Christensen's face, trying to force the mayor to meet her eyes.

"It does not matter. Who I sleep with is none of your business," the mayor said repeated, but the notch of superiority had slipped. "Now, get out before I call the regulators."

"Call them," I said with a grin. "I'd love to see how Hanson deals with your chosen bedroom partner."

Mayor Christensen clucked her tongue in outrage. "Never mind, you go."

I directed my comments at Nathan, ignoring the mayor. "At the benefit, Nathan, she said you were scum. Obviously, she doesn't think highly of you."

Nathan's smirk wilted, but he didn't say anything.

"For all you know," Jane said to Mayor Christensen, "he could've killed Mandy."

Mayor Christensen rolled her eyes. "First Hanson, now

Nathan? You two don't know anything do you? Next thing you know, I'll be a suspect too." She laughed. "And to think someone said you were the best..."

"Are you?" I asked, not smiling.

Jane growled in frustration. "Fine. I'm done!" she spat, turned on her heels and walked out. "Mandy deserved better than this. Better than you!" she said as she started down the stairs.

The mayor glanced quickly to the door where Jane had stood and back to Nathan. "You called me a bitch?" her tone nasal and offended.

Nathan shrugged. "I was tryin' to throw her off our scent, babe."

She stiffened. "So," she said to me. "There you have it. Now you can leave."

"Listen," I said, staring her directly in the face. "Amanda did deserve better than you. Between the two of you, you know what happened to her and I want the truth. Start talking or I'm going to start talking about your little tryst to the media."

The color drained from the mayor's face. She whispered, "You wouldn't dare. Your contract has a confidential clause."

"Wouldn't I? I am well aware of your clause and willing to refund your fucking currency. This is a game Nathan knows well, don't you, Nat?" I said. "I have several very close friends working at the D.C. Mirror and one in Toronto at the Star."

She sat down, crossing her legs at the ankles. "I-I don't know anything..."

I gestured toward Nathan. "When you dropped Amanda off at the spot by the embankment, where did you go?"

Nathan's mouth was a slash of fury.

"Tell her, dammit," Mayor Christensen said, her voice slightly elevated. "Tell her so she can go."

Grudgingly, Nathan said, "I came back here to see how she was doin'." He nodded toward the mayor.

Mayor Christensen nodded her head in agreement, as she bit her bottom lip. "It's true."

"Then what happened," I said as I leaned back against the wall. "All of it."

"If-if he tell you," the mayor said slowly interjected, "none of it will go to the files? It stays here, in this room?"

"Someone is dead. That someone is your daughter! And all you're worried about is what it'll look like in the news? Listen, I can't promise that it'll stay here. It's up to Captain Hanson," I said. "Hanson isn't one to blab, is he?"

"Don't tell her anything!" the mayor demanded. Her eyes met mine and she said, "Go tell your friends. I have friends too and yours won't be around long to tell much. Either way, I'm a shoe in for the governor's seat. So get the hell outta my room!"

"You won't be after I tell Jesus about your little extracurricular activities with Nathan here, whom you helped muscle in on the Raymen Cartel's business. That will be in addition to the stuff I tell the papers. I promise it'll be racer than what I actually saw..." I said, starting for the doors.

Mayor Christensen's eyes popped. "You-you...All right! Stop! Come back!"

I came back into the room. "You hired the best, and you're getting it," I growled, tired of her already. "Nathan, start talking..."

He peeked at the mayor, his lips trembling. "She knows about the cartel? Annabelle..."

"Shush!" she spat, but it was too late and they both knew it.

Nathan collapsed on the bed, his back to the bed's headboard and his hands folded in front of him. His profile outlined his Romanesque nose and bobbing Adam's apple.

"I came back here to check on Annabelle. Mandy called from the spot askin' me to come and get her. I told her I was busy, but I would send Derrick to get her. Believe it or not, Mandy didn't know about me and her mom and I wanted to keep it like that."

Mayor Christensen closed her eyes as Nathan's voice took on a rough, scratchy quality as if worn out from carrying the burden of the truth for so long.

"...Derrick took her to my house. I got back there sometime after midnight. When I walked in Derrick was still there in the living room, sitting by the couch. Mandy-was- she was on the floor dead. Blood-oh God, it was all over the telemonitor..."

Nathan rubbed his face and was silent.

The mayor lay down on the bed and rolled away from me, toward her windows that looked out over the entranceway up to her home.

"Let me guess," I said finally seeing the pieces fit themselves tightly together. "Amanda threatened to report you and Derrick's drug operations to Hanson to fall back in favor with him or to embarrass him. Either way, Derrick had to kill her to shut her up."

Nathan nodded, a sickened look on his face. "That's what he said. I believed him."

"Nat, she was raped. This wasn't a drug hit. The gun blast didn't hide that," I said to Nathan and Mayor Christensen's shoulders started to shake, a sob escaped from her lips.

Nathan's head bobbed up and down before he said, "I-I didn't know that until you told me at the benefit. I believed Derrick. I had no reason not to...But-but after the benefit I read the autopsy report and it was all there. Every stinkin' detail. So, the other night on shift, I asked him about."

The mayor had balled herself into a tight ball as if trying to protect herself from the news.

Nathan didn't want to talk at first. The words wouldn't come, but now they rushed out of him like an old rusted nozzle on a bathtub.

"He didn't wanna say, you know. He even tried to tell me the same ole story. But I told him about the autopsy report...So, I -well, anyway, he said he picked her up like I asked him to. She was a mess. High on Zenith...He told me that Mandy had passed out. He was turned on by her; she wore that denim shirt and a mini-denim skirt. He said the skirt had hiked up, revealing…" Nathan swallowed hard. "…and… and he raped her. He laughed, said he knew she wanted it." Nathan's face distorted into disgust. "Said she woke up midway through it and threatened to tell Annabelle and Hanson. He panicked and killed her. Shot her in the temple, after he beat the living shit out of her. God, I loved her so much…and this piece of shit wipes her out! Just like that! She was my best friend!s"

Nathan words faltered and he sobbed, his head in his hands as if was too heavy to hold up on its own. The mayor clucked her tongue and swore.

"I didn't know any of this until after Mandy was found," the mayor chimed in. "Nothing."

I had no way to prove that Nathan didn't kill Amanda or that Derrick did. Sure Nathan had an alibi, the mayor, but how far would she go to protect her lover? Her image? All the way to perjury? Probably not. The governor's seat was vacant and Christensen wanted her big butt in it.

It wasn't his alibi that made me believe Nathan. It was his eyes. They were bitter and hurt at Amanda's demise. Such a savage death for a young girl would wound the hardest of hearts—except the killer's.

I crept down the staircase and met Maria at the foyer, leaving Nathan alone with the mayor.

"Jane is still waiting for you," Maria said, her voice low and hushed. "Follow me."

We walked back to the sitting room and there Jane stood, her back to me, facing the fireplace. "She confess?"

"She didn't say anything. But Nathan stated it was Derrick who killed Amanda and raped her. She threatened to tell," I said, aware that my own voice held a certain level of weariness. "I'll call Hanson and have him pick Nathan up tomorrow. I doubt even Hanson will agree to arrest him at the mayor's mansion."

She turned around to face me. The corner of her mouth twitching in earnest aggravation.

"And Aunt Belle?" Jane said, her voice calm and somewhat neutral. "She's innocent in all this?"

"I guess that's up to Hanson," I said. "She didn't do anything but neglect her child and put her own ambitions before Amanda's welfare. If the story breaks, it won't go well for her plans to be governor."

Jane snorted as she turned away from the fireplace. Although her face crinkled in worry and anger, the smile revealed her true feelings. "That's enough, isn't it? Let's go."

CHAPTER 38

The ride back to Roger's rental rooms went fast. As soon as we entered the room, I clicked on the telemonitor, needing noise to fill in the emptiness in my chest. Before I could dial Hanson's number, the screen lit up, and a robe-clad Hanson, a pair of glasses resting precariously on his nose, waiting patiently until I answered, popped up instead.

"I was going to contact you," I said, a brief smile on my face. "Listen, about Nathan…"

"We found Derrick," Hanson said, interrupting my beginning spill on Nathan.

"Where?" I whispered.

Hanson took in a deep breath. "In the Mississippi, down the river a bit from where Mandy was found. I'm going to his autopsy right now. What to join me there?"

"Sure, I'll be right there."

Jane had come into the room and stood behind me. "Why do you care about Derrick? Nathan probably killed Mandy and killed Derrick to keep the secret quiet."

An excellent question and one this p.i. couldn't answer. Why did I care about Derrick? I know the answer, knew it as sure as whose name the initials tattooed into my lower back belonged. I didn't like people murdering others. And Nathan had killed Derrick out of revenge, and out of anger. Two reasons that weren't justifiable to me. You can't take matters into your own hands—I mean, without reason. I've killed many people, but all in self-defense, to save my own, or someone else's life.

"This isn't about Derrick," I said, and Jane's eyebrows rose in question. "I'm going to tell Hanson everything, anyway. Why not over a drowned, decaying corpse?"

She laughed.

ꟹ

Despite the advances in technology our society had accomplished since the fall of the United States, the one area to which a human is still important is the role of coroner. A waif of a woman, named Thomasena, carved up Derrick for us to view. Hanson and I stood behind the observation room's double paned windows, while down below in the autopsy room, stainless steel and polished chrome shined. The cause of death had been two laserbeam blasts to the heart. Derrick had struggled against his attacker and lost. Bruises on both hands, around the knuckles confirmed that he punched and fought against someone.

Thomasena spoke into her microphone, describing how much Derrick's liver and heart weighed, his last meal contents and other gruesome details I will leave out, for you may be eating your own meal right now while reading this. Wouldn't want you to get too sick.

Meanwhile, I told him about Nathan's explanation of events leading up to Amanda's death. I left out where we found Nathan and whom we found him with. I didn't want Hanson armed with that knowledge, any more than I would a reporter. Did Mayor Christensen deserve to have her name dragged through the proverbial mud? I didn't know and I wasn't going to be the one who decided. If during Hanson's own investigation, he found out her lover's name, then he may divulge it.

The woman did pay my fees.

And folks don't think I got standards.

"Do you believe, Cybil, that Nathan murdered Amanda?" Hanson asked after my tale was over, his eyes sad and watery.

Perhaps he did love the girl.

"I don't know, Tom," I said. "If I had to place down a bet, I would bet he didn't kill her."

Hanson nodded, face a bit grave. "I will have the morning regulators pick him up and book him until they complete their investigation. Now that he's told you, I don't want him skipping town."

"Captain Hanson!" Thomasena shouted into her microphone. "Sir, you-must see this. There's something in Derrick's throat!"

Hanson cursed silently and left the room. He took the stairs down to the actual autopsy room in quiet steps, his face a blank mask of indifference. I went with him too, even though he didn't ask me to tag along. My abnormal-size curiosity getting the better of me.

The aroma of rotting flesh forced me to gag. I coughed repeatedly as I stumbled to the table. Placing my hand over my mouth didn't seem to help. The odor was lodged into my mind, my nostrils, my mouth and I couldn't rid myself of it fast enough. Hanson seemed immune to the smell or else he was used to it.

Thomasena had Derrick's mouth pried open. Using tweezers, she stuck them into his oral cavity and pulled fabric out of his mouth. She winced as she did so, even though he was very dead.

She held them up toward the bright overhead light.

Hanson grunted. "Underwear."

Indeed, a nice, black lacy pair of underwear, stuffed in his throat. A woman's pair of panties, unless someone was dressing up in drag.

"It was definitely put there postmortem. He died almost instantly from the blasts. There's no blood on these either, but I'll send them over to the DNA lab for testing. We might get lucky."

EPILOGUE

April in D.C. was a cornucopia of cultures. Diplomats from the various territories, the prime ministers from Canada and England, as well as hoards of generals swoop down on the city to collect, exchange and accelerate their political goals. The Old Montgomery college kids were finishing up exams and packing into bars like flies on a dead body. Yes, spring time in D.C. was a haven for violation and slime.

The showers washed most of the visible filth down into sewers and into puddles of murky garbage, but the invisible kind, the kind that lurks a sliver beneath the handsome face of a stranger passing by, that couldn't be reached by rain, snow or hail. That remained.

I sat alone at Big Mike's downtown jazz club. A fat guy in a too tight purple suit was sucking on a saxophone and converting the air into wet, damp unhappiness. The song's sorrow seeped into every pore of my body, resurrecting feelings of grief and loss that I preferred stay locked away in the back corners of my mind. But sometimes, just sometimes, I come to Big Mike's to feel, to be stripped down to my raw, bare emotions. The music provokes, pounds, and perverts my feelings, making me cry and yes, sometimes, making me feel as if I could love again.

Sometimes.

I thought of Trey and wondered where he was…who he was with….

"Thought I'd find you here," said a throaty voice with a slight hint of amusement.

Jane pulled back the chair and sat down in the seat across from me. A tall bottle of Perk clutched in her fist and an already smoking cigarette posed between her fingers.

The waiter came around, and I ordered another margarita.

"Fruity? That's not like you," Jane said quietly as to not drown out the solo.

I nodded. My eyes still on the fat guy at center stage. "Trying something new. It is spring after all."

We listened to two more, slow, steady songs and when the soloist took a break, Jane said to me, "Aunt Belle's ratings are still high amongst the voters. She's definitely going to be governor in November."

"The story about her and Nathan's relationship?" I asked, not really interested, but filling the air until the saxophonist came back on.

"Swept," Jane said with a shrug. "She called couple days ago. Told her to take the attorney general position and bury it with Mandy. I hear Hanson is being talked up to take the spot."

"He's a natural choice," I said, thinking back to Hanson's polished good looks and political know how. As regulator captain, he was in position to be the next attorney general. A smart move on Christensen's behalf to present him as an ally, when in fact they hated each other.

"Here anything from the T.A.?" Jane asked cautiously. She directed her eyes to now, empty stage.

"Maria never found out the connection between the mayor and the Raymen Cartel. With Amanda dead and Nathan in the cradle, there's no one to fill in the blanks. Mayor Christensen isn't going to suddenly tell anyone…"

The waiter dropped off a fresh, new margarita.

I shrugged and sipped my margarita. Besides betraying the little nugget of Susan's trust could get her killed by the Raymen Cartel. The T.A. had enough leaks to sink the Titanic.

"I got this today," Jane said, taking her handheld out of her backpack and sliding it over the table's scarred surface to me with all the cool of a professional private inspector.

I picked it up and read. The DNA on the cigarette I picked up from my stalker was none other than Nathan Martindale. Now a convicted thief, murderer and accomplice, his DNA was no longer protected by the Memphis Regulators.

"That's how your aunt kept tabs on us," I said, with a knowing smile.

Puzzles were great, but only if all the pieces came together. That didn't always happen. Sometimes there were clues I had unearthed and never figured out how it fit into the puzzle. Most of the time, a partial picture is the best I could hope for.

Jane nodded as she lit up a fresh cigarette. "Yeah. He reported us checking in. Probably flashed that stupid reg badge to get our room number and stuff."

We were both silent for a while. Watching the people in the bar. Investigating lends itself to excessive people spying. It was difficult to turn that habitual practice off.

"I didn't know her at all. I thought we were close and, and…we weren't," Jane said to her beer. She took a long drink and slammed the bottle on the table making her handheld leap into the air from the impact. "I didn't know her in the least. And I should've…I should've listened…"

She didn't have to say who. Every since we've gotten back from Memphis some two weeks ago, Jane's sulkiness and long periods of silence grew shorter each day, but the questions. They remained.

"Does anyone really, truly know anyone?" I said, thinking back to Trey and how I trusted him to tell me the truth, and realizing that I didn't really know him at all. "We all have our secrets," I continued, my eyes meeting hers. "It didn't mean she didn't know you or you didn't know her. You were close to her, Jane, which is why she kept some things from you. To protect you. She didn't want to hurt you."

"Got a message from Hanson today," she said, switching

the subject. The moodiness and sadness still lingered despite the change in topic. "Couldn't get you on the telemonitor."

"No," I said, sipping my drink and trying to avoid a brain freeze. "I'm taking a break."

"Hanson said that the DNA on those underwear found in Derrick's mouth were Mandy's," she said. She took a deep drag of her cigarette. Its butt burned into a bright orange in the darkened bar. "Looks like Derrick really did kill her. Took the underwear as a trophy."

I figured Nathan had killed Derrick when he found out that Derrick had raped Amanda. Their argument at the benefit was a foreshadowing of things to come. I had no proof, only my gut. The proof was up to Hanson and his crew of regulators to unearth. I'd done my part.

"At least they found him," I said with a half-hearted shrug.

Jane stared at me a few moments before moving her eyes back to the stage. "I can't get over it. She's gone..."

She switched back to Amanda.

"If it's any comfort, Jane, she didn't die as a part of larger, more sinister scheme. A desperate man with a lot to lose struck her down. He silenced her, but your love has spoken volumes to her memory. In the greater scheme of things that surrounds the mayor, Amanda's death was a tragedy."

Jane blew smoke rings into the air, frowning through the haze. The foghog greedily sucked it from the air.

"That doesn't make me feel better..."

The spotlight on the stage flickered on and the solo saxophonist was back. He heaved himself onto the stool, placed the reed into his mouth and did what he did best.

Strip out pieces of my soul.

I watched Jane across the table from me. She kept her eyes closed, hearing the music without the distractions of sight. A gentle sway to the raw rhythm, Jane was coiled up tight. Was she still thinking of Amanda? Grief sometimes held on like a nasty cold, defying all remedies.

My mind flipped and recalled memories of past loves, Stephen and Trey, a short few on my casualty list of lovers. Most of them were dead. How long before Trey went from the active to the deceased list?

I couldn't think about that right now.

Hearing the peaceful notes of muted sorrow, I closed my eyes and enjoyed the sensation of being silent.

Catch up with Cybil online at

http://www.cybillewisseries.blogspot.com

ABOUT THE AUTHOR

NICOLE GIVENS KURTZ writes science fiction, fantasy, and horror. Her most popular work, futuristic pulp series, Cybil Lewis blends whodunit mysteries within futuristic, post-apocalyptic world-building. Her novels have been named as finalists in the Fresh Voices in Science Fiction, EPPIE in Science Fiction, and Dream Realm Awards in science fiction. Nicole's short stories have earned an Honorable Mention in L. Ron Hubbard's Writers of the Future contest, and have appeared in such noted publications as Crossed Genres, Tales of the Talisman, and Genesis Magazine as well as numerous anthologies.

Nicole's Whereabouts on the Web:

Other Worlds Pulp-http://www.nicolegivenskurtz.com
Join Nicole Givens Kurtz's Newsletter-
http://www.nicolegivenskurtz.com/media
Follow Nicole on Twitter-@nicolegkurtz
Follow on Facebook-http://www.facebook.com/nicolegkurtz

CPSIA information can be obtained
at www.ICGtesting.com
Printed in the USA
FSHW020832250620
71451FS